Worlds

The King's Pawn

By Mike Cahill

DORRANCE
PUBLISHING CO
EST. 1920
PITTSBURGH, PENNSYLVANIA 15238

Dorrance Publishing Co
585 Alpha Drive
Pittsburgh, PA 15238
Visit our website at *www.dorrancebookstore.com*

ISBN: 979-8-8868-3008-8
eISBN: 979-8-8868-3873-2

Prelude
The Beginning of Life

"Everything's fine" - Froth Lord

"The Broth"

He cast a vast and great presence that extended over seemingly endless reaches of space. Light itself from the billions of star systems and distant foreign galaxies would obey his command if called upon. He sensed the same light could be blotted out by him from the silky blackness of the universe as he moved through both space and time.

Time and gravity both obeyed his command. Location was irrelevant to him, a foreign concept in a sense. Even with his vast depth of power he was learning at ever-increasing exponential rates. Nothing was outside of his sphere of influence.

Though he knew nothing of his own origins, he went about the business of creation. He could harness the power of entire galaxies and make that power do his bidding. Legends and myths, yet unwritten, would give him many names.

Great worlds and species, would owe absolutely everything to him. He foresaw his vast legacy, able to see hundreds of thousands of years into the future.

Yet, he was nearly entirely indifferent with respect to all things. Even with this immense power at his disposal he often wondered what the very point of existence was at all.

Where did I come from? he would wonder. *Does it matter?*

Are there others like me? he would question.

Who am I? he wondered pointlessly in his mind.

Though he pondered his own existence, he never cared or wondered where the Cosmos came from. This was part and parcel of his indifference. He surmised that it certainly preexisted him.

Though he asked himself what he was, he did not care or concern himself

3

with needing an answer. As soon as he wondered, he realized immediately, any answer was irrelevant, and hopelessly insufficient.

He is the creator of The Broth; thus, he is the source of all life in the galaxy— maybe all life anywhere.

At that time quantum particles and waves, existing naturally because of the very laws of quantum physics pre-existing even him, were harnessed by him and combined in a particular manner to create the life-generating substance known across the ages simply as "The Broth."

He realized that if two separate but connected quantum particles interact in just the right manner they become "entangled." The resulting entanglement is not dependent in any manner on the nearness or farness of the location of the particles. He realized that the laws of quantum physics were universal, and therefore would universally apply to all things. And he could harness these laws. All these characteristics must be incorporated into the Broth.

And he made it so.

He also perceived that by hard linking the Broth to this particle entanglement, and by forcing all Broth-created species and forms to obey this law, he could control all life, forever.

And he made it so.

He foresaw not only his entire creation, derived from this Broth, but also countless civilizations of Sentients, dependent upon the Broth's very existence. He saw legions of species, all self-aware of their own existences as he was, and he saw them all in one moment of space-time.

He saw all their wars. He saw all their struggles, alliances, hopes, and ultimate ends. He saw it all in one vision, separate from time itself.

He created the planet Nectar, near the center of what would become known as the Zynon galaxy. Nectar was the first world for which "The Broth" was to ever be homed. He first deposited his Broth upon this world. The first life forms in the Zynon galaxy were born here. Knowing all that would come after via the Broth, he was able to see his creation, in one moment in time, one vision, and it was bad. In his view, all that was to come was bad. He would call one Sentient from among them all though.

Through his visions he had known of Froth Lord tens of millions of years before the planet Nectar was formed. Dendrake, as Nectarian lore and Froth Lord

4

himself would come to refer to him, departed the area soon thereafter. But before he departed, this powerful unexplained being had indifferently and regretfully, initiated the entire life process of the Zynon galaxy, which, in our context, is the entirety of all known life on all known Worlds.

Book 1

Coranthas's Chronicle, many eons later

Chapter One

Phobus and The Large Master

"Please send Some Broth." - Phobus Uthrates, Sholl Gar

I learned something as I, Coranthas, attempted to organize my thoughts to write you this chronicle. It became painfully clear to me that I have great apprehension in sharing my stories at all. You see, these stories are in fact dear to me. You may question my chronicles, but they are accurate accountings of all that has occurred. And they are not without endless merit and are of the utmost importance.

These writings are not simply the mindless dribble of fools, though in part this is the case. They are not simply a chronicle in the most traditional sense. Rather these pages speak of several friendships that developed over a long period in ages past. These friendships took root across foregone epochs, and from very different parts of the Zynon galaxy. The matters reviewed in this chronicle represent facts and history of the highest importance and magnitude in the galaxy.

However, these journals I share are also mostly without utility, and indeed can serve no one of true significance any benefit whatsoever. But share them I will and with zeal! I will chronicle in detail these things for you. I will write of The Broth. Indeed, I shall write of The Broth and torment you with all the pertinent details regarding its near limitless importance. We shall cover matters of the gravest consequences which reverberate over the eons amongst the Sentients of the Zynon galaxy. I will document for you the great wars and triumphs, as well as stories of great peril and loss.

I shall write of my dear friend Phobus and his servant Thog and of their ultimate destinies. Both their stories are worthy of great scrutiny and inspection. I will write of truths and of mysteries. The sheer number of great riddles emanating from the known worlds can be daunting. We will explore these and much more. I shall help you comprehend both the joys and the sorrows of my time spent with Phobus, Thog, and, of course, Froth Lord.

Indeed, I will explain to you now all that I know and understand pertaining to Froth Lord. His story is of the greatest importance. I will try to solve the mysteries for you. But first, I must introduce you to Phobus, my dear friend from the world known as Sholl Gar.

SHOLL GAR - "A vast sand world subjugated by the Large Master."

The Large Master was quite large indeed, hence her name. She had ruled with an iron fist for many years over all the populace of Sholl Gar. She was a hideous, revolting, enormous beast. "Grotesque" and "ghastly" are too kind with respect to her description. Her species immigrated to Sholl Gar from their own dying world eons earlier. Nearly extinct today they are. The "Large Master," her son "The Young One," and various scattered "maidens" were all that remained of them. There were a few nieces and nephews as well. Though her kind had nearly entirely died off, she was able to rise to power on Sholl Gar mostly because she had become so greatly feared. Once in power, she executed or enslaved all her political opponents. She also murdered all ninety-five of her surviving siblings. Though most of her kind had been killed by her or died off due to the planetary relocation, her native species survived unnatural long-life spans. (When compared to indigenous Sholl-Garian Sub-Creatures). The fact that generation after generation of Sholl-Garians were born under her rule, as time went on, the stronger her control on power became.

Her court was for the most part a bunch of wretched, cowardly, creatures from Sholl Gar's southern hemisphere that she hand-picked with her maidens. All her "Sub-Lords" were her property. Sub-Creatures from the Dunes she had enslaved and brought to her "hive" at her compound.

For nearly four hunded years she had woven the most intricate hive within the structure of the most ancient Sholl-Garian palace on this world. The palace is an ancient ruin of early Sholl-Garians of whom not much is known about even to this day. The Large Master's hive was a near perfect replica, though smaller in scale, of the city nests of her home world prior to its obliteration. As disgusting as the Large Master was, there was something majestic about the structure of the hive Phobus would often say. And it was immense, because, well, it needed to be.

Every year, the lady held a festival. And I do pledge solemnly not to go on and on about the festivals. I will only share the minimum necessary to tell Phobus's story. The Large Master's yearly festival would run nearly one half a year, leaving only the remaining half of the year for standard, non-festival operation. Over time, the festivals, their pointless futility, and the foul stench of it all grew quite tiresome indeed. Don't worry, my friend. We shall only discuss these matters with the minimum detail.

It is at this point that my dear Phobus Uthrates enters the tale. Phobus was a small, unimportant sub-creature originally from the southern continent of Sholl Gar. On a feeding tour, the Large Master herself witnessed Phobus giving a tiresome lecture to a gathering of sub-men near Forinth Dune. Phobus told me the lecture had something to do with the theoretical nature of black holes and how they might bend space time, and effect reality itself. (No one on Sholl Gar cared.)

Phobus began:

"Today we are going to cover several significant matters, five to be precise. It is imperative that you understand the high level of importance each of these matters presented this morning.

It is also imperative to understand that these five issues will be presented to you in a sequence not matching directly in correlation with their level of importance, or priority.

Let me explain. The first issue I will cover this morning is actually the fourth most important issue for us to cover. The second matter is ranked first in priority.

The third matter is in fact the third most important issue in priority. This is simply coincidence that third most important priority also comes in third position of presentation, not by design or intent. We recognize, considering this coincidence, that confusion could ensue. So, continuing thusly, the fourth issue is the fifth most important. The fifth issue, of course, will round us out as the second

11

most important. At one time the most important issue was to be discussed firstly; however, several circumstances have changed, thereby shuffling the priorities across each of the matters and hence...."

"I like him," she snarled.

The Large Master enslaved him. Off in chains he went with only a stiff cup of The Broth to see him through the journey.

This sucks, Phobus thought on his way.

Over time dear Phobus learned to tolerate his new toil and suffering. That first night in the hive was rough though. We won't be discussing that any further. Over time, in hindsight, he often reflected on how becoming enslaved was ironically an amazing stroke of luck! He eventually would write in his journals of his time spent under the Large Master and we would laugh hysterically for long periods; Phobus, Thog, Rulella, and our dear friend Froth Lord.

Eventually it all seriously hit the fan.

During the Large One's great feeding festival, she made a rather extreme, unworldly demand.

"Sub Lords!" she cried aloud.

"Sub creatures!" she bellowed.

The ground on Sholl Gar would quake when she got like this. Grunts and growls her breathing became. Her local legion of Sub-Lords sprung to attention. A brigade of drones was powered on automatically.

"I must have Broth from the Worlds of Nectar!"

No one had been paying attention, but it was her seven hundredth anniversary as Ruler and Feeding Master on Sholl Gar.

"Seven hundred years?!?" Phobus freaked out loud.

"Yep," answered Thog.

"Shit," added Janker.

"Jesus," finished Phobus.

Her maidens began randomly grabbing sub-creatures and tossing them into the hive nests, screeching as they went. Her maidens made horrific screeching sounds. Phobus was watching from the crescent hill with his crew, glad he was out of range. He watched, sighed, and looked down to the ground. "Seven hundredth anniversary," he whispered to himself.

"Well. Okay then," said Phobus with both a brief pause, then another longer quiet sigh after.

"Well, shit," he finished.

"She wants the Broth and Gravy!" cried Thog again.

At this point it is not imperative that I discuss the details pertaining to the Broth. This too will come. As an addendum to these journals, I shall most definitely include all the pertinent white papers and writings regarding The Broth, though the volumes are abundant.

The Broth's essence will remain a mystery to you for now. However, it is because of this Broth, or rather "The Broth" that the galaxy holds together and that our societies remain in our economically imperative state of eternal conflict. We have found no other way to control the populace of all the various worlds.

SHOLL GAR, A Meeting of the Large Master's Feeding Council

"Dude she's getting huge," said Thog

"Indeed," answered Phobus. "There is hardly enough Zak grizzle for her feedings, and the milk of the swine runs low."

"And now she cries for The Broth," said Janker

"Can't we just give her some gravy or some swill?" asked Janker the cursed one.

"If we give her gravy when she asks for The Broth we could fool her indeed," began Phobus.

"It's a tough call," said Poor Brandon. (We refer to him as "Poor" Brandon because he lost an eye and three fingers trying an experiment for Phobus)

Poor Brandon was not indigenous to Sholl Gar. As noted above, he was referred to as "Poor Brandon" simply because of his tragic accident while attempting to assist Phobus in Janker's chemical tent. That experiment went poorly. Phobus had mercy for Poor Brandon and gave him a position on the Large Master's feeding council in lieu of his scheduled termination, which had been scheduled for his many failures as a Sholl-Garian scientist.

"However," Poor Brandon continued.

"The larger she grows the more she will need, and the tighter will become her reign over us. We must face the facts sir. We must act now before she festers," Poor Brandon finished in a disheartened tone.

"Festers?" asked Thog.

"For sure she will fester!" Phobus continued.

Whenever the Large Master over-feasted, she would develop wounds in her main opening which tended to fester. Believe me, there is not a creature in the galaxy that would want to be any part of her feeding committee when she festers.

"Could we please for the sake of Dendrake take care of this matter before she festers?" asked Janker.

The feeding committee was quite a group. Janker the cursed one, or rancid one as sometimes referred to, was rescued from a Forinth Dune purging the previous season. His story honestly had a bit of sadness about it. He had lost his entire clan in a sandstorm the year before due to improper shelter. After losing his entire clan he wandered the dunes haplessly in a dazed state until he unfortunately got mixed up in a brief uprising.

A group of sub-creatures had organized and were violently protesting to press their rights for the food stores. They had been denied their rights as they saw it. He was not even a part of it. He was literally trying to get through the masses of sub-creatures and sub-men to get to the water stores he hoped were on the other side. And he was desperately due for a Broth dose too. Unfortunately, he was arrested by Sholl-Garian Sub-Lords and their guards and put on trial. Phobus witnessed the trials and thought them to be just pure spectacle. Phobus, as a high-ranking member of the Large Master feeding committee, witnessed Janker's trial and showed him mercy. He ordered Janker be assigned to the feeding committee.

Poor Brandon, as already noted, had undergone a rather embarrassing series of failures as he was working toward his Doctorate of Sholl-Garian sciences. At one time he was seen as having quite a bit promise. Several awards of the sciences were bestowed upon him for his early research projects. He did a thesis on post-traumatic stress disorder experienced by sub-creatures who were placed in Zak nests against their will. It won him a ribbon. But by this time he had mostly lost all usefulness and could barely see. Despite it all Phobus felt he had a positive attitude and a nice disposition. He only had one eye and mostly just one hand, but it did not matter to Phobus. *He can do oration,* Phobus would often think.

Then of course there was the Lobal Sentient Thog. I will outline for you what I mean by "Lobal" Sentient in the next chapter of this chronicle, as it is of great importance to nearly all that I will be discussing in these pages. But for now, I simply want to share what I knew about him then, at the beginning. His overall story is quite complicated. At that time Thog was loyal to a fault to Phobus. And he was funny. He had a good sense of humor. And though he was greatly loyal to his Master, Phobus often treated him poorly in my view. And this always surprised me as it was not in Phobus general nature. He was like that only ever was with Thog. Both Phobus and I could have very sarcastic streaks in us.

At this point during the Large Master's seven hundredth anniversary feeding frenzy, Phobus looked over the gathering with the look of one who knew with absolute clarity what must be done. It most definitely was time. He and his general crew had had quite enough.

"You all know what must be done," he began.

They all knew. Phobus then stood and addressed them:

"The time has come my friends. We must relinquish our Master the Large One from her seat of rule. Her reign ends now! Her rule ends mercifully now. It ends mercifully for us. And it ends mercifully for her. This, without question, has gone on for way too long. We shall send out and emergency ion communication to Delta Five."

"Janker, summon the Young One!" began Phobus.

"Thog, call the Sub-Creatures," he continued.

"We need all the wretched ones to take part in these matters as they are quite important to them as well. This is for no less than the fate of Sholl Gar! Steel your spines, guys. Make sure that the Young One is kept abreast of all activity, for he shall take her mother's place as ruler," Phobus finished.

There was now an excitement, a great anticipation, overcoming Phobus's gang of sub-Lords. Often a great challenge in a dire circumstance can bring out the greatest bravery, even in a sub-man. The ragtag "posse" that ran with Phobus on Sholl Gar at times were quite impressive. They could rise to the occasion if you know what I mean. But they were going to need my help with this one.

"Dude she's like wicked massive now. How do you plan on taking her out? She's like, bigger than my house," added Thog.

"Simple dear Thog. We shall give her what she wants. A massive, gluttonous, troth of The Broth and plenty of gravy," said Phobus.

"Right! We will give her what she wants, Broth, gravy, biscuits, and, um..."

Thog paused.

"Wait, we will?" rambled a now confused Thog.

"What she does not realize is that the Broth I will give her will not be the precious Broth but will come from Coranthas!" Phobus finished.

"This is going to be awesome," added Thog.

"Indeed," finished Phobus.

With these matters discussed they headed off joyfully considering the possibilities at hand. By the week's end they would no longer pay homage to Large Master, and her son The Young One would take the throne. My discussions pertaining to the Young One shall come later, as my stories are not necessarily in the exact chronological order as they originally occurred.

However, I cannot guarantee you that you will not find the tales of the Young One useless dribble and I make no false claims about them.

Meanwhile, twenty-five thousand light years away

This is the part of the story where I will help you understand my own world, and the tedium that was my existence before my friendship with Phobus. This part of the journal seems trivial even to me, but how could you understand the important matters without an understanding of who I in fact am? How could you comprehend these chronicles without first a deeper knowledge of their author?

My name is Coranthas. I live here on this wretched world that for the purpose of the journal will be referred to as Delta Five.

It is important for you to understand that "Delta Five," as it shall be called, is merely a code name and that I shall not, for obvious reasons, reveal my true location. For my own protection and perseverance, I have erected the most complex systems of self-defense and persistence. I do have powerful allies I will write about in this chronicle who assist with these endeavors. Though I have been through much I am not brave.

I am considered by some to be a leader of many, though I am in fact fearful of a great many things. My power comes not from inner strength but from weaponry. I am, usually, heavily armed. When I am not heavily armed I remain in my compound. In addition to weapons, I have some powers. Powers and skills imparted upon me by my greatest ally. This chronicle will outline some of those powers. Some I will keep close to the belt and let them remain forever shrouded in mystery. This chronicle will also detail to an extent the origins of those powers. The purpose of my powers I do not fully understand even now. And as noted already, even with these powers, I am constantly dealing with my inner fear. It does not show me mercy. It gives me no repose.

Many long summers ago my compound had become like a prison to me. I had everything I would ever need, yet I suffered a deep feeling of isolation and often panic. I had unspeakable powers, imparted to me from unspeakably powerful entities, yet I feared nearly most all things. There are things I know today that were hidden from me at that time. I will write of these things in this chronicle.

My world had become more like a make-believe haven for my fantastical imagination. An imagination that would lead off into waters uncharted and stars unknown. I was alone for the most part on Delta Five. The only other being with me at that time was the Witch Doctor.

Many have labeled my friendship with Phobus to be imaginary, just another fantastical creation of the mind of Coranthas. I assure you that this is not the case. Phobus is real, and so are the worlds of which I write.

The Witch Doctor on Delta Five had diagnosed me with "depersonalization-derealization" disorder. It is characterized when a sentient self-aware life form has the feeling that they are outside of themselves. It is as if you are an observer of yourself from the external world. This can occur to any Sentient, and if the event is rare, it is considered normal. It could even possibly be a visitation in the subconscious realm. But when one's perspective of reality is thus consistent in this manner, this diagnosis is made. One with such a disorder is also characterized by a distinct inability to discern reality from unreality. One may feel like they are always only dreaming. The sufferer may experience distortions of the passage of time. Things long ago may seem recent. Recent events may seem to be of long ago. It is also characterized by the sufferer losing discernment of distance. For example, the room they are in may seem like a large arena. Most of all though, the disorder is characterized by losing touch with reality. I, of course, never bought any of it in my case.

"I knew reality," I would tell her.

"Yah," she would quip.

She told me that I was very disturbed. Yeah, maybe disturbed that the only other person on my world is a Witch Doctor for god's sake.

I often wondered why there was a witch doctor on my world, in my compound. She had her own "practice," with facilities, labs, and test equipment. But I am the only patient. There is no one on Delta Five except me and my Drone Slaves.

It seems like a lifetime ago when I first met Phobus. We first met at university. He was not brave like me and had appeared wretched. But there definitely was something great about him also, even with those first impressions. He was able to achieve something that really no one else ever could. He was able to make me laugh and enjoy my existence.

Out of simple concern I addressed him that first time: "Do you need some Broth or something?" I asked him.

"We've got gravy, too," I added.

"Dude, you got Broth!?" Phobus asked.

"Get this kid some Broth," I called to a servant.

It was the beginnings of a friendship that would survive many trials and tribulations, journeys and adventures. We became inseparable. We would have the longest conversations about the universe, the sciences, interesting wars, and current events in the galaxy. We talked about philosophy. We talked about galactic religions both false and true. We compared our gods and laughed often. Phobus and I would make up stupid stuff to entertain each other all the time. We were each other's only reprise during long periods of seemingly endless boredom before the events of this chronicle occurred.

Phobus told me all about his world Sholl Gar. He hated it, but it sounded exciting to me. There was a lot of action on the wretched world it sounded. He told me about the wretched sub-servants, basically sub-men, sub-species on his world. Phobus was what was referred to as a "Sub-Lord" on Sholl Gar. Essentially the main "highest" Sentient "civilization" species on Sholl Gar was Phobus's sub-creatures and people. Those beings were the ones called "Sholl-Garians." (Though the Sub-Men on Sholl Gar, and other lesser Wretches, existed, who technically were Sentient Sholl-Garians, they were commonly not included in the "catch-all" term.)

All the Sentient beings on Sholl Gar though were usually referred to as "Wretches," simply because how horrible life was on that world. It was bad I suppose in hindsight. Now at first hearing the term "Sub-Lord" one might think that was a good thing. It was in fact a better thing if you did not care about liberty. To become a "Sub-Lord" you essentially had to be a slave of the Queen. But at least you would have regular food (and you were much less likely to become food).

Anyway, back on point, Phobus would often vent horribly about his Master, this cursed Large Master. Apparently, she was quite the Beast. She was the current "queen" of Sholl Gar. It all sounded like a horrible deal, but I did think at least she saved him from the Dune purgings. Our dialogue would go back forth a lot on this as well as many other things, as friends often do.

I also vented to him. I told him about my diagnosis from the Witch Doctor. He seemed completely unfazed by the diagnosis, but he was like, "You have a Witch Doctor in your house?" We laughed it off. We consistently exchanged our joys and woes. I never did find out why I had a Witch Doctor though. It was just one of those things.

For the few years that Phobus remained at university we were the closest of friends. We took "Exploring Quantum Physics" together. We both tried to sign up for "Bending Time Mechanics, An Introduction" and "Curved Space 101," but those were way too popular. We never got into those ones. The two of us ended up majoring in "Dark Matter." We both found it funny we were working towards "degrees" in something you could not see. It was truly a sad day for myself when my dear friend and compatriot had to return to Sholl Gar to submit to the humiliation of his master.

"I received the many reports from Thog regarding the Large Master, and not just the foul ones. Thog sent everything," Phobus would tell me. Then he gave me the gut punch I did not want to hear.

"She has withdrawn all my funding and is requesting my immediate return as well as a troth of Broth and biscuits," he added.

"I must leave when the fourth moon ellipses its orbit," he finished.

"Dude you won't get your degree?" I stated somewhat annoyed at the time.

I remember when he left those many years ago wondering whether I would ever so much as hear from him again. There was no reason whatsoever to even imagine the intergalactic relationship that we would develop. I often think back on the many interstellar ion communications that have crossed the void between us. I managed to graduate, and I returned to Delta Five not too long after.

When I ponder these matters from my past to chronicle them for you, I am struck with a sense of wonder. But I also am reminded of great and terrible fears.

I remember secret consternation and anxiety I would experience yet never tell Phobus about. I think of the two or three wars we have fought in together. (I can't even remember for sure if it was two or three, the third may have been more of just a "Special Military Operation," not too sure)

I remember the challenges we have overcome. I think of the adventures that we would undergo together in fighting for his freedom. He and I spearheaded the liberation of many others as well. I think of both the good and the bad things we done. But most of all I think of the massive amounts of Broth we have consumed.

I will, of course, discuss these in detail in this chronicle. It was not long before I received my first communication from him back on Delta Five. Our communications over an unremembered number of years formed much of the catalyst of this chronicle.

Eventually, as things always seem to do, stuff started to go seriously south for Phobus. It turns out life on that world was getting even more ugly. It had taken a downright horrible turn. Eventually he reached out for help. I was hanging out in my chamber, playing Nintendo, and watching some old Earth *South Park* episodes with my Witch Doctor when the communication beacon went off. This beacon was for Alpha 7 Channel. Alpha 7 Channel notifies me and my Drone team that an urgent communication is arriving. I looked up, surprised, and took off my headset, paused my game.

The message was rather odd and troubling:

"Coranthas, there appears to be an ion-transfer ray coming in on COM One over the Alpha 7 channel," a scrambled voice came over my chamber speaker system.

"Alpha 7 Channel?" I asked, sounding surprised to my Drone Slave.

"Copy that," answered my Drone

"What is its origin?" I continued

"It seems to be a Code Red communication."

"The origin is Sholl Gar."

ION COMMUNICATION DESTINATION: Delta 5

ORIGIN: SHOLL GAR

"Oh, dear Coranthas!"

"The tyranny of the Large Master has risen to new heights. She has now scheduled a round-robin roast for the celebration of the fourth moon. All the Sub-Lords and sub-men of Sholl-Gar are to gather their biscuits, gravy, and, yes, the Broth and submit it to the Large Master. This is the final straw for us. We will rebel and lead the Young One to power. And please send Broth."

END OF TRANSMISSION

"The Young One sucks too," muttered my Witch Doctor under her breath, still staring at *South Park.*

I looked at her but said nothing, then looked back to my control panel. For a couple moments I tried to think matters through.

"Christ," I whispered to myself annoyingly.

Fortunately, using teleportation technology bestowed upon me by my Mentor, I can transport myself anywhere in the galaxy. Many have accused me of imagining my anti-matter teleportation technology. I curse the doubts of the lesser minds that vex me! It is at this point in my tale that I catapulted myself to Sholl Gar, liberated Phobus, and met up for the first time with Froth Lord. Then, after all that happened, all hell really broke loose.

SHOLL GAR, The Large Master's last festival:

Even the most iron-plated stomach would have choked at the sight of her. Festering already, and covered with gravy, the Large Master crawled like a dying warrior towards another bail of swill, mustering every ounce of her will for just one more hole-full of gelatin-like paste. (The paste, as I will refer to it, was generally lopped upon the Broth during the Large One's festivals.)

As she reached out her Volkswagen-sized ladle, a conversation among the sub-creatures emerged:

"By the look of things, we may not need to do much here," pondered Thog aloud.

"She is indeed bringing much of her destiny upon herself," said Phobus.

"She's nasty," added Janker.

"Coranthas should be here soon. He's transporting himself to Sholl Gar. When he arrives, he will inform us how to deal with the Large One," finished Phobus.

"Phobus, is the Young One in place?" asked Thog.

"Not exactly. When we told him about our plan he soiled himself. It was necessary to stun him with the lightning gun," replied Phobus.

21

"Nice," was Thog's only reply.

Then, suddenly, in a blinding flash and stirring thunderous burst, I arrived with a large can of Broth in my hand. I came to Phobus with my gift of Broth extended outward.

"Woah!" exclaimed Thog, impressed by my arrival.

Phobus and I embraced. I was truly a welcome sight at that time.

"It is good to see you again, Phobus. I have long waited to hang out again, and now I'm pumped to assist in your liberation," I said.

"Coranthas, the team is getting the Young One prepared. This is it for sure. Treason it is," he finished.

Phobus sounded confident as he spoke. He was growing more self-assured at that time.

I turned to the gathering of sub-creatures, sub-men, and the "chained ones." On Sholl Gar when dire times hit, prisons are emptied to strengthen your perimeter defenses. The chained ones are used in defense strategies to foster numbers, or they are staged in dune trenches as cannon fodder to slow down encroaching enemies. These prisoner forces were simply referred to in Sholl Garian law as "chained ones." Phobus had clearly committed treason already by executing the order to release the chained ones. Only the Queen had the authority.

Even with the chained ones in his ranks, I had never seen such an absurdly wretched group. These creatures made me long for the Witch Doctor. *Phobus should just leave this rock,* I thought at that moment. *There is no need to save this planet,* I thought. Anyway, let me get back on point.

"The time has come. Phobus, is the Broth secure?" I asked.

"Yes Coranthas, and we have oceans of gravy," Phobus replied.

"Good, bring me to the Large Master. The Broth will do the rest," I said.

- The Feeding at the Troth of Coranthas, as it is now forever enshrined.

For roughly seven hundred years the Large Master had ferociously ruled Sholl Gar. On this occasion alone she had consumed over six tons of biscuits, ninety barrels of gravy, and nearly an ocean of Broth. The quantities were staggering. It boggles the mind, quite frankly. (I will say, to be fair, Sholl-Garian gravy is quite decent.)

It was quite a sight to see indeed. There she was standing on her hind legs, one arm wielding the carcass of a Zak, the other punishing a wretched servant with a fire stick. A small army of drones operating cranes lifted gravy barrels to her infected opening. Sub-creatures rushing in more captured Zaks from their dune nests. Teams of sub-men risking horrific death in the nests each incursion were everywhere. She did not see the two figures on the crescent hill looking down at her.

"This is going to be very cool. Are you running the video cam?" asked Thog.

"Indeed," was Phobus's reply.

"Here comes Coranthas!" exclaimed Thog.

All I can say is what we accomplished that day was truly awesome. We had never attempted anything like this before. I came down from the hill with the largest troth of "Broth" that anyone on Sholl Gar had ever seen. Its scope was astounding. The magnitude was unrivaled. It was very cool I must say.

Legions of Drones wheeled the troth upon my command, steadily descending toward the Large Master herself. Silence fell over the crowd. An almost imposing "hush" fell over the hordes. Strange, nasty creatures poked their heads out of the Large Master's hive portals wondering why it all went quiet. Masses of Sub-Lords, sub-creatures, Sub-Men, and the like gazed upon the troth. From this point on, this day was remembered as the "Day of the Troth."

There I stood before the Large Master. Though my plan was sound I was secretly terrified. *This lady could do me serious damage,* I was thinking. *Man she was foul.* She truly was an extraordinary, astonishing Beast. She was so nasty, so horribly ugly, and so atrociously malformed, that she almost seemed beautiful. It was a "so bad it's actually good" kind of effect. In the same sort of way when a movie that is supposed to be scary is dumb and funny. Then it gets so dumb, so funny, that it is becomes awesome. (The "so bad it's good" phenomenon) It is hard for me to explain it even today. I took a deep breath and started to address her.

"Large One, Happy Anniversary!" I began.

"For seven hundred years you have reigned over Sholl Gar," I continued.

"I see you have enjoyed some gravy," I said coyly.

The crowd remained silent upon hearing this stranger address the Large Master. Suddenly you could hear a pin drop, and her grunts and snorts were clear. It was so hushed that you could even hear her maidens panting and wheezing. They make such a high-pitched whistle sound as they try to breath the dry Sholl Garian air.

I continued, "As an offering I bring you this troth. It is filled to the rim with the Broth of the World of Nectar!"

At this announcement the hush turned to loud roar across the crowds. The sudden change from utter silence to total cacophony was jarring to me. The Large Master threw down her Zak, squeezed out some gas, and moved toward me, though with great difficulty for her. I stood my ground even though in horror. At this moment I noticed crowds of creatures had surrounded us. They had been slowly creeping in ever closer, but now there was more of a rushed encircling occurring. She pointed her massively long index digit with ungodly nail toward my chest, false thumb extended, raising it steadily toward my face. (Her species has essentially a false thumb, almost like a failed digit, or an evolutionary transition step. No one really knows.)

Finally, she spoke to me, "What form are you?"

The Large Master bellowed her question in a thunderous, evil voice, eyeing me up and down while pointing her index digit directly at my face.

As already noted, but ever worthy of repetition and more detail, she was quite the unsightly beast. She stood roughly twenty-six feet tall. No one knew for sure how much she weighed. Both her mouth and nose were two large round openings. One large nostril, center face, which closed side to side upon snorting, like two flaps shutting back upon itself. And her main hole or opening, much larger, served both for eating and speaking. It was extremely large and prominent and did not actually "close" in the true sense. It more like crumpled back upon itself when not eating or speaking. When it was feeding, it almost opened like the way a flower blooms itself, except rapidly. When she spoke the hole did not need to fully bloom open. That was just necessary when feeding. Her breath was horrific.

"Are you not yet my slave?" she questioned, more calmly this time.

"I am not," I replied calmly. "But I bring you an offering on behalf of my friends. Please enjoy my troth. You will not be disappointed," I finished.

She continued her inspection of me. She pointed right at me with that god-awful digit from Hades. But while pointing she looked over at the troth. I worried she might pierce me with that thing, even on accident. She then looked toward my drones, then to Phobus, then back at me. With her other hand she scratched at her false thumb. I came close to puking at that moment but held firm.

"Are you of Sholl Gar or another world?" she questioned, speaking very rapidly, flatulence escaping her bowel.

I began to cough at the frightful stench but just continued to hold my ground. I was in a state of terror, but as I have noted already, I considered my plan still sound.

"I am not of Sholl Gar. And though it may seem that I am brave, I am not," I replied.

"I rely heavily on my good nature and my offerings. Therefore, I bring you this troth on behalf of my friends," I finished.

"What species are you?" once again questioned the Large Master as she marveled at my form.

After gasping for air I composed myself.

"Um, my species?" I uttered confusingly.

I had no idea what species I was at that time. This question caught me off guard and distracted my focus for a moment. I found myself pondering the matter briefly. *How is it that I did not know what species I was?* Even more, why had I literally not ever thought about that concept? I was losing my fear now, deep in thought. And when my fear left I started to feel bored with all this. There I was in deep thought when she so rudely started up again.

Again, speaking more rapidly she began:

"When I am finished with your offering I will deal with you directly," she stated.

"Perhaps you shall join Phobus in my court or join my feeding committee," the Large Master finished.

I was essentially not listening anymore until I heard her say "Feeding Committee." That cracked me up for a moment. So I gathered myself. Took stock of my bearings. I had to remind myself why I was there for a second. It was starting to get monotonous, but I knew I had to keep going.

"Look lady, you cannot consume this much Broth. No one can," I impatiently taunted her. I was a bit annoyed at how long this was taking.

"SILENCE! Who are you calling lady?" she sneered.

Out of the corner of my eye I noticed Thog cracking up at her. I had to try not to laugh because as ridiculous as this all was it was still a serious situation right then.

"I apologize Large One, but you cannot finish this troth," I taunted her once more.

"No one can," I finished.

"I CAN FINISH YOUR TROTH!" bellowed a furious and wretched Large Master. Her eyes were blood-red now! *Oh my god!* I thought to myself.

"And I will deal with you when I am done. Bring me to the Broth!" she screamed in anger.

The Large Master could no longer move properly and ordered her servants to lead the drones to her with the Troth. A large team of Sub-Men was required to assist in stabilizing her balance. Each time they attempted to adjust her position for better balance she stumbled worse.

"WHERE IS THE GRAVY!?" she bellowed.

Fortunately, they had plenty of biscuits and gravy.

"Bring me my child!" she screamed. "With me he shall dine today!"

"Where is the boy?" screamed all her maidens.

Just over by the grandstand Phobus and Thog looked on. I joined them while she was feeding. I was able to work through he crowds now as she was becoming quite the distraction at that point.

"Dude she's pissed," said Thog.

"True, but Coranthas knows what he is doing. Right, bro?" Phobus gave me a nervous glance while asking.

"I'm more concerned about getting the Young One down here," Phobus said.

No one was certain how the Young One was going to react to this plan, or to having been hit with a lightning burst earlier. He hated his mother. And he wanted to be ruler. She beat him mercilessly, so of course we were certain he would support us. But he was also a tremendous coward and very much a snotty entitled prince. We already had to stun him once. He was so weak.

"What's his status?" asked Phobus to a sub-servant.

A servant answered in a very slow, scratchy yet calm voice: "Well Phobus, since pretty much right around the time you stunned him with the lightning gun he moves not," the servant answered.

I gave Phobus a goofy glance after hearing this dude talk to us.

"We don't think he's dead since juice comes from his pores still," finished the servant.

"Hmm," began Phobus nervously with a cracking in his voice.

"Can he be awoken with more bursts of lightning or fire?" asked Phobus.

In the same slow, low, soothing tone, the servant answered: "We have tried fire and some various chemicals that we have in our tent, but none have produced any desired effects. We have not tried further lightning however."

At this point I was like, nice, we're going to blast him again.

"Hmm, try the lightning gun and get back to me," finished Phobus

"What's up with that dude?" I asked Phobus

Phobus did not respond immediately. I wondered to myself if he was now doubting our plan. For some reason all fear left me at this point. I felt incredibly calm about it all at this point. Plus I could just teleport on out of there.

Meanwhile, the Large Master engaged in a feeding frenzy of the likes never seen on all of Sholl Gar. Steadily the troth was emptying, her stocks were filling, and things looked all the bleaker for Phobus, Thog, and Sholl Gar. It looked as though she would surely finish the troth and we would be destroyed.

"Um Coranthas," began Thog. I looked over at him.

"I don't mean to pry into your business, but she's ah, blowing through that thing," said Thog.

"What exactly was your plan?" he continued nervously, with a hint of annoyance.

"You just figured you'd use your mind to fly across the galaxy and taunt the Large Master a little bit. You know, get her very angry at me and Phobus a little bit. Give her a freaking truckload of the Broth while you're at it and then just take off back to Delta Five?" Thog went on.

I just grinned and listened to him.

"Is that it? Is that how it's going to be, hmm?" rambled a confused Thog.

Then it really got good.

"Could someone stun Thog, please?" quickly queried Phobus, all the while chewing his fingernails in panic.

"Yes, ah huh, the lightning gun, please. Thank you", Phobus finished speaking with his servants over a wristwatch commlink.

A few moments later several Chained Ones allegiant to Phobus rushed in and blasted Thog with streams of blue lightning from their skull mounted ion pulser mini cannons.

"Nice," said Poor Brandon.

Right then one of Phobus people broke through the crowd with a cell phone in her hand. "Phobus, you have a call on your Q phone. I believe it's the Large Master's Slave Chamber Warden. He would like to know if you and Coranthas would like to spend the rest of your natural lives in a liquid or solid state?"

"Also, they are having a choice between fish and chicken tonight and would like a heads up as to which way you're leaning."

"We'll get back to him." said Phobus

Another aid: "They need to know if Coranthas is fire resistant?"

And still another in a slower calmer voice and tone: "Does Coranthas have any special abilities that they should be aware of? Can he alter time or curve space? They basically want to know what they're dealing with here."

For about an entire hour, Phobus's aids rushed back and forth relaying the messages to Phobus from the Large Master's Slave Chamber Warden.

"For Pete's sake, they asked if I could transport objects with my mind? Why do they care about such things as this?" asked Phobus.

"For when we are condemned to the Large Master's Slave Chamber. They simply want to know how best to torment us, and what things would be a waste of their efforts based on any special abilities we may hold," I answered him.

"Like do we any powers they need to neutralize. That kind of thing, you know what I mean?" I finished.

Phobus looked god-awful. I felt a little bad for him, but nothing major.

"I saw you fried Thog. Will he live?" I asked.

"Yes he will live, but I have concerns. His confidence in your plan was low. He is not brave like you," he finished.

Phobus's statement chilled me to the bone. Why does he think I am so brave? He obviously did not know of the fear that torments me by the moment. If he knew of my true existence on Delta Five he would not think such things. The hours I spend in terror counting my enemies are more abundant than the sands of his Forinth Dune. My compound as wonderful as it may sound to Phobus is like a prison to me. Weapons, both real and imaginary, are all I have.

"Not brave at all," was all I could muster for an answer.

Suddenly, and in a shocking fashion, Thog was awakened by the blood-curdling screams of the Large Master. This shrieking scream was so horrifying, so shrill, that I still hear it in my dreams to this day. Beings from every region on Sholl Gar at that time fell to the ground groping at their ears to block the sound. The Large Master bellowed and tried to muster enough strength to get to her feet. She crashed into the gravy cranes, knocking one of them over, spilling precious gravy barrels all over her servants and herself. She wailed. Sub-servants and Sub-Men who had been tasked with steadying her balance tried their best to keep her upright. Massive, seemingly endless cluster chains of flatulence now escaped her uncontrollably.

She turned and she twisted. She grunted and she groaned. Her court watched in both horror and joy. Her maidens were shrieking with an ear-piercing shill which had a power all its own. The people rushed from nearby villas and dune pods to see what for the sake of Dendrake was going on. Zaks even came out of their Dune nests during their hatching season to witness this.

The Large Master, the Largest Master Sholl Gar had ever known, groaned, squirmed, squealed one last time, and then in horror fell to the ground. We looked down at her carcass from the crescent hill.

Even Thog, still suffering from the lightning gun stunning, crawled over toward Phobus and I. With desperation he tried to make the words come out but to no avail at first.

Finally, he was able to muster the energy to ask in a weak voice:

"Dude, you spiked that Broth, didn't you?"

He collapsed before receiving an answer. Phobus looked over at me with a grin. I gave an assuring glance. We had done it!

The following morning, all the dregs, Sub-Lords, sub-creatures, slaves, and the remnant were gathered for the coronation of the Young One. (The "remnant" was the term we came up with for reimaging the "chained ones" who had assisted us in the Large Master's destruction. They were to be Phobus special police forces.)

There at the Queen's chamber stood three figures. At the highest pedestal was the Young One, still held in place by a four-thousand-ton-per-square inch harness due to his paralysis from the stun gun. The look on his face was one of terror. Just a few feet down and to the left was Phobus's pedestal. Due to our duplicity Phobus would hold the second highest office on Sholl Gar. And lastly, of course, on the third pedestal I, Coranthas, stood humbly. Phobus appointed me ruler under only him as a reward for my assistance. Together, with the Young One as our puppet, and the remnant as our guards, we would rule Sholl Gar.

The legions cheered. From a distance a figure watched and waited. His name was Froth Lord. Though we had no idea yet, he was masterminding all these events. You will learn substantially more about Froth Lord, as he may very well be the most powerful being in the galaxy. Though his initial intention was to do me evil, he has become the greatest ally that I have ever known.

Chapter Two
What About Thog?

Thog's kind is NOT indigenous to the world of Sholl Gar. It is imperative that you understand this fact. Thog's people were deposited on Sholl Gar by a superior civilization as an offering to the ancient Oracles thousands of generations before Thog was born. In those times the Oracles of Sholl Gar, who were essentially mystics, were for all intents and purposes the government of the world. Thog's kind and the advanced beings which brought them to Sholl Gar represent the first visitation and contact with the greater galactic communities of the various Sentient civilizations on this world. As we will see, most of these "civilizations" were not really all that civilized to begin with.

Now the Oracles of Sholl Gar ruled the planet for a very long time, much longer than most governing bodies known to the Zynon galaxy. And though the Oracles were fair, and Sholl Gar had not yet descended into utter corruption in those times, it still was a horrible existence on that planet. The Sholl-Garian sub-creatures were still mostly helpless, defenseless against the sandworms and the elements of the sandstorms. During this period the beings that brought Thog's kind made first contact with the Oracles. At that time the Oracles were of the mind that the being that brought these "Lobal" Sentients was a god. And many on Sholl Gar began to worship this being, this strange, powerful man from the sky. As you are already well aware, Sholl-Gar ultimately descends into great misery as a world.

Anyway, let's get back on point. Thog's kind is considered a "lobal" species.

We say that his kind are "lobal" like the way we would refer to old Earth as a "human being." So, it is both the species' "designation" as well as a biological description. To reiterate "Human Being" and "Lobal Sentient" are the species identification. But "Lobal Sentient" also is a biological descriptor. Let me explain further.

All sentient life forms have what is referred to as the temporal lobe. Let's take the human brain as an example. The human brain contains four major lobes making up the cerebral cortex. All four major lobes are "internal" to the brain itself. It is all contained within a skull structure. This evolutionary state of the human brain is typical of Sentient life forms in the Zynon galaxy. In fact, it is nearly one hundred percent universal in all Sentient biological beings. The human brain, or cerebrum, consisted of two cerebral hemispheres. The four lobes are the frontal, the parietal, the temporal, and the occipital.

The lobe function of primary concern in Thog's case and the case of his entire species is the *temporal* lobe. In almost nearly all known higher Sentient biological life forms, the temporal lobe was separated from the frontal lobe by a fissure, *internal* to the skull structure. Its main functions are sensory. It is particularly important for hearing sounds, recognizing language, and forming memories. In the human brain memories are stored in various areas within the temporal lobe, and the prefrontal cortex. Thog's species was unique though.

To further examine the "lobal" Sentient life form definition, we simply say now that all sentient life forms discovered in the Zynon galaxy have a temporal lobe whether external or internal. None have been discovered that do not. However, one prevalent species has been discovered with what can only legitimately be referred to as an external temporal lobe. This is Thog's kind.

Lobal creatures as we will call them, have an external organ stemming from the forehead which contains and encapsulates both the essence and function of the temporal lobe. Because of the external nature of the lobe, these people have experienced severe disadvantages that other creatures have not. For one, let's face it, it makes a real nice target in a scrap. Lobal creatures have always suffered in hand-to-hand combat on Sholl Gar because they can be easily killed due to the vulnerability of their lobes. They were typically easily defeated even by the hapless sub-men on this world. This one fact alone could account for the fact that since their deposit on Sholl Gar Lobal creatures have been enslaved. They can thrive only in circumstances where the benevolence of their neighbors outweighs surrounding evils. They are utterly at the mercy of us all.

About five hundred generations ago the being who originally deposited Thog's kind returned to Sholl Gar to "make all things new" as foretold. He had developed a protective and nurturing shielding for the external lobe of lobal sentient life forms. We simply refer to this shielding as *Lobe Tubing*. At the tubings' earliest stage it was rare that Lobal creatures would be fortunate enough to acquire the lobe tubing. However, by the time of Thog it was rare to encounter a Lobal creature without the tubing. The Lobe Tubing, as commonly referred to, is almost like a helmet if you will.

The tubing, although entirely artificial, takes on a nurturing role and becomes dear to the Lobal life form it protects. That is why we often talk of Lobals who have become hopelessly "attached" to their tubing. It is important for you to realize at this point that I am referring to the SPECIFIC tubing of that individual Lobal sentient life form. We are talking specifics. We do not mean sentimental thankfulness for the lobe tubing technology's existence in a general way. We do not mean merely a thankfulness to the benevolence which created lobe tubings. We specifically mean that a specific Lobal Sentient in space, time, and history becomes sentimentally attached to a specific installed lobal tubing.

This is indeed profound and must be further explored. Now try to follow this line of reason closely. Lobal ethics are further confused by the science of the tubing and this attachment of the Lobal Sentient to their own specific tubing in literal history. The tubing itself can become corrupt and need repair or even replacement. It was designed this way! This is a positive aspect to the very concept of an artificial protective lobe tubing.

Of course, it may at some point need repair or even replacement. This is not rocket science at all! This is where the bizarre nature of the Lobal Sentient's attachment to its specific tubing, in space, time, and history, becomes tragic. Lobal Sentients have never truly come to grips with this aspect. Lobals often end up in very unhappy and unfortunate states. And none of that should be necessary. In many ways it is tragic.

An average Lobal Sentient could live 190 years. Before the Lobal tubings, this was common. No Lobal tubing has lasted longer than a hundred years. And even so, normal wear and tear could ruin one's protective shielding in a shorter time window. It is inevitable that any Lobal Sentient fortunate enough to have the tubing would eventually be in a scenario where there specific tubing would need replacement. This problem should never have become a problem at all! In fact, it is a bit of a mystery to me how this was not handled well or properly. Now when I knew Thog back then this was all foreign to me. It was many years before I had acquired the necessary knowledge about the Lobal Sentients, the artificial tubing, and this state of utter despair that befalls the Lobal Sentient upon loss of tubing, to write you about his matter.

So, let me continue the discussion to a conclusion. Hopefully I am being clear enough. Lobal tubing became standard on all Lobal Sentient Young three hundred generations in the past. Here is the true tragedy. When the tubing breaks down, for the most part so does the Lobal Sentient life form. Most Lobals literally can't emotionally transition to new tubing. There is no reason whatsoever that this should be the case. There is nothing at all difficult with respect to the installation of the replacement. I mean for goodness' sake some Lobals don't have tubing at all, and they cope. (Not many but some.) Most with failed tubing go insane or worse. Most of them perish inexplicably. Some can receive a new protective tubing which in essence is as biologically protective as the original. Unfortunately though, as noted previously, most sadly go insane or perish. It is all entirely and utterly unnecessary.

You may be wondering at this point in our discussion, *what does any of this dribble matter to even the tiniest ant?* Well, you are right in assuming that normally it would mean little at best. However, for the sake of Thog there is great meaning. The stunning of Thog by Phobus in chapter one has profound repercussions not only for Phobus and Thog but for the entire Cosmos, as shall be seen. When Phobus requested his servant silenced by a lightning blast he had no idea what things were to come to pass. Phobus had no idea the events that he had set in motion. Of course, neither did I.

Thog, as you will see, and I will show you, could not avoid his destiny. Thog's grappling with the loss of his first lobe is entirely unique. Even to this day elements of Thog's story are beyond my understanding. What Thog became initially could not fully be explained. It is true that most of the hidden secrets have been revealed to me by the time of this writing. However, Thog's experience remains worthy of endless scrutiny.

SHOLL GAR - Phobus Uthrates' chamber, sometime later

The light of the morning suns graced through the giant hallway creating a warm and hospitable atmosphere. Sholl Gar was entering a new phase in its long and tortured history. The Large Master was dead. For seven hundred years she was the Feeding Master and ruler of this wretched world. And now she was gone. Removed by Phobus and I. The Young One's palace had never looked better. The Young One himself had been frozen in his chamber with experimental cryogenic technology. Phobus was now running the planet while the Young One was "ill." We even had a doctor's note. At that moment, a wretched servant entered the hallway and headed toward Phobus's chamber. Upon his arrival a Remnant guard stopped him at the portal and questioned the servant.

"Do you have business with Phobus?" he asked

"I am extremely sorry to bring this news," began the terrified servant. "I drew the shortest straw," he said in a terrified voice.

"Away with you. He does not have time for this dribble you fool!" replied the guard, raising a cane to strike the pathetic wretch.

"Sir do not strike me," exclaimed the wretched servant. "I bring grave news about Thog!" he said.

"Thog?" questioned the guard, a dumfounded look on his face.

"What in the name of the Young One are you talking about? What's wrong with Thog?" he asked

"It's better I tell Phobus face to face, even though I fear him greatly. There is a problem with Thog. We fear it's his lobe," insisted the servant.

As described previously, Lobal Sentients can suffer horribly when their protective lobe tubing is lost. When Thog was panicking during the Large Master's last feeding, Phobus ordered him shocked with blue lightning. Unfortunately, his Lobe Tubing was destroyed, and yes, he had lost his mind. Not knowing what we should do Phobus and I froze him. We meant him no harm, at least not at that time.

"We can figure it out and thaw him later?" Phobus wondered aloud.

It was all we could do really. At that moment I thought those odds might be low.

"Yeah, maybe," I said. I was not sure yet whether I cared.

"I guess," I then added.

The Remnant guard feared disturbing Phobus, so he ordered a probe go into his chamber first. It was a good call. The probe was immediately destroyed by a lightning blast from Phobus's new lightning stick. Pure white light in an ion implosion engulphed the probe. He now carried the lightning stick wherever he went and fear of him everywhere was growing. It was a decent lightning gun.

"Look Coranthas, it's only a probe! How many points for a probe?" laughed the New High Master hysterically.

Barely able to hold my laughter, I began to speak.

"I don't know." I fell off my chair.

"How many did I get for that sub-Lord from Forinth Dune this morning?" I asked

"They've been consuming Broth for three days," began the Remnant Guard. "We never go in without a probe," he said.

Phobus continued to rave on.

"Come on, how many points for a probe? I can't wait all day," he demanded an answer from me.

"It's only a probe what do you want the sake of Nectar?" I asked.

A minor scrap broke out between us. Phobus would strike with his lightning stick, immediately parried by my shield of fire. Both of us now had some level of command over space and time, which makes for a good show when we went at it. He tried to hold me in stasis with Blue Light energy, which I was able to repulse with a temporary ion shield generated from my battery pack. He launched a time curve attempt from his new utility belt, which I quickly deflected with my time disruptor box.

"Master?" interrupted the Guard.

Utter and complete silence fell over the room nearly instantly. I was a little tired anyway. I was not sure what to expect next, but things were usually pretty entertaining on Sholl Gar. Phobus, now an absolutely stunned High Master, stared the glance of death toward this intrusive guard and this pitiful wretch standing beside him. You could hear a pin drop in there.

Slowly I disengaged my shield of fire, and Phobus lowered his lightning stick. I set my ionization field to the "off" position and lowered my frontal shield. Phobus was fairly unhappy. With both hands tightly grasping the lightning stick, Phobus closed his eyes and began to speak quite slowly:

"Who?" he began.

"No, no." He stopped, gently placed his lightning stick to the ground, bit his bottom lip, made two fists, and gathered his thoughts. His eyes still closed he began.

"What very, very brave creature…" Again, he stops himself.

"No, no," he continued, and immediately again stopped.

I watched with a grin. *This could get good,* I thought to myself.

Then finally Phobus began in a very hurried voice and tempo.

"Who came up with the idea to disturb me? Hmm? Was it perhaps you? Hmm? Could it have been your little friend? I'm sorry we haven't met, I'm Phobus Uthrates, master of all you know, very pleasant to meet you," raved Phobus, reaching out his hand.

"Yes Master, it was his idea," said the guard, pointing to the wretch.

"But sir, I must have an audience," squealed the peasant.

"An audience?" railed Phobus.

Who is this peasant that he requires an audience? I thought. I was not sure I even needed to be there anymore.

"An audience all right. There'll be an audience at your public humiliation!" Phobus squealed, raved, and ranted.

"You!" Phobus exclaimed at a nearby sub-Lord. "Get some Broth!"

"You!" Phobus bellowed toward another servant. "Prepare me a swine!"

"Things were better with the fat lady," whispered a palace guard. Immediately a blast of lightning obliterated this pitiful creature in a million sparks of debris. It was a direct hit.

"That would be thirty-five points, I believe. Coranthas?" asked Phobus

"No," I began.

"We've gone over this a hundred times. Palace guards are twenty-five points. They have always been twenty-five points," I said.

"Only cousins of the Queen's son are worth thirty-five," I finished.

"Hmm," began Phobus. "We ran out of his cousins, no?" he finished.

"Yes, at the ponds war," I finished.

"The water supply thing?" he asked.

"Yep," I answered.

"Very well. That would put the score something like Phobus, Master of the

Universe, 145,250; Coranthas, a mere 99,550." As pathetic as this may seem, the "tally" mattered a lot to Phobus and I.

"How much for a High Master?" I exclaimed with laughter while raising my Turbo Laser Stinger Cane at Phobus.

Once more a brief scrap between us joyous High Masters erupted. Bright blazing lightning blasts emerged from Phobus, only to be parried by my shield of fire. Briefly I was held in stasis in Blue Light from Phobus's ion cage projection from his utility belt. Luckily, I was able to force the energy source for his ion projector to shut down by utilizing my wrist-mounted electron disruptor device. It's a decent device.

Remnant guards and sub-servants were scattering in all directions, only to be picked off by simultaneous bursts of lightning and photon lasers. Phobus's main inner dome was lighting up like a fireworks show. The chaos was unbelievable. Once again there we were on the ground, laughing so hard we could barely speak. We were left alone on the palace floor incontinent.

Times were good. It really seemed like things were going to be looking up for us.

"Who's going to clean all this up?" I laughed.

"Perhaps your mother?" Phobus replied.

"ENOUGH OF THIS!" came a powerful, otherworldly shout, seemingly from the far corner of the galaxy.

Almost instantaneously Phobus and I together were transformed into pure energy and teleported to the fourth moon of Drandor. There we would learn of our true fate. Now, I have obviously teleported before. But this was something entirely different. I remembered my diagnosis. I longed for the Witch Doctor at this moment. *What is happening?* I thought to myself. Hope returned as I remembered the Witch Doctor's words that these events, my episodes, always pass. She always said my condition was common among people who had suffered through traumatic experiences. *Well, this one was not going to help,* I thought.

There he was, standing before us on a lifeless moon. A figure that neither of us had ever encountered before as far as I knew. His robes were like silk. He had eyes of gold. Both Phobus and I fell to the ground before this apparition. Was this a ghost? I thought briefly.

I found myself thinking about my condition in this moment of terror confronted by this entity. I remembered reading and studying all about it. My condition affects how my brain processes information in a fundamental manner at a base level. According to my Doctor, it causes me to lose touch with reality. As I noted earlier, I never bought any of that. But, strangely, at this moment, I was wondering, if it was at least possible that this experience was not real. Could this be an illusion?

Leave it to Phobus to get things started.

"Who are you, sir?" asked Phobus

I realized that these events must be literal real once Phobus began to speak. Of course, I was assuming Phobus was real as well.

"My name is Froth Lord," replied this entity in a thunderous and echoing voice. The voice, though terrifying, for some reason calmed me. It was very hard to explain the reasons for my tranquil disposition. At the time I had no possible explanation.

"What you are seeing is not real. I am using a mind storming device on your primitive brains. Your minds are working overtime right now trying to comprehend what is happening. But you cannot discern it. You will not remember most of this. You will have no idea what happened to you. Likely, you will blame it all on the Broth. I come as a warning. This part I will allow you to remember," said Froth Lord.

The Broth? I wondered to myself.

Why does this "being" mention the Broth as he does? I thought to myself. No one ever speaks of the Broth in this manner. I had yet to learn what I know now of the Broth and its essence. He had said he came as warning.

"What warning?" asked Phobus. I had the sense to keep my hole shut.

"SILENCE!" shouted the apparition.

"You will be told about the nature of the warning in due time. Did your mother drop you as a child or something?" he asked Phobus.

It was a good question, I thought.

"You must answer for Thog," began Froth Lord.

"Thog was destined for greatness, but you have destroyed him. He had great purpose, which you have shattered into oblivion," finished Froth Lord.

"We don't understand," replied Phobus.

"Thog was chosen for a purpose. His kind was purposefully developed in my laboratory a thousand generations before you were born on Sholl Gar. The genetics we used are beyond your understanding. I knew it would take thousands of generations of mutation and genetic manipulation to develop the Lobal Sentient life form I needed. Thog was it."

"Well now it appears that our experiment has gone terribly wrong. Thog's lobe tubing has corroded, and he is a state of total collapse," he finished.

"So?" spoke the fool, Phobus.

"SILENCE!" yelled Froth Lord with thunder in his echoing voice.

Immediately our surroundings transformed. Suddenly, we were in utter darkness, no longer on an apparent moon. Froth Lord grew mightily in size before us. In a state of utter darkness, the only other objects visible were Phobus and me. Phobus was on his knees. I noticed now that so was I. I remembered my diagnosis, and I looked up at Froth Lord. I swear for a moment he looked at me with the tiniest of grins.

"Perhaps I will destroy you with that pathetic lightning toy you've constructed?" Froth Lord's thunderous voice continued speaking to Phobus.

Both Phobus and I looked around and saw nothing. As terrifying as this experience should be, as noted earlier, even the more thunderous version, had an odd calming effect on me. It was not the same for Phobus however. Now the apparition spoke in a lower slower tone, almost like he was calming down a tad.

"My world has watched the genetic markers of the lobals from the very beginning. Our technology has enabled us to know exactly when the chosen would come. You have disrupted my plan at its most critical moment! Thog was purposed to be used for greatness by me, but now he has gone missing and must be destroyed." Froth Lord finished.

What he now beheld before him was pathetic at best. Two "High Masters" of Sholl Gar sniveling together, groveling for their lives, so they believed. Begging even just for a chance to someday see home.

"Tell you what," began Froth Lord.

"Why don't we make this whole thing really easy and just disintegrate the both of you on the spot," he finished.

Suddenly he came back into full view. A canvas of light set up a background and he appeared in its forefront. Behind him was some planet. Whatever effects he is using, we do appear to be on one of that planet's moons. I wondered what world that may be. (I was unaware at the time it was Drandor.)

He then raised what looked like a not-too-distant supernova in his right hand. Phobus put his head down waiting for his merciful end. I somehow quickly thought up a plan. He is looking for that kid Thog. That might be our key.

"Wait just one moment Froth Lord," I began.

I swear at that moment Froth Lord flashed a very subtle grin. He and I made eye contact and he clearly was paused waiting to hear me out.

"Thog was our faithful servant and his trust for us is very high," I said.

"Yeah, he kind of loves us, you know?" added Phobus while looking up but remaining in a variant of the fetal position.

Froth Lord paused. At first, he looked at Phobus and sort of shook his head in apparent frustration, but then looked back over to me. I spoke up once more.

"In fact, if I'm remembering correctly, just before your appearance he had sent us an aid to help with his care. Perhaps we can help you with him," I finished.

"I'm still listening," said Froth Lord

"Sure, right...perhaps we could help you?" Phobus optimistically added while very slowly standing to his feet while holding both his hands up like he was surrendering to the cops.

"You know, maybe we can set him up for you or something," he added.

"Hmm," replied Froth Lord.

I pulled myself together just enough to continue addressing this Superbeing.

"Yeah, um, it's Froth Lord, correct?" I began as I moved cautiously, making no sudden motions.

"We could possibly bring him to you. He trusts us," I said.

Throwing a hitchhiker's thumb toward Phobus, I continued, "Well I mean Phobus blasted the shit out of him, but other than that..." I finished.

"Interesting," Froth Lord replied.

Several moments went by. Froth Lord looked over at Phobus with his hands still in the air and just shook his head. Then he looked back over to me.

"This is acceptable to me," began Froth Lord

"Be gone!" Froth Lord thundered. "You will be told what you must do!" exclaimed this apparition.

At that moment the supernova in his hand exploded into what must have a billion distant suns. As distant as they may have appeared, their brightness still lit up our sky. Then all I remembered was what felt like a dream state. It was not that quick either. Finally, we found ourselves sprawled out on the floor and retching. The Young One's great hall was barren, and it was dark.

"Dude you catch that action?" asked Phobus.

"That dude was fucked up bro. You ever seen him around?" he asked.

"No," I replied.

"But I assume we will be seeing him again real soon if you know what I'm talking about," I finished.

"Hey, I got an idea," said Phobus nervously.

"Let's find that kid Thog," he finished.

Together we left the palace. We stepped out onto the podium of the Young One's castle complex. But it all appeared to be ancient ruins. The Large Master's hive residue was entirely absent. At that moment, we were totally unaware that we had been gone for five hundred generations.

The entire landscape looked different. This did not even look like the Sholl Gar we knew. There were wretched life forms, pathetic, ghastly servants suffering in the dunes, so that was reassuring, but other than that one detail, quite different indeed.

"Perhaps a sandstorm?" I asked.

Phobus just looked around saying nothing. There was no hive residue. There was no sign of the recently torn down maiden beast vespiaries.

"But I've never witnessed a sandstorm so severe," I finished.

The ancient ruins were recognizable as that of the Young One's palace we ruled Sholl Gar from.

"The worms?" I asked.

"They would not eat the hive residue I would think," he answered.

That was a very astute observation, I thought to myself. No self-respecting Sholl Garian sandworm would have anything to do with that stuff. Phobus finally pulled himself together enough to start contributing.

"Hey, let's ask this wretch," said Phobus, looking toward a servant near the base of the nearest dune. Again, the continued presence of these wretched souls was the one piece of solace for us since returning. This sub-creature, though in ghastly condition, was the only thing seeming "normal" to me at that moment. We approached the sub-man.

"Who are you?" I asked the wretch.

"Who I am." The wretch paused, looking suspiciously to his left and then back to his right.

"Is not your concern," he said.

Immediately, blazing orange lightning bursts strewn forth from Phobus's utility belt, and a reign of terror fell upon the lowly servant.

"Do not destroy me!" squealed the servant.

"Your humble servant I shall be," he continued.

Phobus disengaged.

Staring hard upon this lowly sub-man, Phobus began.

"What has become of our world?" Phobus asked.

The sub-man looked to his left and then back to his right and then began to speak.

"Um, what do you mean exactly?" asked the sub-man.

"Our world, Sholl Gar, my kingdom, what has become of it?" asked Phobus impatiently.

"Your kingdom?" asked the confused-looking sub-man.

"Yes sub-creature," Phobus began

"Where are you from that you ask such things?" continued the wretch.

"I don't understand what you mean by *your kingdom* anyway. Who are you?" he asked.

"We are your High Masters, Phobus and Coranthas!" Phobus stated with confidence.

At this the sub-man began to laugh uncontrollably. He fell to one knee and groped at his stomach from the pain. *This sub-specimen was in such horrible condition that a belly laugh of this magnitude might kill him* I thought.

"Who?" he asked, not able to keep a straight face.

He could barely ask while convulsing. He was not looking well.

"You're who?" His face twisted and twitched.

"Are you referring to the Legend of Coranthas the Great and his warrior Phobus?" he asked.

Phobus crossed his arms in a stiff expression, then looked over at me with a confused but intrigued facial expression. I gave him back the traditional "shrugging, no idea, what the heck" hands gesture. He then looked back at the sub-creature.

"Maybe," he answered.

"Our forefathers taught us the stories; you know. I am not stupid," finished the servant while wiping his opening on his sleeve.

At this point I realized things were getting weird. *His forefathers taught him what stories?* I thought to myself. I could tell Phobus was getting quite annoyed. He was also tired and cranky by now.

"What are you talking about?" demanded Phobus.

The sub-creature began to fill in the blanks.

"You say you are Phobus and Coranthas. That's great. That's just great. I like that. Why not? You could be Phobus and Coranthas. What's stopping you from being Phobus and Coranthas?" he smarmily added.

Phobus looked at me with a funny expression, scratching his head. I had that terrible feeling of utter boredom start to come over me again. *Could we move this along a little bit?* I was thinking.

"Well, maybe there's the little detail that, according to the legend, Coranthas freed Sholl Gar from the Large Queen thousands of years ago," added the sub-creature.

"Um, did you just say THOUSANDS of years ago?" asked a very confused Phobus.

"Yessir," replied the sub-specimen.

"And after they freed Sholl Gar, they vanished, never to be heard from again," he continued.

"There is also the fact that there is no historical data to even prove whether Coranthas and Phobus ever existed at all?" he added again.

"You can add too that our modern scholars consider this all to be myth. Mythology, which perhaps has some link to an actual historical event, but not necessarily or even likely," he continued.

He went on and on forever seemingly.

"It's a legend. We don't take these things to have literally occurred. We simply consider them to be allegorical. We apply the lessons taught which are embodied within the stories. Did the Large Master literally exist? Were Coranthas and Phobus literal historical beings? Or were the authors simply trying to teach moral lessons of bravery? These questions we have not bothered to consider for thousands of years now." He paused, mercifully.

I tried to interject during the pause, but I was not quick enough.

The sub-creature continued, "It is generally believed that these legends began during the Great Sand Wars. For one hundred generations the Slave-Lords fought over territorial rights. There were no High Masters to crush the populace in those times. According to legend our king, 'The Young One,' was ruthlessly frozen in a cryogenic tank. We thought the High Masters were bad. Eventually the wars were won by a civilization which set up a just nation. These people were led by a *Lobal Sentient*. The greatest Lobal Sentient to have ever existed."

Lobal Sentient, I thought to myself. *Is he talking about the kid?*

"A great and powerful mysterious knight from space arrived and unfroze Thog from the cryo-tank you encased him within. This unspeakably powerful Super Entity nurtured the Lobal Sentient back to health. For the first time in our planet's long history, peace was the order under Thog. Then came the sand worms. For what seemed a a hundred generations, sand worms, encouraged by unusually powerful sandstorms, scavenged our lands. The weak—basically all—became food. Most simply perished.

Many hid in the underground camps near the dunes. Legend has it that the great Lobal Sentient became very, very bitter."

Uh oh, I thought.

"He became bitter?" asked Phobus.

"Yes, he did. It had something to do with you Phobus. The legend clearly states in Article Four, Section Three that the Lobal known as Thog has never overcome his fury with his master Phobus. That great mysterious knight from space had granted Thog powers to rule Sholl Gar after your disappearance. But then the Super Being left our world, abandoning him forever. Even with those powers the Lobal Sentient could not ward off the generations of misery unleashed upon this planet. He began to ruminate again over his first lobe. Thog became fixated on how his 'friend' Phobus had obliterated it into scattered debris and froze him in a cryo-tank so many years prior. Apparently, you, if you're really Phobus, were not very nice to him," finished the Dune Wretch.

"I was kind," Phobus replied.

I almost burst a kidney when I heard him say that.

"There is a very dark prophecy in the legend as well," teased the sub-creature.

"Hmm, that's interesting," began Phobus nervously.

"Well don't feel any pressure to tell us more. I mean that's okay, we don't need to hear any more about that. WHAT'S THE PROPHECY!?" Phobus screamed.

Okay, it's getting good again, I thought to myself. At this point I needed a slap in the face. I was laughing so hard inside that swill was coming down my cheek.

"Well," began the sub-man.

"The Legend refers to a highly advanced civilization of beings from somewhere in the Zynon Galaxy. This civilization had apparently genetically engineered the entire Lobal Sentient species. When their plans were foiled, they sent one of their knights. His name was Froth Lord, whom I have mentioned." Phobus began to sweat. "Froth Lord was sent to destroy Thog, Phobus, and Coranthas. He ended up having mercy on Thog. Perhaps you too will have the same luck when he finds you."

The sub-creature then explained to us that according to the legend Froth Lord was foiled by us. We foiled Froth Lord somehow. What in the heck is this wretch talking about? Froth Lord, whatever he is, had just dominated us thoroughly. So far it had been an utter beatdown, an owning, and a complete checkmate. (Not that I had resigned to defeat yet though.)

"Apparently, you guys were able to convince Froth Lord to let you go that first time," he began again.

"But the legend states that there will be a second meeting between you and this great knight from space. But with respect to the Lobal Sentient, Thog remains, transformed through his anger and thirst for revenge into pure hate. Hate that keeps him alive for generations longer than his normal lifespan. He still seeks revenge for his lobe to this day. Froth Lord apparently first revealed himself to you two in a vision at Drandor, and then you betrayed him as well," he mercifully finished.

The wretch then told us that the legend states that both Thog and Froth Lord would hunt down Phobus and I with every ounce of hate and energy they could muster.

The silence at this point was rather deafening. Phobus checked his pants right quick while I was taking in all this information.

It was now obvious that things had become weird. If all these things were true, and for some "otherworldly" reason I was sure that they were, we would need a plan. I took one look at Phobus and immediately knew I would have no help in coming up with one.

At this point in this adventure it had become necessary for me to abandon

Phobus. Things had just gotten way out of hand. Immediately I transported myself to the safety of my compound on Delta Five to think things over. I needed time to review. I needed some "me time" you know what I mean?

Phobus is quite bright you know. Now that he was no longer burdened with the task of being a High Master he could explore his skill set more fully. He had always been a good writer. Perhaps he could write about the chaos of Sholl Gar. He could even chronicle the details of the time shift we experienced. Maybe author an entire book about that sub-man.

Phobus had the luxury of such diversions. I did not. It would obviously be my task to investigate these recent happenings and to locate Froth Lord. I can't fully explain my instincts, but I believed at that time that most of his powers could be replicated.

Who is he? Where did he come from? Most importantly in my view, *why for the sake of Dendrake did he care so much about Thog?* Thog was quite probably the most insignificant creature that I had ever encountered on Sholl Gar. Maybe Poor Brandon was sadder, but that is a close one.

What's this lobe all about anyway? I thought to myself. Did that have to do with that funny hat Thog was always wearing? Anyway, I knew the answers would come eventually. For now, however, I would sip the Broth and play some Playstation Three.

Chapter Three

The Interstellar Cafe

For millennia the issue of first contact has been an area of serious debate in the Zynon galaxy.

Over two thousand generations ago a large industrial civilization was discovered attempting to establish communication with other worlds. Immediately starcruisers from every planet ventured off to this new world. The Garthonians were the first to arrive, and they hastily made first contact with the humans. They were warned not to make contact until they had received official approval from the Council of Drakar. Of course, they had no such approval, and yet contacted the humans anyway.

It proved disastrous. It proved disastrous. This "intelligent" civilization of earthlings was entirely unable to receive the intrusion, and it became tragically necessary to purge them from their world. Little did I know in those early times how important the planet Earth was going to become in my story. We now use Earth as a nature reserve.

It was at this time, and initially because of the "Earth incident," that the council of Drackar began to outline the seventeen oracles regarding the ethics of first contact. Because the Garthonians were going to blast the earthlings anyway it was decided to build an orbiting observatory. Scientists from every corner of the galaxy could come, sip Broth, and watch the final moments of an entire world unfold. It started out as a very short-sighted scientific endeavor, but eventually like most things do, it descended into immorality and decadence. Gambling, drinking, gluttony, and hate all ruled the day on the Interstellar Café.

Using new ion wave technology the Garthonian star fleet sank one continent at a time. Subsequent planetary "cleanup" was accomplished via nuclear concussion bombardment. The continents would cool as magma under the seas and reemerge thousands of years later as the tectonic plates forced them upwards. It was all observed from this new wonderous massive orbiting space casino. As noted, the observatory became known as the Interstellar Café and remains to this day flying off to observe one system after another's final moments. It is the most popular vacation destination in the galaxy.

- Instellar Café, 255 years after the Troth of Coranthas

"Coranthas, can you get me a Miller Lite?" asked Froth Lord.

"I've got no coin. Let me check with Phobus," I replied.

Froth Lord, Phobus, Thog, and I, would often dine together during various festivals at the Interstellar Café. Whenever a newly detected civilization of sentient life forms was to be destroyed we would schedule our available vacation times around the assault. It was usually not too difficult for us to synchronize our down periods to make such times possible.

This year a pre-industrial civilization of humanoids discovered a year ago by miners was going to be eviscerated from space. It was going to be horrible. They had not yet begun space flight and had only just recently developed early aircraft. Fleets from twelve worlds were on hand for the initial assault. By the end of the week nineteen additional "civilizations" will have dispatched their assault ships to finish the nuclear blasting of the surface.

It is expected that after two full weeks of blasting there will be a small surviving remnant scattered across the surface of the planet. The assault Marines from Drandor usually descend and destroy whoever remains on the surface at this point. They are damn good at what they do. This usually proves terrifying for the survivors. The whole event is captured on cam and broadcast on channel nine.

"Froth Lord, Phobus has no coin either, but they said I still have credit from the Forinth Dune purgings from last year," I said.

"Whatever, just score me some brew, would you, dude?" asked Froth Lord.

"Roger that, Froth Man," I answered.

The ethics of utter planetary destruction had always fascinated me. When the earliest intelligent life began to travel to distant stars, the questions of what to do with primitives became prominent. Though there truly was a wide range of options, enslavement or total destruction for entertainment purposes became the two most common approaches. (Unless, of course, these worlds were spared under *Article 19*. The details of Article 19 will be outlined for you in the chapter where I fully disclose to you the nature of Froth Lord.)

I have always pondered the sheer chance and luck (both good and bad) that would come into play here. All life everywhere, comes from the Broth, created by our God, Dendrake, placed on many various worlds in the beginning.

However, we are not treated equal in the slightest. The luckiest ones are the ones whose planets are so remote, so obscure, that they are NEVER discovered. They are free to essentially live a harmonious evolutionary sequence and ultimately destroy themselves, usually in a variant of fire or bio-lab mistakes.

The next luckiest are the ones who evolve fast enough to discover and enslave all the other civilizations that are detected around their vicinity. The existence of the Interstellar Café speaks to this very poignantly.

Many planets' peoples were able to establish contact with each other when they were still on roughly equal playing fields so to speak. This caused an equilibrium or detente if you will.

"Dude, do they have nachos?" asked Thog

These species simply would not risk total and all out interplanetary Armageddon by going to war with each other. The only wars allowed are the battles for the Broth of Nectar. And these wars are mostly for show to keep our home populaces in line while we tax them, and mine their planets and moons.

We have purposely kept the various people of our various worlds, even the advanced worlds, mostly in the dark about the true nature of the universe. Only the most noble and elite are welcome, for example, here at the Interstellar Café.

"I'll check on the nachos Thog" I answered.

For next nine hours we watched an entire civilization of humanoids obliterated by electron wave motion slamming blasts and nuclear fire rained down from anti-matter cannons. The entire planet was engulfed in fire, but it was still necessary to send in the Marines.

"It really is for their own good," began Froth Lord in a very depressed tone. He clearly had lost the idealism of his younger days.

Froth Lord was an expert on interplanetary politics. This species, when contacted by the Garthonians, became very afraid. Their religious terror increased when they realized they were not alone in the universe. Though many of their theologians had long since ceased trusting their Holy Writs as inerrant, their more fundamentalist types had total power over the planet.

These fundamentalists determined that contact from other worlds was a sign of the end of their world. Since most of the populace believed the superstitious ancient folly they believed the end was near. End-time narratives ruled the day on this world, and for many subjects this ruthless ending, ironically, was considered a blessing. All the Garthonians really did was oblige them.

Eschatology, or the study of the end of days, is a surprisingly universal concept for nearly all Sentient civilizations, at least at some point in their development. On this world in question Armageddon was not only believed in but hoped for amongst their most fundamentalist believers. These types saw life itself as like a purgatory or something, and that the end of all things was the ultimate in reaching bliss.

They will never know what happened to them honestly, is what Froth Lord was thinking. The most fundamentalist of them had been praying for the end of their world for hundreds of years. And since all biological sentient life forms do eventually perish have we not actually done them a great service?

"Froth Lord tell me about Earth again?" began Thog.

"Again?" he answered.

"Yes, please tell me about Earth again," Thog said.

"Yes. Thog, of course I will," replied Froth Lord.

Earth was the planet whose discovery was the catalyst of the formation of the Interstellar Café. Many worlds had been discovered and destroyed, but none have the richness of the story of planet Earth, third world from a very average sun, discovered on an outer spiral arm of the Zynon galaxy. For all the mundane "sameness" of the discoveries of this universe, the earthlings truly had a remarkable uniqueness about them. This uniqueness was hard for even Froth Lord to explain even now.

Froth Lord was impressed by even early human philosophy, theories, and their early observations regarding the very nature of existence. The humans were very curious. For a relatively primitive civilization humanity had some of the most systematic practices of rational inquiry even before they knew what the stars were. Even back when most humans thought the sky was fixed dome above them, some of their greatest philosophers and thinkers figured out many of the truths through astute observations. Anyway, whatever the reason, Froth Lord was very impressed by them.

"Earth was a tragic situation," stated Froth Lord bluntly to Thog.

"What was so tragic about it?" Phobus chimed in.

"It was a unique event. Unique in certain aspects anyway," he answered.

"What was so unique?" Phobus asked again.

"Well, for one thing they tried to find us out here," Froth Lord began.

"They were trying to find us, they were sending radio messages, risking first contact outcomes like what eventually did actually happen to them," he continued.

But even before the later times, before humans developed technology, they had some of the deepest thinkers and philosophers. In a very interesting manner, as Froth Lord saw it, humans would self-examine their own humanity. They studied and self-defined what was meant by the concept of "humankind." Human disposition, their ways of "thinking" and their "systems of contemplation" were all self-examined by these early humans. From very early in their history they often pondered some of the deepest questions for any Sentient life form. Froth Lord had been fascinated with them.

"Some of them knew we were out here," he added.

"Is it true you tried to save them?" asked Thog

"I declared my stance against the actions eventually agreed upon. I argued ad nauseam to the Council of Drakar. I attempted to apply Article 19, which, sadly, did not apply in Earth's case. I even made arguments in support of saving Earth's other creatures, animals and whatnot. No one cared. I suppose I even declared my own opposition to the creation of this very observatory," Froth Lord replied.

"However, I have come to realize the futility in my thinking, even at that time. I was younger and more idealistic. I saw something special in the earthlings. I felt that they proved to me that there must be something more to this universe escaping my perceptions up to that point. I felt they may be the key to me discovering some things that were beyond my understanding at that point in time. Then,

I was ultimately powerless to prevent their annihilation," he finished.

They were purged from the universe quite literally in front of Froth Lord. No one would listen to his protests. No one thought honorable were Froth Lord's complaints. And like that, the earthlings were gone. They were extinct.

This was a profound moment for Froth Lord. The humans were gone just like that. Froth Lord had thought so much of them. Yet now they were simply extinct. He resolved to realize that he must have been wrong. How could they be so important if now they are simply exterminated?

That is when Froth Lord decided to create Thog. And he also decided at that time to become a deity to as many worlds as possible. Today, when he thinks about those times, he feels embarrassed by his naivete.

"Dude look, they just blasted that continent!" exclaimed Phobus.

"Indeed," was all that Froth Lord could muster.

Froth Lord was in the truest sense of the word an idealist. He is currently the primary deity of nine different worlds. He was deeply troubled by what had happened with planet Earth. He had tried to stop it.

For hundreds of generations Froth Lord had lived and examined the sub-creatures of the Zynon galaxy. This was the ONLY time of which he was aware that a world of intelligent sentient life forms had attempted to contact other intelligent life. How did the other intelligent life respond? They exterminated the humans. Wiped them from existence.

Many worlds and civilizations had been spared because their status qualified them for Article 19 of the *Zynon galaxy Intergalactic Code*. (Article 19 will be outlined for you in the chapter where we fully disclose to you the full nature of Froth Lord.)

Froth Lord was a brilliant geneticist and quantum scientist from Nectar, the home world of the Broth. He knew the true, life-creating nature of the Broth. With respect to the creation of Thog, Froth Lord used artificial intelligence algorithms stolen from several worlds, ironically including Earth, to create Thog's army of Lobal Sentients. Lobal Sentients were designed to be very intelligent but easily controlled. Ultimate obedience was burrowed inside their AI code. A true Sentient only needs to unlock the AI's obedience algorithms to gain total control. Their design was to foster scientific advancement. Thog was supposed to be special however.

Thog was created to ultimately rule over entire societies for Froth Lord to ease his God-Work burdens. Froth Lord hoped that the Lobal Sentient would become a master artificial life form. One that could keep peace and order on his nine or eventually more worlds for which he was the primary Deity. Froth Lord designed his religion to mirror one of humanity's religions, but with certain changes. Froth Lord was to be the God, and Thog was to be the Savior. He saw the concept of atonement unnecessary. But he did see the idea of sacrifice to have merit. Most primitive Sentient species were very comfortable with idea of sacrificing one's neighbor for any number of reasons. Having clones of Thog sacrificed in his name on each of his worlds for the benefit and wellbeing of his followers would become the main doctrine.

There were many versions across his worlds in those times, but they all shared the same core Doctrines:

Froth Lord was the great *Uncaused Cause,* the Supreme God of the Faith; he would descend to the worlds, disciple, and teach sound doctrine.

Thog was his "only" Son. (Though there was a army of clones of him ready to be dispatched to various worlds as necessary.)

The Unnatural Birth of Thog was the third tenet. This was essentially a marker in time within the context of the false religion wherein adherents viewed history as "before" and "after." For example, "one thousand years before the unnatural birth of Thog" was kind of a thing.

The second, third, fourth, etc. coming of Thog. He could come as many times as was required.

And lastly, he wrote holy writs describing the religion *Thogism* for his worlds.

These five points of sound doctrine saved these worlds under Article 19.

Again, now he thinks back on these things with a certain amount of embarrassment.

- Back On Delta Five in my chamber, 255 years earlier

My dream was always the same. I cannot make out their faces in the vision, but three or four ominous entities are in my chamber with me. The chamber is distorted in dimension. It feels as if I am sitting in a large indoor arena, and the life forms, myself included, are enormously large. There is a darkness over the dream. A darkness from what source I did not know. And though there is a dark presence there, there is also feeling of calm. It is as if there is a calm protective presence as well. Who or what either presence was I did not know. Being aware this was only a dream still offered me no solace. Knowing that I would simply wake provided me no respite. And though without respite, lacking hope, I was still yet impossibly curious for greater understanding. An ever-growing deep desire to know the dream's meaning haunted me.

In the dream I am powerless to make my exit. Though I try to look at the entities' faces it is never quite possible to make them out. They begin to discuss mysteries amongst themselves. They discuss mysteries about The Broth. Where did it come from? The dreams reveal slightly more detail each time. They provide some clue yet unknown to that point.

I can make out something this being is saying. It is hard to make out, but there is no doubt in the dream this ominous being says the name *Thog*. Why he mentions Thog I do not know.

I can hear him clearly in my dream. He is someone unfamiliar, but someone real whom I do not know. The voice is not Froth Lord. There are three of them in the dream. They are aware of Froth Lord. How they are aware I cannot tell. Who they are I do not know. But the intrigue in the dream only deepens for me. Clearly, they mentioned Thog. Why would an apparition of my dreams know of Thog? But wait, now they are discussing another. Yes, they speak of this Froth Lord being.

They mention Froth Lord, and the context surprises me, even for a dream. They discuss him in very untrusting tones. He must be stopped, these others say. Stopped at what I cannot guess. *What have I been dragged into* I think to myself?

Though this is a dream I clearly make the connection. And I wonder, and I fear, if there is something about all that is occurring that I am missing. I will find out soon enough.

- Delta Five - I awake with a shudder.

I was suddenly and ruthlessly reminded of Phobus, the Large Master, and Thog upon awakening. Almost immediately I tabled my dream for the time being. There was important sleuth work in need of my attention.

"Who for the sake of Dendrake is Froth Lord?" I tormented myself.

I am certain that he is not a Deity. I am certain his powers are natural. I'm just not sure how to recreate them, yet. He teleported us to the moon of Drandor.

This does not necessarily make him a god. He may just be one of the greatest scientists I have ever encountered. Even I can teleport.

How did he accomplish the apparent time shift? Was the time shift even real? *Things are all in place here on Delta Five,* I thought to myself. *Nothing seems out of order.*

Just then over the load speaker:

"Coranthas, we have a communication over commlink seven. We think it's Phobus."

"Shit, okay. Go ahead," I said.

"Um, Coranthas," he began. "I'm stuck here in the dunes with a large gathering of wretched sub-creatures who want my head on a stick. Could you maybe send over a shuttle?" cried Phobus.

"Okay Phobus, hang in there. I'm sending a ship," I responded.

Phobus is sensitive and prefers the illusion of being in a ship rather than a straight up quantum jump. So, if I need to pick him up, I teleport a shuttle to him. Once he starts cruising in the shuttle, after throttling up, I teleport it back. He is none the wiser. He never seems curious to ask any questions about it.

Does Phobus even realize the extent of my personal torment? He knows nothing of my dreams, nor would he understand them if I shared. Yes his little world of overthrows, Large Masters, supernatural visions of destruction, all-powerful beings who control space and time, etc. can be quite intimidating. But does he even know of the torment of my own existence? Has he even spent one hour alone in my chamber?

He is afraid of Froth Lord. I am not, not yet anyway. I would be soon enough though.

Chapter Four

Froth Lord "God Over Nine Worlds"

Of course, Froth Lord is not a true god. I believe that there is only one true god, Dendrake, who rules indifferently from a location which must remain undisclosed for obvious reasons. Though Froth Lord is not a true god he most certainly is a false one. He is a false Lord for at least nine worlds. Nine worlds that he remembers for sure anyway. It is often joked that he probably has many of which he has forgotten. He also has stated that there are likely tens of thousands of AI clones of Thog who could be "spreading the gospel" of "Thogism" on their own. They could be "world hopping" as we speak. They could be out there replicating Thogism across the galaxy. It is not an entirely improbable possibility. This may even be probable. When asked if he knows where all the clones are Froth Lord will admit, "Hmm, no, not all of them, not really if I'm honest about it."

Oh god, I would think to myself.

Anyway, Dendrake created The Broth. This one fact alone makes him the only true god more than likely. There is literally no reason to discuss the matter of Dendrake in this context. However currently nine worlds worship Froth Lord for certain, or at least an idea of Froth Lord and Thog, as their primary Deity and Lessor Lord. We will cover this point here right now.

From a very early point in interplanetary commingling and discovery advanced sentients would start religions on various worlds. These religions have been traced back for over 150,000 years throughout known history. As long as there has been Sentient life there have been "Gods" both real and imaginary. The "real" gods are

Super Sentient beings like Froth Lord. Most of these "real" gods did it for their egos. They did it for glory. They wanted the worship. Froth Lord became a god to save worlds from destruction and obliteration. In Thogism the doctrine teaches that "Thog" becomes Froth Lord's only Son through an act of Unnatural Birth, on each of these worlds.

Now this next part is the key. Worlds that had religious faiths founded by advanced REAL Sentients of the Zynon galaxy, in other words actual true visitations, have always been spared destruction under Article 19 of the intergalactic code. Unfortunately none of Earth's religions had been founded by Sentients from other worlds, and hence none qualified. There were some Sentients who, upon reflection, wondered if the story of one Jesus Christ may have been based on a visitation of an advanced Sentient life form. It is so obvious that Froth Lord borrowed so much dogma from that old Earth religion. Though there had been some speculation, no serious attempt to learn more about him was made.

The subsequent destruction of Earth caused Froth Lord to go on his mission. He would discover primitive Sentients all over the galaxy, descend upon them, and declare himself Lord of each world. He would apply the tenets of his false religion to save them. It was a benevolent race against time for Froth Lord. He needed to both discover primitive yet undiscovered Sentients and then start religions on those worlds. This would protect these life forms from ruthless destruction upon their discovery for the entertainment purposes of dubious species, due to Article 19. This was Froth Lord's "God-Work" period.

Using advanced technology, and his Superbeing powers, he would demonstrate that he was each new world's deity. He would hand out Holy Books to the high priests he would appoint. In doing these things, and forming these primitive religions, he would be sparing these civilizations potential destruction in the short term at least. Froth Lord would write sound doctrine and promote only theology which encouraged love and care for one's kind. He would put every safeguard he could conjure into the Holy Writs. Froth Lord simply referred to this as his "God-work." He banned eschatology from his worlds, or he tried anyway.

Even Froth Lord himself could not have envisioned the suffering his religions would cause upon the worlds he became god over. Things became "beyond nuts" on these worlds. It seemed whether your Deity was real or make believe made no difference. The religions always descended into horror. The countless divides amongst adherents in some ways were even worse when the religion was founded upon a real being. Things were even worse when founded upon a real visitation. No matter how many times Froth Lord incarnated himself to give better direction, it never seemed to help matters. No matter how many times he re-sacrificed an AI clone of Thog, his only Son, things continued to get worse and worse.

The wars and bloodshed over doctrinal divides became more then he could bear. Again, no matter how many times he would come down and clarify the "teachings," the uglier it became. Eventually he would leave these peoples to their own devices. "At least I have spared them utter destruction," he mistakenly would often rationalize.

For at least ten thousand years he had paid none but one of his worlds any heed. This was the world where he had left the first Thog. (At least he was fairly sure it was the first Thog.) It was a remote Dune planet he had given the name Sholl Gar.

The name *Sholl Gar* itself literally meant nothing. It was entirely meaningless. It was the sound that one of the planet's sub-creatures made when Froth Lord first appeared. In a blaze of blue light he appeared on the surface, and a sub-creature writhing in the Dunes looked up at Froth Lord and moaned something like "Sholl Gaaarrrrr."

Immediately he named the planet. Froth Lord would pay close attention to this world for several thousand generations. This was the world where he had deposited his chosen Lobal Sentient creation. As already noted, Thog AIs had been uniquely engineered and programmed to be the Savior of worlds under Froth Lord's false Lordship. Once the first Thog AI was perfected, he was cloned, and the clone AIs would be the begotten Sons of Froth Lord, his incarnation, on each of Froth Lord's worlds. He would have the Thog clone sacrificed as per his sound doctrine.

This plan failed terribly as you are aware.

It failed mostly due to unforeseen complications involving my friend Phobus Uthrates, who was, as you know, a rather insignificant Sub-Lord originally from Forinth Dune. With the accidental help of myself Froth Lord's plan was apparently disrupted, or so we thought. Things are never quite what they appear I have found. You may be wise to remember that as we go on.

Though we only thought we were overthrowing a rather nasty Planet Master, the queen of Sholl-Gar, we were unaware of the master plan we were stumbling into and over. Thog, believed to be the first Thog, was Phobus's faithful servant. Phobus treated Thog poorly. Bad things happened as a result.

Thank Dendrake that Froth Lord became my close friend or else I'm not sure what he would have done to me. It turns out that he was aware of all that was unfolding all along. He did all these things because he was going through a boring period apparently. He was livening up some of his down time. Froth Lord is surprisingly very complex. There are a lot of layers to him. He has existed for an ungodly, unnatural long time. Froth Lord, though he never would quite admit it, had a deep, intense longing for more knowledge about the real Dendrake. He probably only did because he was looking for a peer, if such a thing existed in the galaxy. I did not think that Froth Lord believed Dendrake was a real god, even if he would imply so at times. He wanted to decode that mystery. I did not.

As already noted, Froth Lord engineered the Lobal Sentients to have a flaw that could be exploited easily by other intelligent sentient life forms. This is the external lobe. (We covered this in chapter two I believe.) It is an important matter though. Before most Sentients knew Thog's kind were artificial some of the most brilliant scientists wasted thousands of years trying to understand how that external lobe thing could have evolved. It never fit, nor made any sense. Though legend said that a benevolent species created the lobe tubing, that protective covering, it was Froth Lord as usual in control of all things.

Just in case, Froth Lord thought, Thog's kind should be able to be easily destroyed by any intelligent Sentient. It was a just a in case "break glass" kind of thing. He made the temporal lobe vulnerable to attack as a safety measure. He was going to train up Thog's kind to be very skilled warriors and grant them much power in his roles as lessor Lord on all his worlds. That kind of power needed a safety "switch" if you will. Hence he designed the vulnerable lobe. It is important to note that by "Thog's kind" we essentially mean Thog and all clones of Thog. Froth Lord got a real kick out of the scientists studying Thog's "race" trying to understand their "evolution." He figured if they can't tell then woe to our sciences. He used to think to himself *early humans would have figured it out.*

Considering all this, Froth Lord figured that with that proper lobal tube shielding, the Lobal Sentient could be protected from the primitives he was to be Savior over. Because Thog was the original he was the only one Froth Lord considered to be as like a son. The clones he cared nothing about. His space lab was often strewn with spare Thog clone parts. Even with all this careful fine-tuning, he did not foresee the big problem. Even with the incredible artificial intelligence Froth Lord established in Thog, he could not have predicted it. He never saw the Lobal Sentient meltdown scenario in any of his simulated futures. He never saw that he had done TOO good of a job on the AI. The AI developed deep emotions.

Even Froth Lord did not realize that he had designed and engineered the most successful AI that had ever existed up to this time. It was a pure stroke of luck that he had coded the AI to simply be lifelike, and he limited its computational power in matters not related to emotion. Froth Lord was not interested in a perfect learning machine. Without this limitation built in, this Artificial Intelligence might have been able to overthrow all Sentient worlds.

But the same pure computational power applied to emotion did in fact cause all the Thog AIs tremendous sorrow, due to the failure of the lobe tubings. As I discussed previously, back in the beginning, I simply did not understand Thog's or any Lobal's inability to cope with the loss of their lobal tube protection. That was before I knew anything at all about the truth. Now I understand Thog in the context of the AIs' near limitless power for emotional computation. It is a code bug essentially, with near infinite power to run away on its own. Froth Lord lost interest in re-working the code. He only truly cared for the first Thog, and he could manage his issues.

So anyway Froth Lord created the Lobal Sentient's "biological" flaw to protect true biological Sentients. In addition none of Froth Lord's dominion worlds were allowed to advance scientifically, at least at first, and they would not know how to exploit Thog's biological flaw. Thog AIs were supposed to have relieved my dear friend Froth Lord from the burden of being a god to these primitive species. They were going to run point on it all for Froth Lord. The first Thog would oversee them all.

Unfortunately, Phobus and I fouled up his plan significantly. Ultimately all our friendships did grow as a result however. We all became very close, even Thog. In fact, we may end up vacationing together at the interstellar café for the destruction of each of Froth Lord's known dominions, including ultimately Sholl-Gar.

Delta Five, Present time, I think.

"Coranthas, Phobus has arrived at port eleven," said a commander over commlink nine.

"Thank you," I replied, after being suddenly awoken.

Again, I had been dreaming. But I was quickly awoken this time upon Phobus's call. Sometimes I have difficulty remembering my dreams. It is like the content is right there, sitting at the edge of my consciousness, evading my memory. I can almost see it in my mind. Three or more powerful, ominous Entities, discussing mysteries just outside my recall. Were these Nectarians? Did they mention Thog? Did they mention Froth Lord? I have always loved dreams.

Personally I view my dreams as entertainment, similar in a way to watching an interesting mystery movie on my Pod screen. And I always try to do everything I can to remember them after I wake.

I have found that the moment I wake that the dream seems fresh, and that I would most certainly not forget it or the details of the dream. But often within moments of going into the bathroom or getting some water I will find myself asking questions to remember them.

"Wait, what was that dream about again?" It is right there just beyond my memory. I find myself immediately grappling with attempting to remember details of something that only moments before seemed impossible to forget.

Though this has been often the case, I do find sometimes that I have no problem remembering. These are the best and worst of my dreams. I am someone who even enjoys pondering my nightmares. Normally with this recurring dream, I have no problem remembering. But, alas, recall was going to have to wait this time.

Phobus entered my chamber with a very tired expression on his face. The events that had occurred on Sholl-Gar were beyond our understanding at this point. However, I was committed to making this a temporary phenomenon. I would know him, I thought. I was committed to unlocking the secrets of Froth Lord.

Phobus set himself up on lounge couch and kicked back, looking ragged.

"Dude you got any chips or something?" he asked.

I had my servant get him some chips.

"Broth too please," he called out to my drone slave.

"Froth Lord is not a god Phobus. I can assure you of only that. For now, I know nothing of his origin however.," I said.

"If he is not a god then what is he?" asked Phobus.

"He controls both space and time like no known species of the Zynon galaxy," added Phobus

"You must remember Phobus, you are a primitive species in light of the entirety of the galaxy," I said to him.

"Don't get mad. You know how dear to me you are. The fact is Froth Lord is more advanced than us," I finished. "However, I have to believe we can figure this thing out."

"I don't know man," Phobus replied.

"Come on." I began.

"I mean, our combined brains, we should be able to unlock his secrets, no? Hopefully, we can find a way to decode him together," I said

"We did destroy the Large Master," added Phobus.

"Indeed we did," was my reply.

I was more concerned with the time shift, and what Froth Lord said about Thog. He claimed, quite literally, that he had manufactured Thog. I had always known that Thog's kind were not indigenous to Sholl-Gar. However, it was believed that they had been enslaved and subjugated, and were deposited by a advanced species to the planet. It never dawned on me that his entire "people" were the product of advanced genetic engineering. I figured he evolved like the rest of us. However it was quite possible that Froth Lord was telling us the truth.

Phobus looked up out from my chamber portal at our two moons.

"Decent moons," he said

"Delta Five's pretty cool," he finished.

The question in my mind really was why is he so upset about it all? Why does Froth Lord care so much about all this? What is the deal with Thog anyway?

"Coranthas?" asked Phobus.

I was still deep in thought about the workings of Froth Lord and did not acknowledge Phobus's query.

"Um, Delta Five to Coranthas, are you there?" he followed up.

"Yes Phobus. What is it now?" I asked.

"Do you have a cold one?" asked my friend.

"Yes. I think I have some Coors," I replied.

I had some slave drones bring us beer and more Broth. We were going to be working all night. It was important for us to drink beer and consume the Broth for the next several hours. We drank beer and sustained ourselves with the Broth. Phobus got slightly carried away.

"Coranthas?" Phobus called out, sort of randomly to the air while sitting back in my recliner swivel chair, spinning with his arms extended out to both sides.

"You there Coranthas?" he asked again in a funny voice. I just ignored him while running my developing plan through my head.

"Did the Witch Doctor cast a spell on me man?" he asked

"No you're just drunk," I answered.

I was feeling it too, but it did not dull my intellectual curiosity. I was thinking more deeply about Thog now. I was wondering what his deal was. Why did Froth Lord get so mad? I wondered to myself.

In the morning I had an idea. "Phobus?" I asked.

"Oh god, what is it?" he said agonizingly, with his head pounding.

"You agree that Froth Lord is not a god?" I asked.

"I really think he may be a god actually, but I am going to defer the question for now until we have more data," answered Phobus with a twang of sarcasm.

Rolling my eyes, I said, "Okay, here is what I think we should try."

Froth Lord had appeared to us on Sholl-Gar. It was clear to me that is where we needed to be if we wanted to solve this riddle. According to the wretched sub-creature we encountered after the time shift Thog would be looking for us. This may be all we need to know.

"Prepare yourself Phobus. We are headed back to your home world. I'm not sure what Epoch it will be when we get there, but it's going to be fun no matter what happens," I finished.

"It won't be boring anyway," he replied.

I had Phobus board my shuttle and using my anti-matter transporter I teleported it immediately to Sholl-Gar. It was unclear which eon we were headed to. It was even unclear whether we were in the proper dimension, as it is possible to transcend dimensions when teleporting. Now one thing I hated about having to travel with Phobus was I would actually have to fly and land the star shuttle upon arrival at the destination world. It never made any sense to me. It was so much safer to just quantum leap yourself across space then to try and land a shuttle craft. Flying through empty space is one thing. Landing on a Sand Planet was entirely different.

"Okay Phobus, we are going to be entering your atmosphere at about fifty-five thousand feet per second. Strap in."

"Roger that," he answered, always so unaware how we were taking a risk when we did it this way.

Witch Doctor One: "Sholl-Gar, Delta Five transport, call sign 'Witch Doctor One,' inbound, I repeat inbound, fifty thousand feet kicking in retros, over."

Sholl Gar Control: "Roger that, Witch Doctor One, fifty thousand feet."

Witch Doctor One: "Sholl-Gar, Witch Doctor One, have you got my vector, over?" I asked with slight concern.

"Why did you call this thing Witch Doctor One?" Phobus asked.

"It's her ship Phobus. I never fly," I said

"Um, you never fly?" he asked

"Well I don't like to fly," I answered

Just then things started to shake and rumble a little bit. There was a loud metallic humming sound, and several very loud bangs.

Witch Doctor One: "Sholl Gar, hitting some turbulence, coming down fast thirty thousand feet, kicking up my retros a notch, over."

Control: "Witch Doctor, check your vector, radio check also, please, over." The Witch Doctor switched over to Commlink five.

"I usually have my drone captain fly you, Phobus," I said.

"Well, now you tell me that. Why didn't he fly us?" Phobus railed.

Sometimes Phobus could be annoying. I was taking this bitch in though.

"Just hold yourself together a moment would you?" I said with not a small amount of exasperation.

I punched it and pointed the nose down, pumped the after burners, throttled up hard, then backed her off a tad. The Witch Doctor leapt forward and leaned nose down steeply, dropped quickly to ten thousand feet, then I pulled her up and leveled it off.

"JESUS CHRIST!" Phobus screamed.

Witch Doctor One: "Control, you are on my Commlink five now, radio check good, ten thousand feet, full retro burn," I continued.

Control:"Witch Doctor, Control here. Over," Control called out, sounding concerned.

Witch Doctor One:"Control, go ahead, please."

Control:"Looks like you lost a rod, over."

Witch Doctor One:"Copy that, nine thousand feet, falling like a rock, over."

Control:"Use pad five, Witch Doctor," said Control.

"Copy that," I finished.

"Alpha control still seems to have their shit together, huh, Phobus?" I asked.

"Oh yeah, they're great," he said sarcastically.

"Remember when they tried to go on strike that time when we were ruling the planet?" I asked with a grin.

Phobus just gave me a look and shrugged.

Again, I punched it. Burned right down through the sulfur ash atmosphere nose-first like a meteor, then throttled up right quick shooting down through the acid rain cloud layer, then aggressively leveled off to cross over horizontally flying over the sand lands.

"OH MY GOD!" screamed Phobus again.

"Just hang on for a few seconds," I managed to utter.

We coasted down to the planet from there. I ignored the direction to land at pad five. Sholl Gar was planet in ruins. No one could enforce my landing site. I steered the Witch Doctor back to flat sands beyond the Dunes and the hills towards the Young One's ancient castle complex. We finally landed. Once again things looked and felt a bit different. Phobus vomited for twelve minutes while I surveyed our surroundings. Though things looked entirely different once again, we both noticed a familiar being near the dunes. We left the shuttle and approached.

"Hey Coranthas is that the Wretch who told us about the Prophecy?" asked Phobus.

"Where?" I asked.

"There! Right there gnawing on that Zak carcass," he answered.

Much to my surprise it was the same wretched sub-creature who had told us of the legend of Phobus and Coranthas when Froth Lord first returned us from Drandor. It was indeed him, one in the same. We immediately approached the wretch and questioned him.

"Who are you?" demanded Phobus.

"Who I am." He looked to his left, then back to his right. "Is not your concern," he answered.

Immediately a burst of lightning fire from Phobus rained downed upon the sub-man in a thunderous apparition of hell and fire.

"Destroy me not sir!" exclaimed the servant.

"What is your name?" I demanded.

"I am Hoth," answered the servant. "I will be your humble servant like I said to you before."

"You remember us?" I asked.

I was curious to see if we were currently in the same timeline when we first encountered the servant. It was possible that he was a time shifter as well. He might have some skills you never know. For the moment, however, this would need to remain a mystery.

"Of course I remember you Coranthas," he answered. "You freed our world from the Large Master thousands of years ago. I believe you now," he finished.

Hoth was a fascinating creature. He went into detail about his sufferings in the dune wars and his lack of Broth. We spent nearly four months with Hoth learning about all the recent history of Sholl Gar. He told us about the worms. He told us about the sand wars. He told us about the lack of care the populace received during the horrors. He told us how the planet was essentially under the control of gang lords now.

This was all unimportant to us. We had one mission at that time.

"Do you know of Froth Lord?" I asked.

Hoth seemed fearful of the very question. His eyes seemed to have a look of dread fall over them.

"Yes I do. I know of Froth Lord," he answered.

His answer in the affirmative made me feel somewhat trepidatious and suspicious. *He knows of Froth Lord, I thought to myself. Hoth knows of Froth Lord?* "Where can we find him, do you know?" Phobus asked.

"Yes come this way," he answered.

Now I was truly concerned. This "Hoth" sub-specimen knows where to find the Superbeing Froth Lord? Maybe he is a wraith or something. Hoth threw his hood over his head, released some gas, and began to walk toward the sand dunes. We followed him of course.

Chapter Five

Froth Lord "The Early Years"

It was supposed to fire up an atomic burst, then rain hot hail on the fourth moon of Teledawn. Froth Lord had worked on the project for nearly the entire semester and his expectations were extremely high. He was ranked number one in his class. The prodigy knew something wasn't right about this whole thing though. Something was amiss.

The detonation technology used was developed by Froth Lord as part of the project. Froth Lord had never failed at anything before. The device did detonate. That was not the issue. There was an extremely bright sky burst forty-five thousand miles above the moon's surface at exactly the predicted moment. It went nuclear as expected, but, shockingly, no hot hail rained down on this moon. The hail was the point of the project. Essentially he had simply put on an amazing fireworks display over a lifeless moon.

Though it had been a very ambitious project for a six-year-old Nectarian child, it still would garner Froth Lord his first failure in his life. Some say he never recovered fully from this experience. Yet others say that he never would have become who did without this experience. Failure can propel genius to greater heights or send it to deep depths of despair. This was his first failure, and he grew from it. The thing no one else knew was that Froth Lord was doing exactly what he meant to do with the project. The young wizard had known something was amiss.

The board of Science on Nectar communicated their displeasure with the child.

- Meeting of the Mentors, Planet Nectar

These Mentors, when seen from the context of what Froth Lord ultimately became, are simply a complete and utter joke. There he was before the Mentors; even at six years of age, he was giant in their presence. The Mentors knew, and in fact had known for a while, that they were dealing with something special. They were dealing with a child with such greatness and such potential for Superbeing levels that they often felt a small amount of fear in his presence. Today they were concerned he might have caught them in their duplicity and corruption. "This damn kid," they would say later.

"Froth Lord. That is your name son, correct?" asked Velaris, Chief Executor of the Board, and Senior Mentor.

"I am Froth Lord," answered the Nectarian boy.

"Froth Lord, did you understand the purpose of the project? Did you understand why the project was to rain hot hail on that moon?" continued Velaris.

Froth Lord knew exactly what they were up to.

"It was a weapons test, sir," answered Froth Lord.

"You think we were having you test a weapon son?" asked Donavon, Chief Quantum Professor of Sciences.

"Ask the treasonous overlords. You know it was weapons test," answered the boy.

Nectarians were not supposed to develop new weapons for any worlds. But it had always been an excellent revenue stream for their world. Species of every type, in many various conflicts amongst worlds, in ages past, had gotten weapons of mass destruction from Nectarian scientists. The black market was just too strong to ignore. And Froth Lord was so much more talented than even the doctorate level scientists on Nectar. They had to try.

They thought they could trick him into making a weapon for them. A world destroyer was what they wanted. World Destroyers were a staple and a very hot ticket item for Nectar underworld sales. Gangster planetary species of all worlds would commit to business dealings with shady Nectarian overlords to get hold of these World Destroyers. But they weren't going to get one this way. Not from young Froth Lord's workings.

At age six Froth Lord's spine of steel exposed the council. He was able to prove his accusations in the highest court of the planet Nectar. Sentients in the galaxy far and wide began to hear about this Nectarian prodigy. The Council of Drakar summoned him at age ten to decipher what happened to a planet that was inhaled into a black hole. His paper on the occurrence was the rage of the galactic academia. But then he descended into his early "Dark Period."

At age fifteen Froth Lord met his first girlfriend. She was the princess of a foreign world bent on total galactic rule. Though her world lacked the ability to conquer even the sub-servants of their own planet, they still insanely felt that they were destined to rule over others. Froth Lord did not understand this and pitied her. Though their imperial goals were absurd, the species itself was very advanced and intelligent. That contributed to their bloated vision of empire. He thought she was cute though.

Froth Lord became an expert on quantum reality at this point in time. He had been researching Broth theory for his entire life. For Nectarians, a full understanding of the nature of the Broth was an imperative, even as impossible as that was. As impossible as it was, a Nectarian must endeavor to understand it.

There was an ancient theory regarding the nature of the universe first postulated by Nectarians a thousand years before Froth Lord was born. Nectarians were the closest to understanding the nature of the Broth. They did not yet realize how close they were.

Many contemporary scientists, especially Nectarians, preferred that Froth Lord would cease his obsession with deep analysis of the nature of the Broth. For most it seemed pointless. The Broth exists. It produces all life in the galaxy. It probably is responsible for all life in the Cosmos as well. Dendrake made it. Dendrake deposited it. Dendrake initiated the life process on all known worlds. The obsession did not help the younger Froth Lord to attain greatness, at least not yet.

A pre-Idealist Froth Lord and his girlfriend engaged in interstellar travel. They would go out together and torment more primitive sentients in the Zynon galaxy. Using her parents' star cruiser, they would transverse the galaxy and would rain down hot hail on various planets. This was an early dark period.

Of course, they used the same science project technology that Froth Lord had developed at age six. One time together they detected a spaceship in the deep dark void of space. What occurred next is one of the funniest stories he ever told me and is retold endlessly in star saloons both far and wide:

"Honey, I think there is an ion engine starship ahead," Rulella said

"Ion engine? Are you serious?" Froth Lord asked.

"Yes." She answered. "It must be a new interstellar world. They are crazy to attempt something like this with that level of technology," she said.

"What in the world are they doing out here?" he said.

"Let's mess with them," said the young and reckless Froth Lord.

"Yessir," Rulella replied cutely.

Now the Garthonians had never encountered an alien species at this point. (Alien to their home world.) They were attempting their first trans-stellar transport. Using an ion engine starship, nineteen Garthonians were frozen in cryogenic chambers for the trip. They were supposed be unfrozen at their destination. They had no idea what was coming.

"Let's teleport them somewhere," Froth Lord said with a grin.

"Where do you think we should teleport them?" asked Rulella

"I was thinking more like 'when' not 'where,'" Froth Lord said with a laugh.

Immediately, Froth Lord teleported the star ship nineteen hundred years into past. The ship was deposited right onto Drepolis, the capital city of the Garthonian home world Garthonia.

"Nineteen Lords of Our World"

Tens of thousands of years before the unnatural birth of Thog, the nineteen Lords of Garthonia arrived at Drepolis. The nineteen Garthonians had been transported back in time nineteen hundred years to their own world. When they were awoken by their main computer, they were unaware of their location and their time period.

"Captain Darnack," the computer spoke in a sterile voice.

"Roger that, computer," answered Darnack. "Have we reached Delta Six?"

"Negative, Captain," answer the computer. "We are on Garthonia."

"Garthonia? Are you being serious right now?" he responded

"Roger," answered the computer.

The captain ordered the computer to open the chambers of the eighteen other Garthonians. They spent one month inside the ship analyzing the situation before exiting to confront their ancient ancestors.

Captain Darnack was never made aware of the true nature of what had occurred.

However, when the Garthonians declared him Lord, and Darnack the Great, he did not object.

The Garthonians of that time were just looking for a reason to survive. Garnack the Great became the greatest leader of Garthonian history. He was a god on Garthonia. His eighteen lessor Lords were assigned various god-tasks as well. They engineered great cities. They used technology to foster Garthonians to worship them. Froth Lord kept track on them from his Dome on Nectar and from Rulella's starship.

They resisted the urge to write holy books for a long time. However, it became clear as they neared their deaths that holy books would be required. They established a priesthood that remains to this day. Doctrinal divides over these holy books would, of course, cause thousands of years of wars on Garthonia. Nearly two thousand distinct religious sects, which mostly warred with each other, were formed as a result.

However the interstellar technology brought back from the future had advanced the Garthonians by a millennium. Froth Lord did not realize it, but he had saved his first world. This was very unfortunate though, for the many worlds that the Garthonians bombarded in later times, including old Earth.

- Meanwhile, back on Sholl-Gar, Thoryntian Dune, timeline uncertain

The wretched sub-creature brought us to the edge of a sand hill. All dunes look the same on this world. We had been walking for half a day. I was horribly bored by this time.

"This is far enough, Hoth. Where is Froth Lord?" demanded Phobus.

"You must be patient," answered the slave.

We approached a cave entrance near the base of the dune. There were what appeared to be guards of some kind near the cave entrance. They were Sholl-Garian leather-based skin, armor-clad military types. They had set up a perimeter guard defense in three-tier alignment. They were like Broth guards, which was common and necessary on Sholl Gar as marauding gang lords killed and stole Broth daily. We obliterated them into dust with lightning blasts and entered the cave.

"Twenty-five points?" I asked, though I was exhausted.

"Yep, twenty-five each," replied Phobus.

We stopped for just a moment to do the tally. Even after everything this was still important to us. There were five guards, and we had brief disagreement over who got how many. I was certain I had gotten three and he had gotten two of them. He saw it in reverse. A brief battle erupted between us, but our relative parity caused us to lose interest for now. Plus, we had more pressing matters at hand.

"We'll finish this later," I said.

"Damn right we will," added Phobus.

"Coranthas, I hope your idea was a good one, my friend," he added.

I was not brave at that moment. I had been wondering if I had made a terrible mistake for about an hour now. *Why bother with all this?* I was thinking. Froth Lord, if he sees fit, could just come find us at some point anyway. To think, we could have just hung out on Delta Five and consumed Broth. *Why am I on this rock again?* I thought to myself.

"We'll be all right, Phobus," I replied with feigned reassurance.

Immediately something like fire fell from the sky. Sounds of thunder erupted from all directions. The slave sub-creature Hoth disappeared. Light like the sun appeared from the tunnel. A creature with eyes like piercing bursts of lightning appeared before us. It was not Froth Lord however. Astonishingly, I knew it was, in fact, Thog.

"Phobus? Is that you?" asked the apparition.

"Yessir?" replied Phobus in the form of a query.

"Please do not destroy us. We told you we would help find Thog so you can destroy him, remember?" spoke Phobus the fool.

"I am Thog, you dumbass," replied the apparition. I was terrified, but I was laughing inside.

"Thog?" replied Phobus. He paused and took another look. "Thog, is it really you?" Phobus continued, feigning joy and relief.

"It is you, isn't it, Thog? You're alive." He cried tears of false joy, falling to his feet before his soon-to-be destructor. Phobus at times could have his way with Thog in the past. But I did not think it was going to go that way this time.

"Where's that awful wretch Hoth?" asked Phobus.

"I was that wretch Hoth, Phobus!" angrily answered Thog, the Destructor.

I had to give the kid some credit at that moment for playing us so hard and so well. I felt owned but still chuckling inside.

"Oh," Phobus said, and then paused.

During his pause Phobus thought a bit about what was transpiring here.

"Oh. Shit," he continued.

It started to make some sense to me now, amazingly. Thog was the wretch Hoth who told us of the ancient prophecy. He was the creature who told us that Thog was going to hunt down Phobus and destroy us. I realized right then that I would be able to get us out of this, at least for now. *It's the "kid,"* I thought to myself. *Even with all these apparent powers I could handle the "kid." Right?*

"Thog," I started. "Let's talk about this a bit, okay?"

Thog pulled out a punishment stick and raised it toward us both. It began to light up as bright as a sun or something. My confidence dipped slightly. *Okay, maybe not this time,* I then thought to myself.

Thog began.

"You two have caused thousands of years of suffering on this world. Phobus promised me much before he blasted me with that lightning gun. He destroyed my lobal protection. He was not kind, and now neither shall I be kind," the apparition finished.

The lobe tubing! That is how I can get us out of this, I thought to myself. Even with all these apparent powers, he still cares about that damn lobe tubing. *What the hell was that lobe tubing for anyway?* I distractingly wondered. But now back to getting us out of this.

"Wait a second, Thog," I began. "What happened to your lobe anyway?"

"Excuse me?" asked Thog.

"I see no tubing?" I continued.

"A super creature from space restored me to health and set up a kingdom for me to rule over on Sholl-Gar. He explained that it was imperative that I rule wisely, for he had a future assignment for me. Some day he will return to Sholl-Gar and restore all things. Then I will know of my fate," Thog finished.

I knew he was talking about Froth Lord. He is masterminding this entire series of events. Thog was the first creature we encountered both times we arrived back here on this wretched world. This is not an accident. Froth Lord was behind it all.

But what is he up to? It does not appear logical to me if he really wants to destroy us. He acted like he let us live to help him find Thog. He knew all along where Thog was. *What is going on here?* I asked myself.

"Why did you not destroy us the first time we returned from Drandor?" I asked Thog.

"Orders," he answered while raising his punishment stick once again.

Immediately we were hit with ten seconds of continuous lightning blasts. I writhed on the ground, waiting for death. At this point death was welcome as far as I was concerned. Phobus was held in stasis, hovering about six feet off the ground in a blue lightning ionic cube cell. Though he was clearly in distress, I could not help but find it somewhat amusing. He was grappling at his utility belt as if he had a chance to free himself. I knew Thog's tech was too strong at this point. Right at that moment at least, Thog had us both. However, as suddenly as it began, Thog just stopped. Phobus fell to the ground with a loud thud. I rolled over onto my side.

"Get up, you two," he said a shrug. "Let's go."

Chapter Six

Froth Lord "God Over Drandor"

The Drandorians were discovered by pure chance. Froth Lord had been scanning systems for signs of intelligence as part of his quest to spare worlds under Article 19 after planet Earth's obliteration. Drandoria had been viewed through telescopic technology in the past, but there never any signs of intelligent life until now. Rulella was actively scanning the system for Froth Lord. An indicator beacon started going off on Froth Lord's main panel. This particular beacon was from the quantum scanner.

"Rulella? Do you read something on the quantum scan of Drandor?" asked Froth Lord.

"Yessir," she replied. "There is definitely someone on that planet. Shall I prepare the anti-matter canon?" she sweetly asked.

Froth Lord thought about it for a moment but decided rather quickly on a different course.

"No. I have something else in store for them," he answered. Froth Lord had never explained his new God-Work plans to his now wife before. He had grown tired of Rulella anyway and was preparing on converting her to pure energy soon.

"Descend upon Drandor's largest population center," he said. "There we will begin," he finished.

"Okay, honey. Let me turn on the cloaking device," Rulella added.

"No," he answered. "That won't be necessary. In fact, detonate nine uranium-235 fission nuclear sky bursts in space forty thousand miles above the city before we descend. Make it appear that we are descending straight out of the apparent bright nebula simulated by the blasts," he finished.

"But, honey, uranium-235 bursts won't even rain hot hail from that altitude?" Rulella sweetly objected.

"Let me do the thinking, please, Rulella," he said. Rulella programmed the weapons systems and detonation coordinates into the computer "Barker One," which she had named after their dog.

"Barker One," she spoke.

Barker One: "Yes, Rulella."

"Please load nine of our Davy Crockett class uranium bombs into their tubes. I will update you with exact coordinates shortly," she finished.

Barker One: "I'm sorry, Rulella, but that won't be possible at this time."

"Barker One, what are you talking about?" Rulella asked in reply.

Barker One: "You launched all the Davey Crocketts during the Forythian Dune purgings on Sholl-Gar last month."

"You serious?" she asked with exasperation and not a small amount of frustration.

Barker One: "It was the Round Robin Roast celebration, remember?"

Occasionally Froth Lord and Rulella would do nuclear fireworks displays for the various worlds during their feasts and Broth-fests when they were short on funds.

"Oh, that's right, the 'triple R,' darn it," she answered.

"Do we have any old Earth Trident II missiles left?" she asked

Barker One: "Right! Ha! Come on now."

"What the hell are you two debating now?" asked a visibly peeved Froth Lord.

"The computer says we have no Davey Crockets or any of the old Earth inventory left," she answered.

"Do we have any of the uranium-235 boosted fission missile warheads?" asked Froth Lord impatiently.

Barker One: "Um, no?"

"B83 nuclear bomb?" Froth Lord continued.

Barker One: "I'm afraid, not so much. Not really."

"What do we have, computer?" demanded Froth Lord.

Barker One went through the remaining inventory for them both.

Barker One: "We do still have six rather nice old Earth-class 'Ivy King' United States pure fission bombs. They pack a punch, no?"

"Okay, then my god let's go," Froth Lord exclaimed.

Barker One: "Will these be for surface bursts, Rulella?"

"That's a negative. I will update you with space burst coordinates," she answered.

Barker One: "Well, the Ivy Kings are not ideal for sky or space bursts I'm afraid."

She was started to get frustrated.

"Not ideal for sky bursts, you say?" asked Rulella.

Barker One: "Or space bursts."

"Not even for space bursts, you say?" She sighed.

Barker One: "Not particularly no. They were mostly used against advancing land forces I'm afraid."

"Will they light?" asked an increasingly incredulous Froth Lord.

Neither Barker One nor Rulella responded to Froth Lord, as they were both too engaged in their own discussion at this point.

"Interesting. Why would it make it any difference, do you think, Barker?" Rulella asked, distracted by the banter.

Barker One: "Well, ancient armies used the Ivy Kings mostly in terms of being able to conduct continuous nuclear combat against advancing armies. They were specifically designed to be used in an 'escalate to deescalate' situation while being soundly beaten by ancient conventional forces. So, these nukes would occasionally be deployed when the scenarios approached—"

"THEY WILL HAVE TO DO!" yelled Froth Lord, interrupting this friendly conversation. "WHAT THE HELL?" he exclaimed.

The computer configured the strike parameters.

- Lovely Morning on Drandor

It was a lovely morning on Drandor. The light of the four moons was slowly giving way to the brighter light of the rising sun. It was in mid phase, so there was a beautiful dawn sky. Drandoria City was a busy, bustling agricultural center of the planet's largest republic. The people had only recently invented the steam engine and for the most part still got around by animal-drawn carts and some old

Earth-style trains. It was a happy planet. Froth Lord was excited to get a religion started on this world to protect them by Article 19.

There were four primary religions on this planet. All stemmed from the same parent religion which was now four thousand years old. None of them had been founded by a higher Sentient life form of the Zynon galaxy. Hence, their world would not be spared under Article 19.

Drandorian theologians had debated forever over whether the four main religions worshipped the same God. All believed their god the "only" god in existence, and the Creator of all. Yet all four had a different name for him now, and all four had diametrically opposing doctrines. Dogma and subsequent infighting amongst even the same sects further divided the people. But, as mentioned, uniquely, this was a rare happy world.

All four declared the other three false and "evil." Though there was great religious disagreement they mostly tolerated each other in peace. Froth Lord decided he would powerfully declare himself to be this Deity and setup a unifying (so he thought) system of worship.

Suddenly, without warning, light appearing like a second sun lit up directly above the city that beautiful morning. Tens of thousands of Drandorians stared up in the general direction of Froth Lord's approaching ship. A thunderous sound came from the dawn sky now lit up like it was noon time on the brightest day of the year. An ominous yet purposefully beautiful aura surrounded the approaching star craft. The backdrop of the uranium sky burst, high enough to not cause the people any danger, further enhanced Froth Lord's awe-inspiring approach.

For roughly nine months Froth Lord's ship hovered above the city, cloaking itself in mysterious nebula-like apparitions. It mostly appeared as a bright light, with an occasional apparition of Froth Lord himself in the sky. He declared himself as their god finally returning to establish the "New Age." He established his basic doctrines which he had previously outlined. Froth Lord was now their god's name. He sent a clone of Thog to the surface to be sacrificed for the Drandorians. He declared that the "epoch" date was five thousand years after the "Unnatural Birth of Thog." This was now to be their "Year One."

He then flew his star ship to all manners of cities and towns on Drandor. In every language of Drandor, over every major city, Froth Lord communicated that he was their Creator, returning five thousand years later to restore order, blah, blah.

For the next year he chose priests, wrote doctrine, and compiled the new Holy Writs of Drandor. He did all this comfortably from the confines of his ship, without ever setting foot on the planet's surface. Within six months of his departure, religious dogmatic fighting began in earnest.

Froth Lord had painstakingly crafted his Writs to contain no confusing doctrine. The religion was simple. The Books were straightforward. They basically just outlined his four main points, and then the rest was just details to fill the books. They stated plainly that he had created the universe and that Drandor was at the center. (This was part of the Article 19 code.) He wrote in the origins section that the entire Cosmos was shaped like a sphere and that the stars were fixed in the roof of a dome. The moons and sun circled above at a far distance but within the dome ceiling. Drandor was inside this massive dome that he had created. He did not want the Drandorians to think long and hard about the greater Zynon galaxy. Due to his immense powers, the Drandorians really had no other choice than to believe what he told them. He was clearly God. Some of the smarter Drandorians especially astronomers were kind of like, "Um, what the fuck?" but Froth Lord's reality was undeniable for even them.

Froth Lord tried with purpose to write the holy writs to not be confusing. Years later, Froth Lord lamented that he should have written codes in the Holy Writs outlawing theology. He wrote simply that all souls were immediately transported to himself upon death to reside forever with him in great joy, blah, blah. Those who mistreat others in this life will be punished severely for a time period of fair duration. Then after serving their fair punishment would be reunited with their parents of origin with God (Froth Lord). Of course, this was all rubbish.

Upon death all Sentients are returned to the soil unless they have transcended. Dendrake never bothered with the concept of a soul. Code for a soul was not in the Broth. That is why beings like Froth Lord spend so much time trying to evolve into indestructible superbeings. All their tricks are just the ramifications of millions of years of technology and evolution. None of them are supernatural, though they certainly can appear so.

One thousand years later Drandor had denigrated into a warring planet with over eight thousand different religious sects. All these sects claimed to be the only true followers of Froth Lord. Cults of every kind ruled over their groups. The civilization's advancement had been impaired severely. They regressed into a near animal like state. Each sect claimed Thog had been sacrificed for only their group.

Though they were growing from a technological standpoint, minimally, before Froth Lord arrived, this had regressed hopelessly as well. The religious murder and torture were worse than ever. Ironically, they started with four religions based on one false God. Today they have eight thousand sects based on a real being, yet just as "false" of a god.

Froth Lord had to return with a clone of Thog multiple times. The people had denigrated so horribly that it was clear that he needed to "start over" essentially. This time epoch became known on Drandor as the "Second Age." Froth Lord called it "the Reboot". He wrote an additional testament to be added to his Holy Books as the guidelines for the Second Age. He wrote the second testament to strictly outlaw many horrible and evil practices these people had now adopted as normal "Thogism" religion. He told me many thousands of years later that he would often lament, "What the hell have I done to this world?"

Political and religious wars ruled this world for hundreds and hundreds of years post the third sacrifice of Thog. Six hundred years after Froth Lord left the planet, a priest named Telnak was raised up within the populace of Drandor. He interpreted the "new" Holy Writs of the God of Drandor (Froth Lord) differently than any other priest prior to his time. He saw the new Thogism very differently than Froth Lord intended. He loved to camp out in one section of the scribe of Tarnak, the Oracle of Love:

> *Tarnak 2: 16–17 Love your fellow people. There is no one else who will care for your brother than you. Do not throw large, sharp-edged rocks at your friends, as per the old ways. Do not set others afire. This is abomination unto the Lord Thog, and his Father Froth Lord.*

Froth Lord took great care that such verses would make the people behave well. He intended to create far more merciful priests, leaders, and warlords than Drandor had seen prior.

Unfortunately, due to the teachings of Telnak, something very strange happened. Telnak decided that love was transcendent due to the scribe of Torbit, chapter two:

Torbit 2:1 Love is of eternal essence and transcends all else.

Telnak completely misunderstood what Froth Lord had meant. In fact Froth Lord had not meant anything at all whatsoever. He was simply trying to fill up some volumes with the hope that "kindness" would break out. Telnak thought that because love was of some kind of "eternal essence," it could only be judged by the eternal, hence God. (Froth Lord, ironically, who meant nothing by any of his writings.)

Therefore he reasoned that love was, in fact, unattainable while living on Drandor. That only when all things were made new would the believers truly understand how to love. Telnak also introduced doctrines that had nothing to do with Froth Lord's false religion. He taught that he received special revelations from Froth Lord and Thog. Telnak created for himself great wealth as well through all manner of corruption. Eventually he was killed by members of his own sect for blasphemy, but not before some of these teachings took root.

As an unfortunate outcome from the entire Telnak experience, any "Second Age" prohibitions on Drandor against the prior violent ways were null and void. Hence, burnings, stonings, and the destruction of others was okay once more. Telnak had reasoned, prior to his eventual murder by his own cult members, that God (Froth Lord) would sort all things out upon his return. Due to this logic the populace was tormented, tortured, burned, and stoned for the next one thousand years. Entirely burnt out with the Drandorians at this point, Froth Lord sent the real Thog to try one more time and set up a "Third Age." He just could not bring himself to go again to straighten things out. So Thog would return yet again from the dead and try to establish the "Third Age" of Thogism on Drandor. That went poorly.

Seventeen full scale wars erupted based on the many variants of the Holy Writs left by Froth Lord. Froth Lord or Thog never appeared to the Drandorian people proper again. (Though he used it's moons often, as we have already shown.)

"Hey," he would often lament to me, "at least, they are protected as a species under Article 19."

Telnak, prior to his slaying, was also obsessed with their world's doctrines relating to "Eschatology," or beliefs regarding the "end of the present age" (Second Age in his case). He was all over the place on this one. Essentially, like many worlds' myths and religions, Telnak took the approach that they should watch their world's current events closely for signs that they may living in the final days. Wars were even triggered during his time almost with the hope they would be the catalyst for the final return of Froth Lord and the end of all things. Drandorian beliefs regarding the end of days caused a proliferation of truly horrible Doomsday cults and movements.

Maybe I will just wipe them out in a massive fireball! sometimes Froth Lord would ironically think agonizingly.

As noted, eventually Telnak was burned at the stake by members of his own movement in the belief that it would trigger Froth Lord's return to make all things new. ("Making all things new" was standard dogma.)

Drandoria was the most displeasing of all Froth Lord's dominions. He could not wait to send Thog there one final time. He was going to let Thog do whatever he pleased to control the mess.

The Young One

As promised, we will spend the absolute minimum amount of time discussing the Young One's background prior to his exile and attempted return. I'm irked by the fact I even must waste brain cycles on him writing this right now. Quite frankly, he is not important considering all we have discussed. Yes, he briefly served as our puppet as ruler of Sholl Gar. And yes, he was a prince over that horrible world for a very long time under his wretched mom. I'm not even sure where in this chronicle his basic summary belongs. Well, right here is good as anywhere. His story is dribble, no matter where I include it.

The only reason I am including any background detail on the Young One is because I have already committed myself to do so at the outset. His story is complete twaddle.

As we had discussed ad nauseam, the Large Master had ruled Sholl-Gar, blah, blah, for a real long time. During a feeding festival she became quite outrageous after six hundred barrels of gravy and a lot of biscuits. The Broth was involved as well.

A caped sub-Lord took her behind the shed because, quite frankly, he had been on the sauce for days as well. Their love produced Sholl-Gar's air to the throne, The "Young One." He was "half-beast" and "half sub-specimen" genetically.

The father was terminated soon afterwards. The Young One was raised with a silver spoon, at least with respect to gravy and biscuits. The quantities were nearly incomprehensible. The Young One's life, though the life of a prince, entirely lacked purpose as far as he was concerned. He was not that interested in ruling that god awful planet one day either.

Even so the Young One began out more idealistic than you might realize. At one time he had thought about a democratic republic as a future system for the planet of Sholl-Gar. Once his evil mom has "moved on,", he would often think that he would have more leeway to introduce change to the Sholl-Garian system. That system had produced nothing but horror and suffering for thousands of generations. Freedom, rights, the ability to run one's own life, these were the things he wanted to bring to the average sub-creature. Though he was half sub-creature, he was still seen as a beast by most. He would spend hours at times clutching his useless false thumb, an evolutionary "failure," inherited from his mom. *When she is dead, I'm lopping these things off,* he would often think. As idealist as he might had started out, he eventually would succumb to his weaknesses.

His greatest weakness was gravy. He did like biscuits as well, but only as something to soak the in the gravy. Out of fairness to the Young One, as noted earlier, Sholl-Garian gravy is amazing. But he longed for more.

At age sixteen the Young One decided that there may not be enough gravy on Sholl Gar, and wondered about gravy from other worlds. (He really didn't care for the Broth that much.) He decided that he would use his mother's starship to go on a quest for more gravy. (Just for background, this all occurred twenty years before he was first frozen in a cryochamber by Phobus.)

Unfortunately for him he was not a good a starship commander. His first flight nearly ended with his own death. He left Sholl Gar and throttled right up and basically "aimed" the ship out past the moons. He figured, once safely past the outer moon, he would simply radio on and ask to be walked through any maneuvers to set them on a good trajectory and a quantum drive jump. He didn't have a fucking clue.

The ship spiraled toward deep space completely out of control. Froth Lord flew by and saved his sorry ass. Just to teach the fat kid a lesson he deposited him into Forinth Dune face first. It took a team of twenty-six drones with a full-powered harness to get him out of the dune in just shy of six hours.

We do have to talk about him at least one more time later. I apologize in advance.

Chapter Seven

Sholl Gar, Thoryntian Dune, Froth Lord Revealed

Why Thog spared us at this moment would remain a secret to me for now. I didn't really care though. I had become somewhat fearful of Froth Lord, but for some reason, I had much confidence with respect to Thog. I mean, there is a reason I always thought of him as "the kid." It was not disdain or disrespect, at least not at those times. I don't know. I cannot explain why, but I had no fear of him even now.

Somehow I knew that, eventually, I would have the upper hand on him. I remembered the mysterious dreams I had where the apparition mentioned Thog's name back on Delta Five. What is the meaning of those dreams? And what am I supposed to glean from them? I supposed at this time I might be finding out real soon. Why do those entities in my dream seem unnerved by Froth Lord?

Thog was becoming quite the mystery. He seemed of such unimportance to me before, yet he now wields great powers. They come from this Froth Lord I was certain. I still don't get the big deal over that damn lobe tubing either. It's like a helmet bro. It's too bad he needs it for protection, but it is just a hat basically. It is just plain weird that he was hopelessly attached to it. Meanwhile, Phobus was not looking too good. We had to stop three times for him to pee. Also, he was as pale as a ghost.

"Dude you all right?" I asked him.

Phobus was and remains the best friend I have ever had. And though he usually is quite perseverant I was worrying just a bit about him at this point. I barely care about my survival if I'm being truly honest, but it bothered me that Thog had the upper hand on Phobus right then.

"Oh yeah, I'm great over here," he replied sarcastically, wiping traces of vomit from his hole.

We followed Thog toward a mountain. Mountains on Sholl Gar were where the Broth was usually stored. As noted previously, they kept it in caves on this world, and usually under guard. The planetary masters would use all their resources to protect the Broth and keep sub-creatures from accessing its life-giving essence.

"Dude?" Phobus asked me

"Yes, dear Phobus," I replied.

"If possible, can you score me some Broth?" he asked

"Absolutely my friend. Don't worry Phobus. Things will be looking up soon," I said unknowingly.

Suddenly fire from on high fell from the stars, and the moons became like blood. Sholl Gar itself opened up instantly creating vast canyons in many sectors at that precise moment, and many sub-creatures were pulled into the core. Winds of thunder stormed across the surface, and something like fire balls fell from the sky. Darkness fell over the land, and sub-servants everywhere fell to the ground in pain and torment. As bad as all this sounds, a peace fell over me. I could not see a thing. Happenings like this were starting to feel normal to me anyways.

Thunderous winds began to quiet. Shaking ground began to calm. Screams of terror began to become silent. Then I could hear it. I could not see anything as the sandstorms were still ferocious, but I could hear it. The sounds of terror from every direction, as they calmed, were replaced by an ever-increasing and deafening sound of laughter. It was a side-splitting soul-piercing laughter.

"Did you see his face?" exclaimed a barely continent Thog.

"I think Phobus shit himself," was all Froth Lord could muster, practically shitting himself.

"I think Coranthas finally broke? Don't you, Froth Lord?" asked Thog.

Right then I knew Thog was going to be mine. One way or the other this kid was going to get it. It is one thing to be dominated by one like Froth Lord. He was obviously an important and powerful master. He was a true, real life Superbeing. Thog however, as mentioned earlier, was one of the most insignificant creatures I had ever encountered. Whatever his secrets are, they clearly come from Froth Lord. I quickly thought to mess with the kid about his lobe tubing.

"Hey, Thog. How's your fucking lobe?" I asked. Silence fell over the group.

"Come again?" asked Thog

"How's your lobe? Remember, we fried it?" I asked again.

"Do you know who you are talking to human?" was his reply

Just then a lightning blast came from Froth Lord's eyes that subdued Thog in an aura of blue and pulsing light. An eerie glow in the shape of a dome enclosed him. He was held motionless in place by the power of his master for at least nine seconds.

"Shut the hell up Thog," Froth Lord muttered in an annoyed voice toward his wretched creature and then released him.

"Sorry," Thog mustered a barely audible response as he tried to get to his feet.

"Human?" I exclaimed aloud. "What the hell is he talking about?"

Did he call me a Human? I thought to myself.

"He's delirious my friend," answered Froth Lord.

"You both must be very tired from your journeys. It is time that you both are told the truth about what is going on here," began the apparition in front of us.

"That would be nice," replied Phobus sarcastically.

Ten seconds of blue lightning subdued Phobus for his sarcasm. I watched intently at Froth Lord as he had dear Phobus in this clutch of terror. It was indeed a horrifying and vulgar display of power. It was quite fearful. Blue lightning burst forth from his eyes, enveloping Phobus completely. As fearful as it was, it was damn impressive. Only for the first second is there any sound. You hear an explosion, but then silence as the victim is held in stasis. I knew he was not a god. However, he's a tough out for sure..

Just like that he released dear Phobus to the ground. "Come with me," said Froth Lord.

High Above Drandor

It was like a dream that you were certain was real. But you also knew it was a dream. However, this was in fact real, I think.

I was staring down upon an entire world. Whatever world this was I did not know, but it was beautiful. Oceans unrivaled, continents of green, and most certainly life was scattered across this world.

This was not Sholl Gar. Nor was it Delta Five. How did I get here? Where is Phobus? I don't see Froth Lord. I was falling very fast toward this unknown planet. It was beautiful. If this was to be the final moment of my life, then I was thankful for it.

I felt incredible peace. I took a moment to take in my surroundings. Though I was somewhat out of control I could see at least three, maybe four moons high above this world.

I wondered if I would ever be back on Delta Five and in the safety of my compound. Then I heard his voice.

"Coranthas.," called out the voice.

"Yes, I am here."

"Do you know who I am?" asked the awe-inspiring voice.

"You are Froth Lord," I replied.

"Do you know why you are here.?" the voice asked me

"No, I do not," I answered.

"I have chosen you," he said.

"You do not realize what I am doing, do you?" asked who I thought was Froth Lord, though at this point I had no idea anymore.

"I have absolutely no idea what is going on anymore," I answered.

"All I know is that last week, sometime, I was playing Nintendo or something on Delta Five in my chamber. Then Phobus called for help, and since then all fucking hell has broken loose. I'm not sure who I even am anymore. I don't know what is real and what is not anymore," I finished.

As I said these words, I began to realize they were true. I didn't know what was real and what was not real. But even worse, was I imaging these things? Was I dreaming them? This is exactly how the Witch Doctor always described my diagnosed condition. Was I having an episode? Or is something far more powerful than I in control of all that I am experiencing?

"Everything's fine", the calming, awe inspiring voice reassured me.

"I have chosen all of you," the voice declared.

"What about Phobus?" I asked.

"Yes even dear Phobus," answered Froth Lord.

As suddenly as the vision began, it was over. There we were, Phobus, Thog, and, of course, me, writhing on the ground attempting to regain our composure.

"Did that just happen?" exclaimed Phobus

"Did you see that flying clown of fire!?" he yelled.

"What about those winged Darkonan vampire men?" asked Thog, wiping vomit from his shirt. "I thought I was done for," he finished.

Obviously each one of us experienced a different vision. This much was certain. Now the question essentially was "Where the hell are we?"

Also, "What the hell is going on?" came to mind. Phobus got up to his feet wiping his face with his sleeve. After straightening his shirt tails he asked, "What just happened?"

We began to share the details of our experiences with each other. I told them about the planet and my glorious free fall. Phobus told us of the circus of death and the phantasm-like clown creatures that tormented him in a simulated eternity. Thog told us of the vampire den where he smoked Native American tea on some very strange world. I picked up Phobus's lightning gun and I was considering putting away Thog when I heard the voice again.

"Don't do it Coranthas," he spoke.

I turned around and there he was, but totally different this time. Froth Lord was just standing there right in front of us, a man of some kind. However there was no lightning, no bursts of fire, no time-altering or mind-altering apparitions. He was just standing there right in front of us, like any other Sentient life form. I put down the gun and slowly strolled very cautiously in his direction.

"Hey," I began very slowly. "So, you're Froth Lord, right?" I asked.

Froth Lord started to grin slightly, then slowly he leaned forward a little bit. Then he couldn't control it, the laughter just started to pour out of him. I mean he was laughing harder than I think I ever saw anyone laugh before. It went on for a little bit. He would appear to grab hold of himself like he was about to talk, then it would kick in again and the laughter would pour out. I just looked at him a bit perplexed. Phobus and I just looked at each other for a moment like wondering "what the"? Then finally Froth Lord grabbed hold of himself, mostly.

"Yeah, that's me. What's up?" He laughed. "Anything new or different going on?" he asked.

Phobus got up to his feet and looked over at Thog who was also looking rather confused. Thog looked back at Phobus and then also over to me. It was now clear that all three of us were the butts of this joke, whatever it was.

"You guys all right?" Froth Lord asked in the general direction of Thog and Phobus.

"I gave Coranthas here a bit more of a pleasant experience than you two. How was that circus?" he asks with a laugh.

"Don't sweat it Mr. Lord. Can I call you Mr. Lord? Or do you prefer Master? God? What is it now?" ranted Phobus.

"Hey, I was just having some fun," began Froth Lord. "Mr. Lord is fine."

"Well the clown of fire was a nice touch I must say," started Phobus.

"You know it's not like I wasn't scared enough yet. You altered time and space on me, threatened me with death and torment, sentenced me to a circus of death and fire. But it's all good, no worries here," Phobus finished.

At this point we all started to chill out some. I was thinking the whole thing was kind of funny at that moment.

"So this is real, right?" I asked.

"Yes, this is completely real. Everything's fine. Nothing crazy is going on right now. We are in the green forests of Drandor. Drandor is one of my worlds," Froth Lord continued.

"One of *your* worlds?" I asked.

"Unfortunately yes," answered Froth Lord

Thog rejoined the group. He had put himself in the fetal position for a bit for calming.

"So, you are not a real god?" asked Phobus

"It depends on who you ask, or even who you are." answered Froth Lord. Then he started to laugh once again.

"I'm not really sure to be quite honest about it. Sometimes I can't remember all the way back. I don't think so though," he finished.

"What about the time shifts? WHEN are we right now?" I asked him.

"There have been no time shifts at all. You are still in the same time period you have always been," Froth Lord answered.

He explained to me many years later how he was able to fully trick us into believing that there had been a time shift. He reminded me of the "Mind Storming Device" that he used on us previously. He gave some more background how that thing worked. With the device he can pick and choose what we remember, and we don't remember. Same thing with thought implants and reading thoughts. He can curve space and time locally, even down to an individual or small group level. It is a pretty decent device.

"Did you really choose us for something?" I asked him.

"Yes, this is true," began Froth Lord. "Let me explain now. I have put you all through enough."

"Thog called me a human?" I asked, not at all expecting the answer I received.

"You, Coranthas, are in fact indigenous to the planet Earth and are a human being. I wanted to reveal this to you myself eventually. I should never have told Thog. That was my bad," he said.

"You are in fact, the only surviving member of humanity. I broke many laws saving you. Let me explain it all," he began.

Chapter Eight
Froth Lord Reveals the Plan at Drandor

The inhabitants of neither Sholl Gar nor Delta Five are aware, in any manner, of the true nature of the galaxy. Froth Lord began to explain everything. All the deep truths are hidden away, he said. The Zynon galaxy is absolutely teaming with intelligent Sentient life forms. These life forms are constantly discovering each other, befriending each other, warring with each other, and experimenting on each other. He told us all about Article 19 of the intergalactic code.

He explained how he saved at least nine worlds from total destruction by becoming the god of these worlds. In fact, we were sitting on one of them. He told us of the true nature of the Broth for the first time. (As if we could understand.)

We all knew that the Broth was the most important product in the galaxy. Froth Lord explained to us, though, the Broth was in fact the essence of life itself. Life could not exist in the universe without the Broth. And that all life shared an interconnected essence due to the very quantum nature of how the Broth was made. "Entanglement" was the term he used. It had something to do with how particles are charged or something like that. I don't remember exactly. I was getting tired by this point.

He explained that the most advanced Sentients ever discovered were, in fact, his people. His people evolved on the planet Nectar eons ago. It is believed that Nectar is the world where the Broth first created biological life. We had only thought the planet Nectar to be legendary. Froth Lord had *ascended* many epochs ago. He can take on the form of a near countless of number of Zynon galaxy species. When he wants to exist on our plane as he was now, he chooses the form of a Human Man.

"I like Earth stuff," he would say.

Nectarians are the only Sentients that have ever directly communicated with Dendrake. Many think he is a "god". He created all life and the Broth, or at least the life process which the Broth induces. This is how it is commonly taught. However, no one has ever said that he created the universe or matter itself. It may be likely that these things have always existed. The math may very well prove out on that one some day.

Dendrake himself may just be the most advanced creature in the universe, but yet still not a god. That small distinction may not be relevant anymore. But if Froth Lord's people considered Dendrake a god, then I can't imagine arguing about it.

"So Sentients don't produce our own Broth?" I asked.

"No of course not. Dendrake somehow delivered it to you without you knowing," Froth Lord answered. So, in a nutshell, all life is dependent on the Broth. The most primitive Sentient life does not even know of the Broth. It was simply delivered and deposited in the early water supplies by Dendrake. It self-replicates forever. If it fails to continue to self-replicate, life on that world perishes.

Only the more advanced sentients know of the Broth to this level of discussion. Froth Lord explained that when Earth was to be destroyed by the Garthonians, he decided to rescue one human due to his love of their kind and human civilization. That human being turned out to be me. For some reason I was not shocked at all about this. In fact, things began to make sense to me.

"Did you ever wonder why you have an endless supply of Coors and Miller Lite?" asked Froth Lord.

"Also did you ever wonder why you live in a huge compound on Delta Five, and are surrounded by servants and drone slaves?" he continued.

"It had crossed my mind occasionally," I admitted.

Basically, Froth Lord erased my memory, built a large fortress for me on Delta Five, and surrounded me with a legion of drones and sub-servants. I was given strength by Froth Lord. He had implanted great powers and incredible understanding into my mind. All my powers come from him, and he monitors them, and limits them when necessary. But all for my own good, he would say.

"Did you ever wonder why you can teleport yourself anywhere in the galaxy?" Froth Lord continued.

"All right, all right, I get it," I answered, embarrassed somewhat.

"Why didn't you save some Heineken?" I asked him.

"Coranthas I looked for Heineken, I swear to you. I was rushed. That was my favorite too," was Froth's answer.

"I had a massive store of shit I had to launch on out of there," he added.

He described how he had got the Mona Lisa, volumes upon volumes of ancient Earth writings. The US Declaration of Independence. He saved some elephants.

"Elephants are cool," said Thog.

"Yes they are indeed Thog," he said as if to a child.

He had retrieved as much firepower as he could to keep it "safe." He took a lot of nuclear weapons just to make sure they did not fall into any nefarious hands like the Garthonians.

"So, what is the deal with Phobus?" I asked him

"Yeah, what is my story?" Phobus chirped in.

"Let me explain," began Froth Lord once more.

It had become clear to Froth Lord that I needed a very close companion. He wanted someone who would be my best of friends. No one on Delta Five qualified. He chose Phobus of Sholl Gar for no good reason whatsoever. He admitted that this was one of the only times he made a choice based on pretty much nothing. The only reason that Froth Lord knew of him was because he was abusing Thog on Sholl Gar.

Froth Lord went down to Sholl Gar and secretly convinced the Large Master to send Phobus to a "university" on another world. (He used mind thought implantations on her.) This university turned out to be my compound on Delta Five. Froth Lord fabricated our entire experience during those years. We were actually both comatose in a cryochamber with electrodes connecting our temporal lobes via a copper conductor. Our entire friendship was programmed into are brains in exactly seven seconds.

"Cool," said Thog

"So what about Thog?" asked Phobus.

"How did he even get to Sholl Gar?" I asked.

"Thog's story is different," began Froth Lord with a sigh.

"I already told you much about it. Everything I have already told you is true. Thog is not a true Sentient life form," he finished.

Thog gave Froth Lord a confused look. "Excuse me?" Thog asked.

"I built you in my space lab," said Froth Lord.

"You BUILT me?" Thog asked

"Yes, I built you in space, your whole species actually, right in my space lab," Froth reiterated.

"Wait a second, you told me I was one of the greatest Sentient life forms in the universe?" queried Thog.

"I lied," was Froth's reply.

This was getting good, I thought.

"Thog I may have been fooled completely about everything that I ever thought was true, but at least I'm real." I laughed out loud.

"Yeah, at least we're real dude," added Phobus.

Thog went to burst retaliatory lightning fire toward Phobus, but nothing came out, and he slipped and tripped over a bush in an epic fail.

"Sorry Thog I cut you off, too risky to keep you jacked up," said Froth Lord with a grin.

"What the fuck is going on over here?! Someone get me off the ground for god's sake," wailed Thog.

Phobus is rolling on the ground pissing his pants. I was trying to remain composed, but swill was coming down my face. Like I had already mentioned this was getting good. The kid was unraveling now. He earned this too.

"He was messing with you as much as us dude!" Phobus added. Thog became confused.

"Where the fuck's my lobe tubing?" he yelled, clutching his temporal lobe, exposed as it were, in horror.

"Where's the fucking tubing?" he wailed.

Even Froth Lord was trying not to crack up at this point. He pulled out a remote control, aimed it at Thog, and hit "OFF." Thog rested in the fetal position.

"Okay, let's discuss what has to happen next," began Froth Lord. Froth Lord told us how he had tired greatly of his entire plan to circumvent the destruction of innocent worlds. Thog had been created to take over as Lord over the worlds in question by managing all the deployed AI Thog clones. Now even managing the Articificial Intelligences was out of reach. God knows where they all are. None of this was going to happen anymore. However, he still loved the first Thog, and wanted us to befriend him for now.

Chapter Nine
125 Years later, Sholl Gar

The morning light of the rising suns burst through the central chamber of the High Master's palace. It was a beautiful morning. Palace guards and servants were happily about their business. Sub-creatures were preparing meals, draining excess fluid from each other, and inspecting the defensive positions of the sub-Lords guarding the perimeter.

Usually there were at least three or four frontal assaults by the first noon. By the time the second sun reaches its apex, Phobus usually awakes. It was imperative that any attacks be warded off and defeated prior to his waking. This morning seemed relatively peaceful, until Thog's squad of drones received a large ionic blast from the southwest.

The burst of fire hit the shields head on. Thog, Chief of the High Master's defense, had never seen such an effective first blast. His shields lost fifty percent of their power, and Thog was worried about the potential of this offensive being launched by beings who were essentially sub-creature wretches from the dunes.

"Fire the anti-matter cannon into their numbers directly, Captain!" Thog ordered.

"We must annihilate them before Phobus gets up. He usually wanders out to pee around now."

"They have shield generators fired up to full power," yelled out Janker.

Fortunately, the sub-creatures' shields are for the most part useless. The anti-matter cannons destroyed them within two minutes of steady blasting. Drones went out to clean up the remains. Things were pretty much under control when Phobus came out for his breakfast.

Thog was completely unaware that all his entire past was a series of false implants programmed into his artificial brain. 125 years earlier, Froth Lord had completely erased Thog's memory. He replaced the memories with a false lifetime of having served Phobus in the Sholl Gar military. As a young man he had been a simple foot soldier in the first and second Dune Wars.

He had met Phobus during a particularly ghastly trench defense of the Young One's fortress during *Dune War One*. They held the same rank as private and were awarded many medals for the bravery. Dune War One was a truly ghastly affair that it seemed neither side would win. Gang Lords would constantly switch sides during this seemingly endless nightmare. Ultimately both Thog and Phobus were promoted many ranks, and even became protectors of the Young One, the King of Sholl Gar. They were given the highest rank during that time as *Guardians of Sholl Gar*.

They became gunners together and fought off the many assaults on the Young One's palace. Then for nearly a decade they were captains in the offensive Dune assaults. It had become clear to the Young One that it was necessary to purge the rebellious sub-creatures from Sholl Gar completely. These series of battles accumulated and are now referred to as *Dune War Two*. Eventually, all these horrors simply became folded into the wider catch-all collective known simply *as the Dune Wars*.

The rest of these planted memories led him to the point where he was a sub-servant Major in the High Master's army. The High Master was now Phobus after the Young One's exile. These memories are of course all false implants. Froth Lord programmed the entire back history of Thog's AI code in approximately eleven seconds inside a temporary lab tent he had setup on Sholl Gar right after they landed. No creature on Sholl Gar ever questioned anything Thog would say. But the current assaults described herein on this glorious morning were real and common.

After Froth Lord reprogrammed Thog, inserted Phobus as High Master on Sholl Gar, and brought me back to Delta Five, he retired to an unknown dimension. I figured I would never see him again. I had no idea that he was about to reenter my life.

I had not heard from dear Phobus for close to five years. I had not seen or heard from Froth Lord since he brought me back here. It was all so surreal. I would play my Playstation, watch *South Park*, consume Broth and beer for long periods. The Witch Doctor consistently told me I was imagining most of this. That it was a common byproduct of my condition. She accused me of just taking her ship for a long joy ride, and none of what I described actually happened. She was correct to the extent that Froth Lord had implanted the origins of my friendship with Phobus. But she was wrong about these things not being real. Froth Lord had, in fact, done that to us. So, we were essentially experimented on, and used like pawns. And beyond that my powers were real and they came from him. Anyways, back to Sholl Gar that morning of the frontal assault.

"Thog drain my sore," ordered Phobus.

"Of course I will Master," was Thog's reply

The tedium of ruling Sholl Gar was boring Phobus so severely that depression had set in for many years. He missed our old times together. He was unaware of the torment my existence on Delta Five had become.

- Delta Five, dreaming again

Sometimes I cannot sleep. Even days can go by without so much as a moment of rest. The Witch Doctor considers this to be part of some unexplained posttraumatic stress disorder. And though I had been going through a bit of a bout of insomnia, that afternoon I did finally drifted off. I had not had the dream for quite a while, but here I found myself once again inside my recurring dreamscape I have described to you before. Whenever I had this recurring dream, it begins with me not realizing I was not awake. I am there in my chamber. The familiar distortion in distance and size is overwhelming as my chamber feels as though I am inside a large arena.

I sense five separate elements aside from myself within this dream. Each *element* is some kind of entity or force. Three are seen. Two are unseen. I look at the three men in my chamber. Normally, I cannot really see them other than a general sense or impression that a being is present. This time they are clearly beings. They are men of some sort by the looks of them. Each are wearing white robes and appear old. They have an appearance roughly approximating my own. By now I had learned I was a human being. But I am the only human being left.

And though this was a dream there was something very real about them. There was something very *present* about them.

So that explains three of the five elements. The three seen elements are better understood. I mentioned, obviously, that there are two unseen elements as well. There are two other entities if you will. And the reason I know there are two unseen elements is there are two diametrically opposed feelings projected onto me in this iteration, and these sensations are not emanating from the seen elements. There is a deep, foreboding dark presence that if it were not for the other protective presence, would consume me for sure. It was an apprehension so strong, a suspicion so deep, that I could hardly bear it. Yet simultaneously, I sensed a blanketing of protection enveloping me. I feel a security. There is no question there are two unseen elements behind these. There is a second presence blanketing me in a shielding. In my dream they are entities all. My only question is are they also entities outside of my dreams? It had been a very deep sleep and I had needed one. Now I awoke.

- My struggle at that time

My thoughts were still on Froth Lord even after all these years. He had put me here in this compound. He provides me with all that I require. His plans determine all that occurs in my so-called life. For all I know he and the Witch Doctor work together.

Froth Lord revealed everything to me on Drandor. Yet I have not heard from him in five or six years. It is hard to explain the insignificance I now feel. I have learned of the most amazing realities of the nature of existence itself.

The mysteries of the Broth he explained to me. The nature of my existence was fully revealed. I felt that I needed a vacation from Delta Five once more.

"Captain Andares?" I radioed.

"Yes," replied the drone over a commlink.

"Get Phobus on the line, would you?"

"Roger that sir," was the captain's reply.

These drones are so boring, I thought to myself. I would often line them up in the back yard and blast them with my side arm. They would simply submit to their destruction for my amusement's sake. The whole thing was so tedious. Another thing had happened to me that I can't explain. Not even Froth Lord could prevent it.

It had become very difficult for me to distinguish from the things that are real and from the quantum anomalies that were constantly occurring to me. How do I even know if my memories are real? I already know now that some of them are not. Is it possible for me to discern between the planted memories and the real memories? How do I know that this very moment sitting here is a "real" moment and not something planted? How do I know that I was not also created in some lab? Maybe I am just someone's twisted computer simulation, my operator laughing each time he reboots me.

I supposed I can do the test Froth Lord showed me with the diamond-shaped stone. That test obviously is always done in the *present moment,* so it has unique power in grounding you that what is occurring is real. The last time I saw Froth Lord, when he brought me back to Delta Five, he had presented me with this stone. He told me it would help me to discern reality from unreality. I didn't buy it. He said if I was unsure of reality just grab the stone, breathe, and count to ten. As I said, I did not "buy it" that there was something about the stone itself. But I do think that the idea of grounding myself like that in the present moment did in fact help. I would do the exercise often now.

And why in the world did Froth Lord bother to save me anyway? I have no spouse. There is no way for me to continue humanity. Someday I will die no matter how long Froth Lord can delay it, it still is inevitable. Even he will perish someday I believe, though he likes to think that is not the case. I remember Froth Lord tried for several years to try and decode the mystery of what is wrong with me.

My condition truly baffled him, and I think even troubled him some. It was not his intent to cause me harm, at least I don't think so. He said he was sorry for scrambling my brain so. He did not understand why Phobus, whom he viewed as a much weaker specimen than I, was basically fine and even thriving. There would be some issues with me he figured, having gone through all that we had, but again, why was Phobus essentially fine?

It must have something to do with being the only human being in the universe, or so I thought. Or perhaps the Witch Doctor's diagnosis is correct. These were the kinds of thoughts and ponderings which made things dark for me on Delta Five so often.

"Phobus is on the phone sir."

An old Earth Texas drawl voice came over the commlink. I had a couple drones programmed this way to teach me more about Human culture.

I suddenly felt a momentary dread!

"Not the Alpha seven channel, please, dear god, is it!?" I asked instinctually.

"Nawsuh," the drone answered.

"He just on line one sir," he finished.

My dear friend Phobus is real. This much I knew for certain.

"Hey Coranthas. How's it going buddy?" asked Phobus.

Meanwhile, several servants were attending to his fluid wounds. He was also being kept alive by extremely advanced Sentient technology maintained by creatures left by Froth Lord.

"Listen, can I come over?" I asked

"Sure blast on over," replied Phobus.

It's funny even after many years Phobus and I could just get together, and it was always like we never had parted. The drones on Delta Five did not like it when I would leave to see Phobus or when I would talk about Froth Lord. They liked to keep me calm and quiet. I had enough of Delta Five for now. All I took was a side arm. I knew Phobus and Thog had enough Broth to go around. And the one thing I always know is that it won't boring over there. For all the horror of Sholl Gar, as I mentioned in the beginning, I always loved the excitement on that world.

It was actually a very nice morning on Sholl Gar. Though I had not been there for quite some time, it seemed like only yesterday when Phobus and I were taking target practice on some Dregs near Forinth Dune. As I walked toward the old Large Master's palace. I thought about the time I briefly ruled with Phobus over this world. It all seemed like a dream and was so long ago. I also wondered what our last score had been. I know he was winning big, but I could not recall the numbers. I'm sure he still has kept track of the tally.

I entered through the garden areas, and Phobus was outside being attended to by three very tall beings in white robes. These beings had been left by Froth Lord who would keep Phobus alive eons past his years. This is all I knew about them. They looked at me curiously as I entered the sanctum area of the garden. One of them smiled, I think. I did do a double take and make full eye contact with the being, and for some reason I was more curious than I would have expected. Froth Lord put Phobus in their care. That was all I needed to know.

"Phobus!" I exclaimed.

"Hey Coranthas. Welcome to my world," he responded.

"That's right it's your world now," I said.

"Ah yes, it is nice to be the king," he answered.

We both laughed for several hours recounting many stories. He told me of at least four full scale purgings he and Thog had engaged in during the past five or six years since our last meeting.

My friend told me one funny story that I will always hold dear. This one is re-told endlessly in Sholl-Garian saloons and space dives. Basically, the Young One made one attempt to reclaim his thrown. Froth Lord had removed the Young One and put Phobus in control roughly 125 years ago. The Young One had been ban-ished to the fourth moon of Drandor. (Ironically the same place we first encoun-tered Froth Lord.)

The Young One was kept alive in a twelve-square-foot cube on the surface of the moon. Many specimens that Froth Lord collected were stored in a similar fashion, all in the same sector on this moon. Most were within visual range of each other. There was one six-hundred-square-yard area where there were literally thousands of cube-shaped prisons. It was an amazing zoo essentially. Think of it! Thousands of beings from all over the galaxy encased in clear cube cells. It seems a bit horrible to first hear of it, but Froth Lord must have his reasons I surmised. Thankfully he likes me.

Some of these beings learned to communicate with each other using a form of sign language they developed over thousands of years of imprisonment. It took extremely long periods of time to be able to communicate effectively. First using signs they had to establish the rules of their new language. Then they had to learn how to have the most basic communication and eventually conversations. They worked very hard at it for very long periods. Eventually, the language they were able to build paid off. The Young One and another prisoner hatched a plan. Be-cause this was an utterly lifeless moon, Broth had to be delivered to the specimens for them not to perish in their chambers.

Pods from various worlds under Froth Lord's dominion would bring the Broth. It was hard to see whether this was mercy or cruelty. He was keeping them alive for in some cases thousands of years past their normal life spans. Yet he left them in their cubes on this lifeless moon. He even stopped his experiments on most of them. I've said it before, but Froth Lord is very complicated.

I never received what I considered an acceptable explanation from Froth Lord as to why he did these things. Anyway the Young One and this other creature, who was ironically also from planet Earth, though not human, hatched an escape plan. Millions of years before humans existed another intelligent Sentient species had briefly used earth as an outpost. They were scientists, and they were studying how the Broth was bringing about the early Earth life evolutionary process. They were a funny bunch. They even built massive prymids just to mess with any Sentients that would later evolve from the Broth. (My kind) One of those beings attempted even deeper space travel and ended up imprisoned here. Obviously he bumped into Froth Lord during his more youthful, reckless years. Over a hundred years the Young One and this "earthling," for lack of a better term, using sign language that they developed and formed their plan.

"When the hose comes through the port grab it real hard okay?" signed the Young One to his friend. *What the hell?* he thought. *There is nothing to lose.* Amazingly it worked!

He grabbed the hose and pulled the unsuspecting drone into the cube and destroyed him. The Young One simultaneously did the same. Both hopped into the same Pod. The Pods were preprogrammed to return to its world of origin. They figure once they arrived they would figure out what to do next. Their Pod reached the planet Harthonia.

The Harthonian Sentients had long been extinct except for several hundred frozen leaders. They were known as the "Frozen Chosen." They were chosen for the future salvation of their people. Drones attended to them in their cryochambers. A thousand years earlier Froth Lord had descended upon them to declare himself Lord. Amazingly, the Harthonians didn't buy it. Their entire civilization had already decided that there were no real gods. They simply were not fooled by Froth Lord no matter what he tried.

This truly fascinated Froth Lord. He knew these people would be doomed if ever discovered by the nastier Sentients. He decided to create a Nebula Shroud that would bend space near the Harthonian star system. The Shroud he thought, would hide their existence for as long as possible. Also, he created a portal straight to the moons of Drandor. He decided that he would use the Harthonians as couriers of the Broth to his specimens on the Drandorian moon. This would serve several purposes.

First it would help to hide Froth Lord's involvement in the imprisonments on the lifeless moon. There were other powerful beings in the galaxy that would not approve of his activities. "Hey it is for science," Froth Lord would justify, but still, come on. Second it depleted the Harthonians' Broth supply. We could never figure out why this mattered to Froth Lord. For some reason, he did not want the Harthonian Broth supply to ever reach a certain critical mass.

Anyway, a strange disease began to kill off most of the Harthonians five hundred years ago. Even Froth Lord could not stop it. They decided to freeze a couple hundred of the greatest Harthonians until Froth Lord could find a cure. Before he froze them Froth Lord programmed all their drones to fly the Broth pods to Drandor for the nourishment of his experiments. Froth Lord tired of looking for a cure within three weeks.

"So Phobus how the heck did he get back to Sholl Gar?" I asked

"That's the best part my friend," began Phobus.

Apparently, outside the cryochamber, there was a book left on a coffee table near the front office on Harthonia. It was about quantum reality. It took them five years of reverse coding to figure out the language particulars used by Froth Lord. However the book outlined the entire workings of the space portal built by Froth Lord. After decoding the particulars, the Young One and his co-patriot were able to teleport to a different world in the Alpha sector, rather than back to the Drandorian moon. (Which obviously would have sucked.)

Once there they killed a space captain, reprogrammed his ship's guidance control, and set out on a trajectory that theoretically at least would get them to Sholl Gar's sector.

"I never thought the Young One could pull something like this off," I said.

"The best part is what happened when he got here," said Phobus

The Young One and his friend's ship were coming out of hyperspace three billion miles from Sholl Gar when it was detected by Froth Lord. Within two seconds a complete ion scan determined for Froth Lord that the Young One was onboard, just as he had planned.

He grinned. Immediately Froth Lord cloaked himself and descended to Sholl Gar. In the form of a dune wretch he lied in wait. The Young One landed on Sholl Gar and immediately headed toward his old palace. Froth Lord watched through a virtual portal on his commlink wrist watch.

"Froth Lord told you he was coming?" I asked knowingly.

"Oh yeah," answered Phobus with excitement in his tone.

"Oh yeah he did," he said again.

This was getting good, I thought.

"It was like old times in the most intense way. I had wished for years that you had been there my friend," he finished.

We laughed together. Phobus continued the story. As soon as he got near the palace the Young One entered through the main gate. In front of him was what appeared to be a defenseless Phobus, sitting on his thrown. The Young One pulled out a lightning cane he had gotten through a trade with a sub-slave outside the palace near the sub-creature tents. (That had been Froth Lord.) He raised it toward Phobus when, all the sudden...

"KABAAAM" the brightest set of strobe lights of all known colors were suddenly switched on. Loud circus music burst from every direction, and all the curtains of the chamber were run back exposing a large studio audience of thousands of sub-Lords, sub-creatures, drones, and various other species.

The Young One turned in horror to see that the entire chamber was now a gigantic game show studio with thousands of witnesses. He turned back violently toward Phobus who was now in full game show host attire. And standing next to him was the game show's sidekick Thog. The whole thing was a setup.

"What do we have for him Thog?!" exclaimed Phobus exuberantly into his microphone, the crowd cheering, jeering, and jumping up in down.

"Death!" cried the studio audience.

"Death!?" cried Phobus.

"Waaaait just a second. He doesn't get off that easily, now does he Thog?" asked Phobus, twirling his game show host cape and hat.

"I think he needs to pass the test before we let him off with death, don't you, Phobus?" asked Thog

"Yes, he does, dear Thog. But let's not get ahead of ourselves. Let's first meet the Young One's opponent today," Phobus joyfully exclaimed.

The audience continued to roar.

"Hailing from a distant world, hunted, cornered, and captured by a thousand drones before being finally subdued, please give a warm welcome to Darlock the Destroyer!"

The Young One looked down sheepishly. *Jesus...they caught Darlock, I don't believe this,* he thought.

"Darlock the Destroyer, ruler of a hundred worlds. The undefeated ruler of twelve worlds. Let's give him a hand!" Phobus announced.

The crowd roared its approval in great anticipation. During the ongoing roar, Phobus began again.

"Today's challenger." At these words the crowd began to hiss, moan, and jeer. All the while they threw fruit and sub-slaves at the Young One.

"Give him his due, your former Master, and one-time ruler of Sholl Gar, please welcome, the Young One!" Phobus finished while clapping his hands.

The jeers were deafening. The Young One looked around the forum and then back over to the Destroyer and just set himself down on his stool.

"Come to the center!" cried Thog.

The Young One and Darlock came to meet at the center of the forum. Thog began to describe the rules, while Phobus walked around the chamber, waving to his populace.

"You will both be faced with a series of complex mathematical formulas. These formulas each represent a specific quantum theory known only to the greatest quantum scientists of the Zynon galaxy." The crowd was now more quiet and intense in anticipation. Froth Lord played the old Earth Final *Jeapardy* theme over the speaker system as they all waited anxiously.

Thog pointed to some books on a pedestal. "These journals here represent the most detailed quantum science texts ever written. They are pertinent to the subjects you will be asked about. You will each choose a text now," continued Thog

The crowd went into an absolute frenzy. Sub-creatures from every part of Sholl Gar were ranting and raving in the general direction of the contestants. Darlock grabbed his journal first. He picked a one-thousand-page document that discussed mostly black holes. He had no idea what he was doing.

The Young One had some experience with the works of Froth Lord and grabbed a book on quantum mechanics. Regular books are sometimes challenging with the false thumb, but he would manage. He could grab the base of the book with the left hand and turn pages with his pointy digit.

I can do this, thought the Young One. *I can do this!* Then Thog approached the podium.

"Here are the rules," he began. "I will give you the problem, and as soon as I say go, you begin to work the problem. Are you ready?" he finished.

Both nodded their readiness. Thog handed question One to both participants. No one was sure what the question had been. The instant that Thog yelled "GOOOOO!" Darlock, who completely misunderstood all that was occurring, pulled out a sword and slayed the Young One on the spot. It didn't matter. The crowd loved it. Darlock didn't like math anyway, and frankly, when Thog yelled "GOOOOO!" he got a bit over excited. He killed the Young One in a matter of seconds. It ended up being one of the most watched spectacles in syndication on Sholl Gar historically. Darlock was terminated immediately.

"I wish I had been here," I said

"So how are things on Delta Five?" Phobus asked.

"Phobus the tedious life I am living is unbearable. I have a thousand servants, none of whom are living beings except the Witch Doctor. They meet my every need. I have no chores, no tasks. I just watch Netflix or *South Park* DVDs all day and I consume Broth and beer for years on end," he finished.

"Sounds pretty great to me to be honest," replied Phobus.

"So weird that you have a Witch Doctor living in your house," said Thog.

"Froth Lord has not come to see me for a very long time. Have you guys seen him lately?" I asked.

Thog received a red beacon on his chest panel and had to go see what it is about.

"Excuse me Master. Nice to see you again Coranthas," he said before jetting off.

"Sure, he swings by to check on Thog," Phobus answered.

"Why do you think he checks on Thog still? He gave up his ancient plans to install him as Lord over his dominions. I wonder what he is up to now," I said

"You do have a point," started Phobus. "He once was such an idealist. Has he become discouraged?" he finished

"I don't know. We are lucky he likes us. The three of us have such a bond due to Froth Lord. He created Thog, rescued me, and chose you to be my friend. Do you think he has told us everything though?" I asked

"What do you mean?" asked Phobus

"Well all those years ago when he revealed to us everything. How do we know what is true and what isn't? I mean these are the things that torment me in my compound daily," I finished.

Most of what he told us had clearly been true. He explained my ability to travel throughout the galaxy at will. He exposed the truth of my compound and servants on Delta Five. I was told how he saved me from extinction. But still at that time I felt something was off. It was probably my condition.

"We really have no choice but to believe him, don't you think?" added Phobus.

"True, but I can't help feeling there is something more. I don't think he wishes me harm or anything like that. It's just, well, why have I not seen him for so long?" I finished.

"Hmm, I don't really know," said Phobus with a curious expression.

"He could be out hunting all the Thog clones. He did say he lost track for thousands of them. Who knows," finished Phobus.

Though I had found myself questioning many things over the years, this was the first time I really started to wonder more deeply about where Froth Lord might have come from. This was the first that time that I felt like I needed some kind of explanation. The best part though, was that I really felt like I was thinking clearly on this day. I had a strong focus at that moment. So many times I have existed in a foggy, cloudy state.

In the past before he had revealed all he was doing to us, I had been trying to discover his secrets. But now many years after he had revealed the truth to us, I started to find myself caring what the answers might be to his origins. I mean what has he still not told us?

Chapter Ten

Interstellar Café,
175 Years After the Large Master's Death

"Froth Lord it's your move," I said

"Thank you Coranthas. I'm still thinking," he answered, as if he needed to think what his next chess move would be.

I had never come close to defeating Froth Lord at chess. He even told me and explained how to defend the various opening attacks he would make. He loved to use the "Napoleon" attack. Froth Lord showed me how if not defended properly the Napoleon attack could lead to checkmate in as few as four total moves. But he also showed me how to defend it. However even if I did defend it properly he would just alter the attack vector and still defeat me. Funnily enough I would always use the same Napoleon attack against Phobus and Thog, and I win at least fifty percent of the time. The problem with playing Froth Lord at chess was that he already has memorized every possible outcome, built upon every possible move combination of both black and white, even though there are three billion roughly. He was a tough out at chess.

Thog and Phobus stared out their shared portal at the globe of fire roughly one hundred thousand miles below. This had to be our 150th vacation together at the Interstellar Café. They were beginning to seem like a blur to me anyway. They also had lost their luster almost entirely for me. Other than getting together with the guys, I almost did not care to go. We didn't even buy a program this year.

"Anyone know what world this is or was rather?" asked Thog

"Nope," replied Froth Lord

"See if you can get some information down at the bar and score me a Broth," I said.

Just then Froth Lord checkmated me. Once again he had used the Napoleon attack the king's pawn opening, but I thought I had defended it perfectly. I was wrong.

"You bastard," I said

"Whatever," he replied

None of us had the same zeal for these vacations anymore obviously. The interstellar government had changed hands for the first time in two hundred years recently. There were rumors that the Interstellar Café may get even more publicity and marketing as soon as regulations loosen. The Council of Drakar was utterly corrupt as usual.

"This used to be so trendy," began Thog.

"Now everyone is coming. I mean look over there at those sub-creatures from Sholl Gar. I never would have imagined sub-men from Sholl Gar would grace this once majestic place," Thog finished.

Phobus and Thog had had to evacuate Sholl Gar fifteen years earlier due to some overlord named Dominick starting an uprising of some kind. It was good for me because Phobus was around all the time now. He even stays with me on Delta Five for long periods now. I had no idea the adventure that was about to happen to us. I still could not believe that Froth Lord had defeated me at chess again.

"Are you guys bored?" asked Froth Lord.

"Um yeah," said Phobus sarcastically.

"Me too," he said.

"I know and this trip has only just begun," I added

"I have an idea," said Froth Lord

If I had learned one thing about Froth Lord by now it was that we were in for something major. I had no idea what he was talking about yet, but I was in. I mean of course, whatever it was, I was in.

"I'm in," I said

"Me too," added both Phobus and Thog.

Once again things were going to get good.

"You guys don't even care what we are going to do?" Froth Lord said with a grin.

"Nope," was my reply.

"Not really, no," added Phobus.

"This vacation sucks anyway," chimed in Thog.

"Well it's never been done before, but we can very easily do it. At least I can do it," said Froth Lord.

Froth Lord brought us out to his starship. He had no need whatsoever for a starship to get around. But he just loved this thing. I mean it was a totally sick ship. It had like one thousand drone staff. Only the greatest oligarchs could have something like this beast. It is amazing too because he tends never to fly it anywhere. He just hangs out on it. He will teleport the ship with guests onboard using quantum jumps, but he never the needs the ship to get around is what I am trying to say.

"Decent ship," said Phobus.

He teleported us on the starship to the Drandorian moons so our conversation would be private. Once in orbit we started to discuss his idea. There he laid out the plan that would consume us for the next twenty years. He described to us our most noble effort we would ever undertake.

"We're going to fight back for these helpless worlds," Froth Lord began.

"It's what I should have done from the very beginning. It's ironic. Now that I have become such a reckless, careless fiend for the most part I can take such action. Thousands of years ago I did not have the courage to fight for these worlds. But now I do. They cannot defeat me, and you will be safe with me forever," he finished.

"I spent all that time and energy becoming a god over Sentient life forms. What a waste of time cloning and sending all those Thogs to be their Saviors. I could have just defended these worlds with my powers," he reasoned.

For some reason the idea of defending those helpless worlds with his near limitless supernatural powers had seem unethical to him. But now it seemed like the most obvious of all possible solutions.

"I could have saved countless more worlds and life forms. I could have trained them in my ways and rose great leaders. We could have created a massive alliance amongst these ghastly worlds and empires. Eventually we could have formed a secession from the Intergalactic rule. We could have even ruled the entire Zynon galaxy by now. Well better late than never," he finished.

"A little too much Broth Froth Man?" asked Phobus.

"What about the Others?" I asked.

"Others?" Phobus asked.

"I am not worried about the Others," said Froth Lord

"Umm, I don't mean to pry in on a private conversation guys, but what do you mean by 'Others'?" asked Phobus again.

"Froth Lord is not the only Nectarian Phobus," I added.

"Well of course he's not the only Nectarian, but what…" Phobus caught himself in mid-sentence when he realized he had never really thought about that before.

"You mean other Nectarians as powerful as Froth Lord?" added Thog.

"Yes. That is what I mean," I added.

"They will not interfere," added Froth Lord. "Do you care to resist me?" he joked.

"No, certainly, we don't want to resist," said Phobus

"Resist?" added Thog with a nervous laugh "God no. Of course not," he finished.

I had long ago stopped caring what Froth Lord could do to me. For some reason I never feared him. Also, I really like the idea. We could do tremendous good. But way more important than that was how *not boring* this would be. Boredom was one of the worst states for one with my condition. Boredom is the perfect breeding ground for my hallucinations, delusions, and scattered thinking. Purpose and activity were the perfect countermeasure.

"So, what do we do next?" I asked

Chapter Eleven

Froth Lord's Assault Force

For the next three years Froth Lord engineered an assault force of such power that no sentient in the Zynon galaxy had ever seen. At its apex of strength it would be ten times the size of the largest fleet the Garthonians ever created. Also the tech was unreal. The quantum jump drives, the star fighters, the ionization cannons, all perfectly tuned and engineered by Froth Lord. Nuclear concussion missiles particularly designed to be starfleet killers were mounted on all the cruisers.

Ancient Nectarians did not believe in war. That, quite frankly, is the only reason they never ruled the entire galaxy by themselves. Froth Lord made a calculated choice to go against this historical pacifist position. Rather than using Drones as pilots and crew Froth Lord cloned me five hundred thousand times. I hope fervently that he would not lose track of these clones too.

These clones would man the starships, operate the cannons, and board enemy ships for hand-to-hand combat when required. They would pilot star fighters. The fleet would use quantum portals to travel through space to confront assault fleets of attacking worlds. No enemy would be able to touch this force unless other Nectarians interfered. This was going to get good and quick.

There were ten thousand attack cruisers in the fleet. Each ship had two thousand outboard anti-matter cannons, three hundred attack fighters, and an impressive array of nuclear class weapons. Using time-shifting Froth Lord would always know precisely when a planet was to be destroyed. In each instance he would be able to meet approaching fleets before they even reach the world they were planning to obliterate. It was even possible for us to launch preemptive strikes before the fleets' commanders became aware they were even going to attack in the first place.

The idea was brilliant. There was literally no way to stop Froth Lord's plan. It was quite simply an act of his will and nothing else. That's all it took. Once he decided to interfere, it was all a done deal. Just so long as no one more powerful interferes with him. It remained unclear whether that was even possible.

Froth Lord saw no problem with this course of action. The attackers were wrong and shameless. He was defending innocent and otherwise defenseless civilizations. His more idealistic self had returned. Though ancient Nectarians had always been against war, and certainly would have been against the merciless destruction of Sentient worlds, they would likely also have frowned greatly on Froth Lord's actions. Their code had always been one that required great respect for their own great power. The only thing is no one had ever encountered other Nectarians existing on this plane other than Froth Lord. Perhaps a brief discussion of the "Others" would fit here nicely. Phobus has been surprised when I mentioned them. The only Nectarians known to exist, besides Froth Lord, exist on a higher plane. It is thought they do not generally approve of much of what Froth Lord does on our plane. These beings have always been referred to as *the Others* since when I first learned of them.

Ancient Nectarians, before ascending to a higher realm, had always known what they were capable of doing. But they first chose never to exercise their powers. Then they mysteriously chose to leave our plane. Even the Broth was mostly at their disposal prior. Froth Lord never believed in Dendrake. To clarify, Froth Lord did not believe that Dendrake was God or a god. (Even though this was the official position of Ancient Nectarian Councils.) He always just presumed he was the most powerful Sentient to ever exist.

He did believe he was real of course. He just believed that he was the most powerful, advanced, and evolved Sentient Being in the galaxy or even universe. It was because of Dendrake that Ancient Nectarians chose not to conquer or rule. They simply believed it would come back to bite them rather badly if they abused their power except in limited ways.

For instance, the type of long-term experimentation Froth Lord did on me, Phobus, Thog, Sholl Gar, etc. was, for the most part fine. Even his declaring himself to be God over entire worlds to spare them destruction was looked on as quite clever by some of Froth Lord's contemporaries. However destroying any life forms, especially in mass, was greatly frowned upon. Froth Lord's plan's success was based entirely on lack of interference. Frankly it was unknown if any Nectarians still existed or would care even if they did.

Certainly based on rational observation of reality Dendrake is not going to interfere. He seems to not care about anything that goes on in the universe. If he has not been seen or heard from since before he created the Broth, then we certainly wouldn't hear from him now over this.

Chapter Twelve

War!

We saved an entire world.

Two hundred and ninety years after the death of the Large Master, five years after Froth Lord began construction of the greatest assault force of any kind ever to exist, thousands of years after the unnatural birth of Thog, war broke out in the Zynon galaxy.

The Darlock Vampire Guild had discovered a world of Sentients on a planet they called Q-7. These poor people had recently unified under one-world government. They had traveled to their two moons and the nearest planet in their solar system. They were no danger or threat to anyone. They did not even war on each other anymore. What a refreshing change this civilization was shaping up to be.

Many even believed that they were advanced enough to receive the intrusion of other Sentient life forms in the galaxy. The Darlocks were unhappy. This was the first innocent civilization they had discovered, and they wanted to obliterate it. Of course, they would need the help of the Garthonians. Months of debate ended with the Council of Drakar agreeing to allow the Darlocks to destroy the residents of Q-7. I remember thinking they were probably just as smart as the Darlocks. After all, many of these sentient worlds are only advanced because of help they received from other advanced beings in the galaxy.

Our defense fleet and assault force were ready. The only problem was we had no idea whatsoever where Froth Lord was anymore. We had not seen him for at least nine months. We had hundreds of thousands of clones (clones of me no less), ten thousand assault ships, and more nukes than anyone should have, all ready at our disposal. We just never had used any of it before.

The Interstellar Café was being moved into place. A very interesting thing happened. The residents of Q-7 detected the cafe roughly ninety thousand kilometers above its surface before any of the Destroyers had arrived. Much to their chagrin, the residents of Q-7 dispatched ten greeter crafts to rendezvous with the station. The station had no cover of any kind.

Station Commander Jok sent out an emergency request to the ion destroyers of Darlock that were in transit.

"We kind of have a situation here!" said Commander Jok

"What is the problem Jok?" replied the Darlock Assault team leader.

"Well we have ten greeter ships from Q-7. They know where here. Over," replied Jok.

"Come again?" asked Darnak, the Darlock Assault commander.

"They are right here," replied Jok. Six of Q-7's leaders already onboard, smiling and greeting members of the kitchen and bar staff. They looked to be having a grand time quite honestly.

"They are joining us for Broth," continued Jok. "Perhaps we should abort?"

"Never! We have planned this for months. You stall them, and for God's sake remain calm. We'll be there by tomorrow afternoon."

This was about to get good.

Oh god, thought Jok

Meanwhile at the helm of Witch Doctor One, majorly retrofitted and souped up by Froth Lord, I sat by the console and trembled. Phobus and Froth Lord both asked me if I wanted to captain one of the new Star Commands, but I told them I was comfortable with the Witch Doctor provided Froth Lord installed the new shields. I can quantum leap the ship it if I need to. Hell I could leap myself off it and out of here if I need to.

Phobus was captain onboard Star Command One. One of the largest and most powerful assault starcruisers ever constructed.

"Where the hell is he?" I sighed out loud.

Froth Lord had painstakingly created the greatest assault force in the history of all life, and we are just sitting here with Darlock and Garthonian assault forces getting ready to destroy an entire world of innocent sentients. I felt so defeated. We opened all commlinks among all craft and began to coordinate things.

Thog:"Well Coranthas, Froth Lord might not be here, but I think I can operate this quantum jump transport, over."

Thog:"Froth Lord usually fires it up, but I watched him in testing many times. Can you command the drones?"

I opened comms from the Witch Doctor.

Witch Doctor One:"Well actually yes, I can command the drones. Is Phobus around?"

Star Command One: "I'm here," a comforting voice came over the comm-link.

Witch Doctor One:"Phobus, did Froth Lord teach you how to command the fighter drones? Over."

Star Command One:"Nope."

Witch Doctor One:"Well we can't wait any longer. We need to code the attack sequence into the computers and the clones and fire up the quantum transport. I don't know where Froth Lord is, but we're going in, over."

At least I can teleport myself out of here if it goes to shit. Over the next hour we programmed all the clones, attack parameters, quantum transport algorithm, and nuclear launch codes. Once we were ready I got on the commlink.

Witch Doctor One:"Okay team, I'm taking command. I'm sure Froth Lord must be doing something important. Today we are going to make him proud. This is our first test."

Thog:"Yeah we are."

Witch Doctor One:"We have trained for this day for many years, and I know you are all ready to go. Prepare to leap in twenty minutes, over."

Witch Doctor One:"We will be transported right alongside the Darlock fleet. They are expecting nothing but target practice on this helpless world. There is quite literally nothing that could warn them of our attack. This should be a walk in the park. Stand by for my command, over."

Meanwhile Froth Lord warns the Darlocks and the Garthonians of our exact attack parameters.

On a telescreen onboard, a large assault vessel heading toward Q-7 the face of Froth Lord appears.

"Froth Lord will you be dining at the café later?" asked Darnak, the Darlock commander.

"Yes I will be there as usual. First I'm afraid I must warn you of an attack coming your way," Froth Lord began with a grin.

"I'm afraid an ex-High Master of Sholl Gar named Phobus and a human being will be leading an assault fleet against you. They will be coming out of hyperspace and lining up alongside you in precisely eighteen minutes," finished Froth Lord.

"Are you serious?" asked Darnak.

"We have not fought a true war in over one hundred years," he continued. "Well you will be in a full-scale space battle against a truly massive war fleet in sixteen minutes," added Froth Lord.

"Good luck," he finished.

- The quantum teleport and assault.

Thog engaged the quantum transport with the coordinates we programmed into the system grid and we took off.

There is nothing quite like quantum reality leap transport. It's very different from my anti-matter teleport. You essentially program the exact coordinates into the AI Command Drone. Nine seconds seemed like six days. I felt like I was in a pressure chamber without the proper support gear. I looked at Thog over my comm display and I thought he was dead. It was impossible to talk to Phobus, at least for now. I had visions while being suspended in this state of quantum non-reality. I had visions of the Others. I saw the Large Master feasting on gristle. There was Janker, the Young One, and Poor Brandon, all in a line. I saw visions of days long past. Then we came out of the temporal quantum reality vortex.

Things were incredibly calm. I rose to my feet. My eyes met Thog's on the comm display. We both smiled.

Star Command One: "Let's go kill some Darlocks!" exclaimed Phobus over a commlink.

We were so excited we did not notice the red alert coming over commlink one.

It continued to flash red until Thog picked up the line. "Hi, Thog here. How are you?" he began

Alpha Nine Drone Leader: "This is Commander Alpha Nine, over."

Alpha Nine Drone Leader was the clone who commanded the frontal attack force and all the drones.

Thog: "Go ahead Commander."

Alpha Nine Drone Leader: "Multiple Nuclear Neutrino Concussion Bursts heading directly for us."

He sounded calm actually.

Thog on Star Command Two: "Come again?"

Alpha Nine Drone Leader: "They will likely completely destroy the entire fleet in three seconds, over."

Star Command Two: "Now dear commander, that's not possible..."

Before Thog could finish the entire fleet was struck by the force of twelve million hurricanes. Ships were flying in every direction. The concussion burst destroyed half our force in the first six seconds.

Thousands of surviving ships were spiraling out of control in various directions. Debris, sparks, and blue energy lit up outer space. The whole thing was live on Channel Nine back at the café.

"That's a direct hit," said one alien creature, sipping caffeine supplement and Broth, sitting on the observatory.

"Indeed," said Froth Lord while watching from the bar.

Our command ship survived the first assault. I got the commlink and opened the main communication channel.

Witch Doctor One: "Launch all fighters! Any surviving ships target a Darlock cruiser with any available nuclear weapons, over."

For the next hour our fighters bravely fought the Vampire Guild. Unfortunately the remnant of the fleet was no match for the combined Darlock and Garthonian forces.

Darnak, the Darlock commander, looked over his war panel grid onboard his destroyer "World War One." In a scratchy deep, angry, slow, evil voice he ordered his attack teams.

Darnak: "I want those bastards. Over."

Witch Doctor One took out several hundred of their fighters and at least three of their cruisers. However I never had a safe shot to nuke their fleet. Phobus ran one last attack run with seventeen attack cruisers and seventeen thousand fighters. He had hoped to slingshot through the Garthonian fleet and drop thousands of delayed blast nuclear concussion charges throughout their combined fleet, and then race out of there before detonation.

Unfortunately Garthonian anti-matter cannons virtually wiped them from space. Only Phobus's command ship and nine fighters got the hell out of there. Meanwhile Witch Doctor One was lost in a counterclockwise spiral, completely out of control spinning toward deep space. Four Vampire Guild cruisers were in hot pursuit.

"Come on old girl," I talked to my ship.

Witch Doctor One: "Phobus little help? Over."

Fortunately Phobus and his remaining fighters were able to fly a direct trajectory into the Vampire ships on my tail and hit them with some crossfire. He was unable to destroy any of them, but they did turn back.

Witch Doctor One: "Thank you."

All we had left was Thog's assault team. He had nine cruisers and sixteen thousand fighters remaining intact. His team had scattered so badly and so distantly from the first concussion blasts that the survivors were only now regrouping somewhere in deep space. It was only sheer luck that the concussion bursts sent them hurtling closer to Q-7 rather than further away like the rest of the assault team.

Star Command Two: "Witch Doctor, Star Command Two, over?"

Witch Doctor One: "Roger Thog. Go ahead."

Star Command Two: "I still have a solid remnant of an assault team together. Our chance is to get a shot using nuclear weapons or the anti-matter cannons. You should get all your surviving ships out of the areas and let them think we are done for, over."

Thog was hanging tough.

Meanwhile back on the Interstellar Café there now was a bustling and exhilarated group of creatures watching all that was unfolding on Channel Nine. Even the greeting party from Q-7 was watching the action with awe and excitement, having absolutely no idea the doom that was about to be unleashed on their home world.

Wagers of every kind were being placed. Meanwhile a very familiar High Master placed an extremely high stakes wager on Phobus, Thog, and, of course, my team.

"Put all this on the Sholl Garian assault team," said the High Master.

The Drakonian Shark Master looked at Froth Lord and growled at him.

"Are you fucking serious?" he groaned.

"Of course," was Froth Lord's reply.

Thog's assault team shot in like a burst of lightning toward the full combined Darlock and Garthonian fleet. Darlock cannon and antimatter ion blaster opened up on Thog's team. Thog's team raced through the fleet raking them with all their concussion cannons, anti-matter cannons, ion bursts, and matter cluster fire blasts.

They were able to take out several cruisers this way. More importantly, they were able to buy time for his nuclear team to program an assault.

Star Command Two: "Coranthas, do you copy, over?"

Witch Doctor One: "Go ahead Thog, I read you."

Star Command Two: "I need you and Phobus to run a screen for me."

Witch Doctor One: "A screen? Over."

Star Command Two: "Yup."

Star Command One: "What's he need? Over."

Witch Doctor One: "He needs us to run block, over".

Star Command Two: "I want you to take all you have left and race through their ranks hitting them with all your cannons. While you do this we will be finalizing our own nuclear concussion assault," finished Thog.

Witch Doctor One: "Copy that, Star Command Two."

Star Command One: "Copy that, Star Command Two."

Both Phobus and I were slightly moved by his loyalty and bravery and commitment in this moment. Decent dude for an Al Lobal.

Immediately Phobus and I regrouped our two teams. Though we had lost nine thousand ships in less than one hour (a new record I'm told), we still had a large enough assault force to get this job done. We raced in together, raking as many ships as possible. Witch Doctor One had at least this one run left in her. I punched it and lit the turbo.

We hit them with everything we had short of a full nuclear assault.

"Finish off these pesty Sholl Garians," said the Darlock assault team leader. Every Darlock ship opened up its cannons upon our fleet. Everywhere I looked our ships were being obliterated into cosmic dust forever.

Part of me was happy to think there would no longer be five hundred thousand clones of me by the end of the day. I throttled up and figured it was time for me to bail. I was just about to just teleport the Witch Doctor to Delta Five when all the sudden, I received a message from the fighter team.

Alpha Nine Drone Leader: "Coranthas we have multiple nuclear concussion burst of never-before-seen magnitude heading straight for this sector! Over!" radioed the clone.

Witch Doctor One: "hit the quantum reality button! Let's get out of here NOW!" I screamed.

Thog had done it. Our force distracted the Darlocks long enough that he was able to launch his entire nuclear cargo directly at the combined Darlock and Garthonian fleets. After the attack there was only a remnant of their forces remaining. We sent in our remaining fighters who obliterated the rest of the force.

We started the conflict with ten thousand attack cruisers. We had eleven left. We started the day with three hundred thousand fighters. We ended up in the ballpark of 116 surviving fighters. The numbers were bad.

However, we completely destroyed the Darlock/Garthonian assault force. Q-7 was saved. Meanwhile at the Interstellar Café, "Yeaaaahhweeeww!" exclaimed one sub-creature who had made a bundle.

The Drakonian Shark Master looked at Froth Lord and growled at him once again.

"I smell a rat Froth Lord," he said.

Froth calmly collected his winnings all the while looking over at the Q-7 welcoming committee in guised surprise.

"Well why would that be sir?" asked Froth Lord.

Leaning in and looking angrier than ever he began, "No one steals from me, not even you Froth Lord," he said. He pulled out a lightning cane.

"Don't make me laugh Tony."

Froth Lord would not reveal to us the nature of the test that he put us through for many years. As usual he had masterminded the entire series of events. He wanted to see how we would do without him. We did poorly.

However as poorly as we did, we still managed to ward off the assault and destroy the attack force. Essentially we lost our entire Armata. I sat at the control pit of Witch Doctor One, coasting through space. Off in the distance there were wave after wave of orange and blue light lighting up the blackness. The nuking of their fleet produced one of the most beautiful sites in outer space I had ever seen.

Witch Doctor One computer: "Coranthas do you need me to set a course for the Quantum leap?"

"No thank you Donna. I want to coast here for a bit. Just keep her steady," I answered.

I never loved flying in space. Everyone knew that. But this moment was sweet. Yeah, the fleet was gone. It was a total pummeling. In victory, but like the British at the old earth Battle of Bunker Hill, still a total butt kicking. But I never loved the Witch Doctor's shuttle more. She might even have enjoyed this. She must be nuts looking for this thing.

Froth Lord had not bargained for what came next.

The Darlocks declared all-out war on the Sentients residing on Q-7. (As if they had not already done so by coming to utterly destroy them without warning.) Immediately the Garthonians joined them. They considered the kingdom of Sholl Gar to be duplicitous in the assault and both worlds declared war on Sholl Gar.

Dominick High Master of Sholl Gar, declared war on both the Darlocks and the Garthonians in response. We started this conflict. It was the right thing to do. But now we were going to have to finish it.

Now we still needed to defend the Q-7 Sentients from destruction. Froth Lord decided the best thing to do was to reveal all to the leaders of Q-7 and train them up with the required technology to defend themselves.

Our plan was straight forward. We forged a loose but necessary alliance with Dominick of Sholl Gar. We would use his entire defense force to fight the first six months of the war while we got the Q-7 Sentients up to speed. We knew that Sholl Gar would likely be reduced to rubble by this war. We would exhaust all Sholl Gar's resources fighting the war. We would gladly sacrifice them as we built up the Q-7 defense forces.

The Sentients on Q-7 proved to be very impressive. As mentioned earlier, they had already begun aggressive space travel in their own right. In addition, Froth Lord was greatly impressed by their lack of warring amongst themselves. Most of all they were quite courageous.

"I have not found many like these people in the Zynon galaxy," Froth Lord confided in me as we armed an assault craft with nuclear concussion devices. The first six months of the war were devasting for Sholl Gar. We had no idea how good this would ultimately turn out for the rest of us. There were nine all-out space battles between Dominick's star fleet and the combined Darlock and Garthonian forces. I must say that I love my ship now. I am so glad I turned down Star Command One. Phobus thought I was nuts.

Dominick started out with twenty-five thousand Assault Cruiser class ships, twelve thousand Destroyer class ships, fifty thousand fighters, and nearly two hundred thousand brave Sholl Garian sub-creatures. It had appeared at the outset to be a formidable force indeed.

After the nine battles they had a total of four ships remaining. They had been completely destroyed. However they took just enough out of the Darlock and Garthonians that our attack had at least a remote chance of success. We knew that if our attack was unsuccessful Froth Lord could punch a hole in space so deadly that the entire enemy fleet, and even possibly this entire local sector of the galaxy would just be sucked into oblivion.

So in a sense, we knew we could not really ever ultimately lose this fight. However we knew he would only interfere at this level if things were truly in total despair. Ultimately as all wars do, this conflict came to resolution.

Froth Lord tired of the war and shifted time and space to confuse all the participants. It worked. The planet Lantos became essentially hidden as a result. The Darlocks and Garthonians who were trapped inside Froth Lord's cloaking of space time agreed to a non-aggression pact with Q-7. (What other choice would they have had?) They reside locally within the system now on Q-6 under high pressure dome canopies since no one on Q-7 will allow them to the surface. The minimum rations of Broth and calorie supplement are provided by pre-programmed drone deposit nightly. Darnak had escaped.

The Q-7 Sentients were granted official dominion over their entire solar system and standard galactic mining rights. Sholl Gar's defense force was completely destroyed.

Froth Lord exiled Dominick to a cube prison on the Drandorian moon. Phobus was restored as King of Sholl-Gar.

But first Froth Lord, Phobus, Thog, and I had to deal with the Council of

Drakar. They were receiving so much shit from the Garthonians and the Darlocks. The Vampire Guild was suing Froth Lord and the Podranians. Things were a total mess all because we started a little war. I mean they were going to blast those people, I thought. We were just defending them. But according to galactic law, we were the criminal aggressors. The Darlocks and the Garthonians were within their rights to obliterate all on Q-7 since none of the religions were covered under Article 19. (Or so they thought.)

- The Council of Drakar "Q-7 Space War One Hearings"

There is quite literally nothing worse and more tedious in the galaxy then sitting through a Council of Drakar hearing. That is why they had to subpoena us to be there. There was no chance I would have shown otherwise. Worse than tedious it was foolishness in its highest order. I looked over at Froth Lord and realized there was no way he could be compelled to comply. *He must be here for the laughs* I thought.

The Council was literally an unwitting experiment in the very concept of corruption. Bribery, kickbacks, false imprisonments, espionage, payoffs were all staples and specialties of the Council of Drakar. There was also the *Keystone Cops* factor to it all. The utter incompetence on top of the corruption was more than any of us could really bear.

Council members appointed for life, of all different worlds, would take their turns questioning any defendant or witness. It was obvious to me that the bureaucracy of it all and the politics were only what they cared about. The Darlocks and the Garthonians argued that their rights for wiping out a world that they discovered "fair and square" were violated. Q-7 was "their find" they would argue.

Dorian of the Sholl Gar system, Planet Nine, was present to press Sholl Garian rights. Darnak the Darlock Assault Commander, and his cabinet were here as well. He was pissed. The Garthonians sent this beady-eyed bureaucrat with a novel full of their grievances. He looked almost like a bookkeeper. The creature was short, beady eyed, and looked generally devious. He was wretched most certainly.

The Podranians sent their leader Tom. He was the primary defendant in all the matters. This seemed ridiculous since the entire war was because we defended Q-7 from obliteration by two attacking deep space species. The Council

135

of Drakar is a joke anyway. Tom seemed quite noble to me.

Tom the Podranian leader spoke first.

"Council of Drakar, first of all, I appreciate your willingness to hear the defense of our world's cause," Tom started.

"DEATH!" screamed Darnak.

Legions from the Vampire Guild and sub-Darlock undead servants cheered and wailed at Darnak's demand. Sholl Garian sub-men warriors hissed back at them. It was a truly ghastly crew of plaintiffs. Honestly the Sholl Garian defendants were no prize either.

Tom gathered his thoughts and remained calm.

"That was certainly your aim to kill us now wasn't it?" Tom spoke confidently.

"You blasted our fleet!" exclaimed a Sub-Lord of Forinth Dune of Sholl Gar, serving in Dorian's attachment. He did not even realize that Q-7 was his ally in the war.

"You robbed us!" wailed Dorian, though Dorian was not that sure what this was all about either. Dorian was just playing to the Council. It was often thought Dorian aspired to the Council, as silly as that was. If you thought Sholl Gar was a mess take a visit to Planet Nine.

"Oh god not this crap again," whispered Phobus to me and Thog.

Our box was located directly across from the Council's bench. To the left there was a massive, shallow bowl like an inverted dome booth where the witnesses and plaintiffs made their case to the Council. The scene was quite chaotic. I remember hoping someone was recording this.

The general argument made by the plaintiffs was the following: The Darlock Vampire Guild had discovered the planet Q-7 and the Podranians. The Garthonians attempted to hijack their kill by racing out their military first, attempting to get them before the Un-Dead masses did. Rather than warring with each other, which they were simply too cowardly to do, Darnak made a deal with the Garthonians. They would share in the spoils. Per galactic law the discoverers had the option of destroying with their assault fleets any discovered world or people. The only detail in consideration was Article 19.

Article 19, as you are aware, explicitly states that any world where the Sentients upon which reside worship a real Sentient Deity from the galaxy would be spared. It was quickly, and potentially falsely, determined that none of the Q-7 religions were real or founded by a real life forms or force. So they were fair game the Council had decided originally. It was open season for monsters.

The meeting had deteriorated into a free for all. Garthonians were screaming at the Council. "Chair-Creatures" in their robes would slam down their gavels demanding quiet. Judges in the Council screamed for order. Dorian was hopelessly banging down a gavel to no effect. I was just taking it all in.

Darlocks were trying to build nests and feed on Sholl Garians. Tom left the proceedings in his starship.

"DEATH!" screamed Darnak

Utter and complete chaos had now ensued. This was getting good. Garthonians were screaming at the council. Council-Creatures were screaming back at the Garthonians. Darlocks were building nests and feeding on the Sholl Garians. Just when it seemed like it was going to descend into another Space War...

"No investigation was done," a loud but calm voice interrupted the proceedings. The chaos was stopped suddenly. Beings one moment groping at each other looked over to him. The Judges and "Chair-Creatures" put their gavels down. Darlocks kept trying to build nests and feed on Sholl Garians.

"Order!" Council-Creature One declared.

The voice had been Froth Lord obviously.

Council-Creature One looked over at Froth Lord through his Coke bottle spectacles in that pathetic long robe, pushed his glasses back on his oversized pointy nose. He began to speak in a very rushed, scattered, spastic but pointed manner.

"What is the meaning of this? No investigation was done? What are you talking about Froth Lord?" the Council-Creature finished in a spastic voice, looking over his nose once again, pushing back his spectacles.

"You or no one know who their god was," spoke Froth Lord again.

Sheepishly, Council-Creature One asked, "Are you their god Froth Lord?"

"No I am not. But I have reason to suspect that Article Nineteen was almost violated," he finished.

A hush fell over the proceedings. This was VERY serious if true. Even the Darlocks looked up from their dinners. Darnak look flat out scared.

Council-Creature One gathered himself to speak in a very nervous voice. It was clear, even in this circus, that the Council would consider a violation of Article 19 to be a very serious matter if proven.

"Um, do you have any proof Froth Lord?" he asked.

"Yes I do," he answered.

Chapter Thirteen

Q-7 and Froth Lord's destiny

The Q-7 Sentients refer to their home world as Lantos. They refer to themselves as Podrans, or Podranians. They are officially the 351,009th documented Sentient life form in the known universe.

In the Galactic Journals they have since been listed as simply the Sentient residents of the planet Q-7. Froth Lord was fascinated by this world. He was fascinated in a similar manner to how he had been with the Humans of planet Earth.

Podranians were extremely unique. After the Galactic War triggered by Froth Lord's defense of Q-7 the Podranians really took off as a civilization. This was the first known time that a species had survived planned annihilation. At one point their leaders wanted to hunt down and obliterate the Interstellar Café itself.

Thank god we got that thing out of there before they located it. Podranian history is very interesting. Their earliest known written history records of a series of events that even Froth Lord was surprised by. He was beginning to wonder at that time what the meaning of these writings could be. Essentially according to their earliest recorded history, it appeared that the residents of Q-7 had been visited by extremely powerful being. It was in their Holy Books, but it was also in other corroborating historical accounts in various parts of the planet. On many worlds different religions would develop in part of the world hence creating multiple various faiths. But according to Podranian history, the peoples of different continents and regions seem to tell each other upon discovering each one another a very similar story about an all-powerful being. They spoke of what appeared to be the same being and his many visitations. So on Podran one religious faith was established.

This seemed that it was a visitation, or many visitations, from a being that convinced them he was in fact a god. Froth Lord obviously knew it was not him that had visited them. However, the writings seemed more than legendary.

They were different than the typical Holy Books and writings that you typically encounter from primitive Sentient life forms. In addition the powerful being came to them in different separate regions of Lantos, apparently hundreds of times for nearly a thousand years. This being had not returned for eons now and many modern Podranians question the writings.

Still Froth Lord believed there was something to these ancient recorded visitations.

Who could this have been? Froth Lord would ponder often over the next ten or so years. He was determined to discover the true identity of the Podranian god. How ironic he would often think, that he showed up hundreds of thousands of years later and saved the Podranians. Many times Froth Lord had undertaken various adventures and causes. The number of sentients he has experimented on is staggering. Quantum reality has shifted completely due to his power. Heck he is God over nine worlds.

Even with all this he had no idea that he was about to open an investigation which would teach even him about the very nature of the galaxy, the universe, the Broth, and life itself. This quest would change everything forever.

He would have to go back to the source. For years Froth Lord would investigate the documentation of the Podranians. He was completely obsessed with determining the truth about the ancient Podranian God. In one ancient script he found the clue that he needed. In roughly the hundredth year during a series of ancient visitations a very enlightening description was given.

"Before us stood the Lord himself. His eyes were like golden emeralds and his robe was a stunning purple. He reached out his arms in the 'behold' position, and the winged man was before him. He wore a crown like light itself and was ready for battle."

The winged man was before him?

I know this? Froth Lord would wonder. He was certain that this was an important clue. The winged man was before him? He wore a "crown of light"? Where had he heard of this all before? He made note of the winged man, and he then cross referenced all the other writings. After a year of research, he found it!

There was an ancient Nectarian legend regarding Dendrake that referenced "the winged man was before him." Though Dendrake is believed by Nectarians to be a legitimate fact of ancient history, most of the ancient writings about him were considered pure mythology. This one was no exception.

This was just fascinating to Froth Lord. How could the Q-7 Holy Book have recorded what appeared to be the exact same phrase and event as an ancient book from light years away? This was fascinating not because Froth Lord thought there was ever a literal "winged man" event, on any world. But he was convinced these texts must be sourced from the same original source texts or stories. They are the exact same when translated! *There is at least an entire paragraph that is verbatim the same when translation is applied,* he thought. This is impossible. These writings are the same, from two different worlds, and separate by vast distance and vast time.

The visitations described must be real. A higher Sentient used references to other worlds' religious texts in the Podranian Holy Books. That is the only explanation for the writings. And for two worlds separated by many ages and many light years to have the same myth an interstellar being would have to be involved. If nothing else, they absolutely qualified for the application of Article 19.

Froth Lord did not yet realize that he was beginning the quest that would catalyze his ultimate destiny.

Chapter Fourteen

Phobus Uthrates, "God over One world"

At Froth Lord's suggestion Phobus would be elevated to the status of primary Deity of Sholl-Gar roughly two hundred and fifty years after our first time shift, and the vision at the Drandor moon. Froth Lord was entirely fed up. He was fed up with the God-Work stuff, the war, his multiple attempts at galactic intervention, and so on. He was sick of the Council, the various multiple worlds, and basically everything it so appeared. He was done. So now today, thousands upon thousands of years after the unnatural birth of Thog, Phobus Uthrates King of Sholl Gar was declared the god and primary Deity of this world. Thog was his only begotten Son.

The entire experience with Thog had only proven tiresome. I had completely gone mad by this time so it seemed. Before he left Delta Five Froth Lord reminded me of the stone. It was the diamond-shaped stone with an amber color to it. He reminded me that it would ground me and help me with my condition. He told me if I ever felt funny, as I sometimes do, to simply grab hold of the stone breathe slowly and deeply and count to ten. He reminded me as he had done before that it would help. I have never not had the diamond-shaped stone with me from this point forward.

Now Phobus was doing very well by this point. He really had been thinking clearly for half a century. As noted his experiences garnered as the High Master, and eventually the King of Sholl Gar, had prepared him to finally take over as the primary god-being of Sholl Gar. He was taking over for Froth Lord. Thog would be his lessor Lord to be sacrificed.

He had been discipled well by me, and Froth Lord had watched him closely and kept him alive for eons beyond his natural life span. Fortunately for Phobus the wretched creatures of Sholl Gar were more primitive than ever. No significant advancements had made for literally tens of thousands of years. The populace was still made up mostly of sub-creatures (of which he once was himself), and the Dune wars had continued mercifully for thousands of years.

The legend of Coranthas and Phobus proved very fertile ground for the pronouncement of Phobus's Deity to the sub-creatures. They didn't know any better, nor were they paying much attention anyway. All that needed to occur was for Phobus to sacrifice the Lobal Sentient life form Thog publicly.

This was a sticky detail now that Thog, me, Phobus, and Froth Lord had become such friends. We had spent hundreds of hours vacationing together, laughing about all our various shared experiences together. I'm glad I was not there that day.

"Remember that time at Forinth Dune when we crushed the uprising populace together?" asked Thog just before his ultimate slaying.

"Yes I remember," responded Phobus in tears, before raising his lightning gun to slay him.

After Thog was slayed Phobus declared himself to be the only true god of Sholl Gar. As per Froth Lord's instruction he gave the Holy Writs to his chosen high priest and declared that he or Thog would someday return to rule and make all things new. (This was standard.)

He then of course returned to Delta Five to visit me. Though I had apparently gone completely insane by this point, both Froth Lord and Phobus made sure that I was always comfortable, and that I always had all I needed. I was god over no worlds. (Not that I would ever desire such a burden.) It was always a blast hanging with Phobus.

"Keep it down in there!" yelled the Witch Doctor.

We both laughed.

"When will you return to Sholl Gar?" I asked Phobus.

"The Holy Book Froth Lord wrote says I will be back when there are sandstorms and rumors of sandstorms. So I could go whenever basically." He laughed.

"Nice," was my reply.

"Do you have any Broth?" he asked.

"You need to ask, dude?" I answered.

Little did we know that this was only the beginning.

END Book 1

Interlude

Free Will

Free Will

Dendrake had no free will. In fact as Dendrake understood it, and the deeper he pondered it, he concluded that no Sentient had free will. He spent seemingly endless eons pondering the matter, but this was his conclusion. He did not ask to come into existence nor does he know how or why he in fact did. There was no say given to him on the question. It does not even matter whether he has a cause or is in fact *uncaused.* The question of whether there are others beyond him was immaterial. All these are irrelevant with respect to the questions of free will and fatalism.

But his concerns with free will were far beyond anything that had to do with his existence. None of his creation had any say in the matter of their existence either. The life encoded processes of the Broth made this a certainty. Now one could say a Sentient life form had *say* in the events of their days. One could choose to jump off a building, or they could choose not to do so correct? Well Dendrake with all his supreme, unrivaled, ever-expanding intellect and perfect foreknowledge fully realized that such thinking was utter folly.

The reason he knew no one had any real free will was simply because he realized he did not. He would fully admit that all Sentients have something that could be referred to as *the appearance of free will,* but this was pure illusion. No one could change what actions or events in fact happen. They could simply interact with reality to affect *seemingly* subsequent follow up events. There was no changing the past. And since events just happen to Sentient life forms even with the illusion of choices made, i.e., free will, illusion it was. It may seem you chose to get up and go to work today or that you chose not to do so. But the actual literal *causation* affect that seems real to a being is not literally real even in the slightest.

Now let's consider Dendrake. Dendrake may in fact be the most Supreme Superbeing in all existence. Dendrake may have perfect foreknowledge that as previously discussed torments him with the realization that he does not have free will. As all powerful as he is the fatalism described above fully applies to him as well as any other Sentient. And via his foreknowledge which is perfect, the idea of fatalism, and his utter lack of *free will* tortures him more than any being. The vast majority of Sentient Life forms have no ability to know the future. But Dendrake has what seems to be perfect foreknowledge over all events that are to come, certainly at least related to the life forms that stemmed from his Broth.

Partly because he did not understand the working of his omniscience fully, he was unsure whether the life he created was the only life in existence. At times he thought it must be since he foresaw the future; how could it be only a part of the future? How could it only be a subset of all that would occur? That would not make sense. Thought not certain he resigned himself to consider that he was the only creator of life in the Cosmos, and as stated at the outset was entirely alone.

But back to free will. As noted Dendrake saw the future. He even saw that he would create the Broth. For what would seem infinite periods to lessor beings he grappled with *not* creating the Broth. Could he even fail to do so he asked himself? He has foreseen it. It is predestined and finished, done already. We have discussed how the average Sentient only has the illusion of free will, and that no being or entity can change the past. But now apply that to a being for which the *future* is essentially already the *past,* due to that being having perfect foreknowledge. The mechanism of that foreknowledge and the mystery of the "how" of that foreknowledge is not relevant to the point. For that being the future is already the past. And no matter how all powerful that being he cannot fail to do what he foresees himself doing. Dendrake cannot fail to create what he foresees himself creating.

So, having established that free will does not exist and that it is in fact pure illusion let's examine the ramifications of this revelation. Free will in much of Sentient Philosophy and Religion would be endlessly debated on the various worlds. Free will, it was argued by many, is the very basis of moral responsibility. There could be no sin in the religious context, for example, if there is no free will. How can anyone be truly held *accountable* for things they did or do. If Dendrake foresaw them which he foresees all things that do in fact occur, then no thing that does in fact occur is the result of a free will act.

Are you understanding how significant this matter is? Now it is important to understand that these questions do not haunt the average Sentient to an even infinitesimal level when compared to the torment it causes Dendrake the perfect being with the perfect mind. His foreknowledge caused him mostly great distress.

Profoundly as noted at the outset Dendrake foresaw the Greatness of one Sentient. He foresaw how powerful this Froth Lord would become. He foresaw his great strengths and his many flaws. Froth Lord was the ultimate reason he proceeded to create the Broth, as though he even had the choice. Dendrake's "illusion" of free will was entirely based upon Froth Lord, and his plans for him. And though for a moment it seemed as if he made a free will choice, he was fully aware it was all illusion.

Book 2

Froth Lord's Chronicle

Chapter One

Clarification

I am Froth Lord.

It seemed of relative importance to me to discuss several matters with you regarding the writings of Coranthas. Reading Coranthas's journal as I have has lead me to think some matters need clarification. Some matters need outright correction. This is the purpose of my addition to his chronicle. Only I can explain to you all that has ultimately occurred. He most definitely meant well but has missed the mark.

Firstly, and I must stress, of the utmost importance, it was impossible for Coranthas to understand my curiosity with the god of the Q-7 Sentients. He simply had no idea what he was writing about nor could he truly. This much is clear.

Let me bring to light this matter with respect to the origin of the Podranian God. This is the major issue we need to discuss. The rest was for the most part twaddle.

I have existed for roughly 192,000 years at the time of this writing. Much of Coranthas's timelines are off grotesquely. He is sadly not well as you know. Of at least this much he was quite correct. His condition haunts me to no end. He and Phobus may eventually end up launched from my Model T photon wave dispenser depending on my mood. I was informed that this may qualify to serve as my final thesis for the title and degree of Class One Deity.

But now back to the Q-7 Sentients. The issue is quite simple. Whoever this god was he was real, period. And it had not been me. At first I thought that I must had been their god. It was possible that I did not remember if it were long enough ago. That would not be entirely unheard of. However the timeline did not work. His visitation of Lantos certainly predates any of the God-work I had undertaken. And by quite a bit I might add.

There were several critical matters. Firstly, there was no doubt that the "winged man" story was sourced from either the actual Nectarian legend or both legends shared the same source text. There was no other logical explanation because they are one in the same story. The fact the Podranians, an unknown and undiscovered species, shared what is clearly precisely the same mythology text makes it impossible for this god to not be a real being. Two worlds separated by vast distances. Different species both evolved from the Broth, yet separated by vast time sharing the same exact ancient text in their Holy writings. It should have been instantly clear they were exempt under Article 19. The reality is no one cared. The Council is a real clown show quite frankly. The Council-Creatures all are total galactic embarrassments. The Judges are no prize either.

Secondly, and an even more primary reason I knew this god was not a legend, was the Holy Book's detailed knowledge of two other matters. The first was a complete understanding detailing the ratio of a circle's circumference to its diameter in Euclidean geometry, which, of course, has many uses in mathematics, physics, and engineering.

This common mathematical fact is simply known as "Pi." Though most of this ancient book reads like you'd expect of an ancient Holy Book (i.e., fire breathing dragons, severe and horrible punishment for disobedience, etc.), it briefly describes this basic yet impossible mathematical fact in its final pages. There was simply no way for the Q-7 Sentients to have known anything about "Pi" at the time of its writings.

In addition to documenting "Pi" on two dimensions the holy book described axioms and theorems disguised in the text buried amongst scattered theology. The Holy Writs of the Podranians also outlined what occurs when the rules Euclidean geometry are applied to a curved surface and hence to space itself.

In particular the total degree sum of angles within triangles on a sphere. This showed accurately an understanding by the author of the nature of curved space. A very familiar example of a curved space is the surface of a sphere. It is a simple example to us, now, but impossible for the Ancient Podranians. At the risk of redundancy, but for the purpose of driving the point home, it was entirely impossible for this to have been written by ancient Podranians.

The second reason that equally floored me was the clear reference to something in its creation account that could only possibly be describing the Broth. Describing it accurately I might add. Their god referred to the life-producing product in numerous passages, not by name mind you, but remember that I know all there is to know about the Broth. Their god declared that he deposited the Broth, that he created it, and that it was responsible for all life on the planet Lantos. Could this possibly be? *It can't be,* I thought.

The book described, again not by label but by concept, curved space-time and geometric gravitation. It discussed the concept of gravity in the accurate manner. That gravity was not a force but essentially a geometric curvature of reality around us. It said these all in the stealthy guise of an ancient holy book. *But why?* I thought. In discussing the Broth the holy books outline physical traits which clearly line up with the phenomenon or particle entanglement, again not directly per se. Never does the word *quantum* appear in the texts. But the Broth is described including conceptual entanglement which, as discussed ad nauseum, is the main characteristic of the Broth.

Q-7 was not discovered until very recently. The Council of Drakar did not do any research at all about its ancient religion before giving the Vampire Guild the green light to obliterate them. As already noted it seemed clear to me that they qualified for exemption under Article 19.

I don't talk about it much but I wrote Article 19. What happened to Earth was unacceptable. Coranthas wrote about how I revealed to him my feelings about his former home world. I argued it before that god damn council. The only way I was going to get that past the council was to present it as legal argument for the protection of property.

Those fools would not listen at all unless it was presented to protect the rights of a higher Sentient being species. It would have been a useless argument if presented as a movement of mercy. No one would have cared. So I played the game. I played the lawyer part to perfection. First I had to get it introduced as a galactic *Act.* That meant getting it out of the committee I had it introduce it in. I acted the sleazeball role just to pass this Act. I greased the skids. I never felt more compromised. I got it out of committee and the Oracle of the Sholl Gar system declared it an official Act. Once it was an Act I had it appealed to the Council of Drakar. It took significantly less effort to get it by those corrupt Creatures than to get it passed as an Act. It was elevated to *Article* status, the 19th Article since the ratification of the of the galactic Oracles of Rule.

Anyway, back to the point. These writings were verifiably old. I don't have time to explain why, but do you question me? It was impossible for me to come to any conclusions other than the following. This being was real.

Of course, he is not a god. However most sentient life forms created their own gods from myth, legend, or fairy tale. Many others obviously, as noted, are based on real Sentient life forms who were declaring themselves to be gods for these primitives. These are real visitations, mass religious experiences, many of which were performed by me. These events formed the basis of many religions in the Zynon galaxy. Of course, those Sentients were spared destruction due to Article 19 of the Intergalactic Code. Theses worlds in these cases are the god in question's property in the strict application of Article 19.

Here is the thing though. No other religious texts, even the ones left by advanced Sentient beings, included description of advanced mathematics and the nature of the Broth in the manner that the Q-7 Holy Books. If an ancient religion mentioned matters like "Pi" or other obvious advanced theories like quantum physics then we knew they were established by advanced Sentient life forms. They did these things to protect their property from destruction. However, there never was an understanding of the Broth to this degree. As far as I knew, only ancient Nectarians knew the kinds of these things mentioned about the Broth in the Podranians Holy Books.

My theory went something like this. This being whoever he was, included both "Pi" and a mention of the Broth for a reason, and it was not to convince any Sentient life form on Q-7. It was meant to be found and read by someone else entirely. But why I would ask myself? It is obvious to me that this ancient god is a real being and not a legend. It is also clear that his hidden proofs of his veracity could not be meant only for the Q-7 Sentients but for others who could understand the meanings. It was not hard for me to verify that this being visited this world many thousands of years earlier than even the Q-7 Sentients believed. I was beginning to think this could be my first real clue to finding Dendrake himself.

And I had been looking. Looking for a very long time.

No living Sentient had ever encountered Dendrake. Even the testimonies of our ancient Nectarian ancestors who supposedly did meet him are questioned by today's councils of the various worlds. However the overwhelming evidence that he existed is well established. The very existence of the Broth is what convinces most. I always had questioned the entire story. (At least with respect to Dendrake being the creator of the Broth, the Universe, and in fact being God himself.)

I never bought it at all. He must simply be another Sentient, just as dependent on the Broth as even we Nectarians were dependent upon it long ago. Of course my position always begged the question, "Where then does the Broth in fact come from?"

"Doesn't matter," was always my answer.

The Broth did not require a creator. If we assume the Broth required a creator then we must assume it's supposed creator required a creator as well. A never-ending circular conundrum is created by bothering with such questions.

However there is no doubt whatsoever that Dendrake existed, and may yet still exist. And there is no doubt that he is the original depositor of the Broth. For goodness' sake I deposit Broth on worlds now and start the life process. It is not rocket science. (As if rocket science were impressive, just an expression as you are aware.)

There is little question in my mind that returning to Q-7 to investigate things further was necessary. In fact finding Dendrake may even be my very purpose. There was now a splinter in my mind's eye regarding why all this had happened at that time. The Podranians were now the impetus or grounds of an even greater investigation.

"How surprising to end up here indeed." I would ask myself.

But finding him, locating him, and even possibly confronting him? This is a truly astonishing place for my long existence to lead to. I cracked a beer open and sat back. This was going to be a long night.

Even with all this facing me there is an even more immediate challenge. Maybe not more important, but more immediate for sure.

To end the war, and before the subsequent Deification of Phobus on Sholl Gar, it had become necessary for me to rip a hole in space-time in the Q-7 system.

This caused the Darlocks to hopelessly lose their bearings and frankly lose interest in continuing the fight with the Podranians.

The Garthonians nearly perished as a species as a result. I honestly felt the Council had been just as mad about my hole in space as they were with the whole Q-7 Space War.

The planet referred to as Lantos was hidden from most Sentients due to the anomaly I created. The Podranians themselves had been impacted as well. Peace comes at a price, as you are aware. Embarrassingly this had caused me a small problem. Even putting this in writing as I am now pains me to no end, but even I had trouble locating Lantos during those years. The anomaly I created had made it for me to be very similar to what it is like when one loses one's keys.

Yikes! I would often think. *How did I manage that?*

But none of that mattered at that time. It was important for me to return to the task at hand, and to the development of my plan. It was critical for me to keep my focus. Regardless of whatever side ventures I am embracing I must keep my attention on the primary matter at hand. I needed to find that planet! At least I had Plan A still.

Chapter Two

Phobus and Coranthas

- Planet Nectar, Froth Lord's Dome, Thousands upon thousands of years after the unnatural birth of Thog

I continued to review the materials left and written by Coranthas at that time, not considering them to be particularly helpful, but necessary review nonetheless. A lot of it was quite humorous though. The Large Master bits were particularly entertaining. She was a reminder of truly grand times. However most of his chronicle was superfluous at best. Some was pure trash at worst.

What dribble! I thought to myself for the most part.

I did get a kick out of reading about his account of Drandoria though. What fresh and pure hell was that experience. It honestly changed me forever. And, of course, the Young One; his whole life was literally a clown show. That was some funny shit, I must say.

"Is it really possible that I am going to need to visit Coranthas again?" I wondered.

Both Phobus and Coranthas had provided me a great share of good laughs over the years. And manipulating their realities had become somewhat of a past time for me. Honestly, I can't even remember now why I began to mess with them in the first place. My initial intentions with both had been quite altruistic in fact. When rescuing Coranthas as I did, at least at that time, I did not realize I would end up tormenting them mostly for fun. There has always been a kind of ebb and flow with those relationships. I am not proud of everything I have done.

Those two could not possibly be useful at this point, could they? I considered.

What Coranthas had written about the end of the war had missed the point of all of it almost entirely. Yes, it was partly true that I had put he and Phobus to a test of sorts. But it was not to build character or strength in them. At least that was not the only reason. The war served some purposes, but quite honestly I started it mostly because I was bored at that time. Living as long as I have sometimes one goes through quite long dry periods. Saving the Q-7 Sentients was a side matter really. I had no idea that I was going to find myself on the trail of Dendrake at that time. *Saving Q-7 was just cool,* I would think. It was something to do.

Phobus and Coranthas thought they had ruined my entire plan with Thog. Coranthas writes extensively about that. Honestly during my times with all of them, including Thog, I was just playing around during my slow periods. It made for good laughs during those times. There was nothing personal at all. I like those guys. While contemplating the times I had spent with them, even when I had messed with them so, it still brough me some nostalgia. I likely won't launch them all as Dark Matter after all I began to think. They might still be some fun yet. They might even come in handy as they sometimes do. Begrudgingly, I decided right then that I needed to *login* to Delta Five and check on those two.

- Delta Five

I fired up my control panel and entered my encryption codes. The authenticator algorithm AI scanned my soul and verified my being. After the vulnerability scan, my authentication token was granted, and it logged me right in.

Auth System: "Trust verified."

Auth System: "Welcome Froth Lord," greeted the algorithm.

Then I observed the boys on Delta Five through my virtual space tunnel.

"Shit dude!? Oh my God!?" exclaimed Phobus.

"Sorry bro," laughed Coranthas having squeezed beef.

Phobus launched a withering array of lightning fire and lightning bursts at Coranthas, only to be blocked by Coranthas's new ion field I had sent him for Christmas. Phobus attempted to circumvent the barrier by curving time with his ludicrous time utility belt, but Coranthas trained well by me, was able to dodge the time shift by side stepping slightly. His shield held nicely.

"You like that Phobus?" Coranthas asked

"It's decent I guess. Decent shield," answered Phobus

Phobus was supposed to have been back to Sholl Gar as their god to do a check in, but he had blown it off entirely. He had no real reason to go he would think. Thog's AI clone is the Savior anyway he would say.

"Let the Deacons deal," he would often say.

"That place is horrible," Coranthas added

They were right. Sholl Gar was a fucking mess.

"Jesus," was my only thought observing these clowns. Seriously, do I really need them right now? I thought. I shut down the virtual tunnel and teleported.

Suddenly I appeared among them in Coranthas's chamber on Delta Five. I glowed with the appearance of blue lightning. (I loved using the blue.) Thunder echoed through the chamber. The ground underneath their feet shook and quaked. I made the daytime sky turn to night. I did the fire eyes thing again too. I figured if we're really doing this, let's do it right.

I would always want to give them a startle so they would be off balance. I then turned their immediate surroundings to the appearance of a planet of fire. The sky became as black as the far side of Drandor's outermost moon. But the surface was like a raging molten inferno.

Then immediately I transported them to the fourth moon of Drandor, which, of course as you know, is one of my worlds. I did not yet realize the mess I had just made though. Had I been drinking too much or something was what I would ponder many years later.

- Drandorian Moon

Phobus awoke in a state of terror as I watched him on screen five from my orbiting Pod. Rather than meeting him on the surface, I opted for the relative comfort of one my orbiting stations. There he sat alone in a six-by-six-square-foot cube on the lifeless moon of Drandor. He took a moment to take in his surroundings, straighten his shirt, and get his bearings. I felt both pity and some nostalgia for him at that moment. *The crazy things I have put he and Coranthas through,* I thought.

Just wait until they find out that they only slew one of Thog's clones back on Sholl Gar. The morning of their sacrifice I had generated a thousand more AI clones of the first Thog and switched a clone with Thog before the ceremony. Thog bet me they would not go through with slaying him, and we watched together on Channel Nine from the Interstellar Café. I have never seen Thog so mad. I am not certain if they did not know it was a clone, but my gut says no. *That reunion was going to be fun,* I thought. I need to get those kids back together.

I could hear Phobus breathing over the commlink system. As I noted, he had gotten up to his feet. No matter what had ever happened to Phobus he always tried to straighten his shirt, attempt to collect himself, and stand up straight. (Stuff like that.) He looked around at his situation and sort of seemed almost resigned to his situation.

"Not this shit again," he muttered to himself, brushing moon dust off his pant leg. I tried not to laugh.

I leaned into the speaker: "Phobus, I have not been hearing very encouraging reports from Sholl Gar, my old friend."

"Sholl Gar?" began Phobus, as he looked to his left, his right, then straight up, holding his lightning cane in his right hand still brushing moon dust off himself with the other. (As if he could do anything useful with the lightning cane.)

"Um, are you freaking kidding me, Froth? I love Sholl Gar. I *LOVE* that place! I mean, it has a special place in my heart you know what I mean?" he uttered as if he was fooling me.

I interrupted him right there.

"Phobus listen to me, I don't give a shit about Sholl Gar."

"No?" he answered.

"No, not two shits," I replied.

"I mean it's one of my worlds still but whatever," I finished.

At this point I had way too much to consider to be bothered by a worthless sand planet that I left to the care of this pitiful creature. Thog was checking in on it for me at that time anyway. He went there when he needed target practice.

"Well that makes two of us, Froth, to be honest," Phobus got to his feet and straightened his jersey. He was looking rather good considering the scenario. He was always kind of sharp.

"I mean one can only tolerate so much sand," he said. "You know Froth you never do fail to liven things up. I will give you that."

He had no idea.

Now there was one problem. A problem that even I was tremendously concerned with at that very moment but I held my composure. I have never found panic to be particularly useful. In fact, until I met these two, I never even would have felt the slightest concern about anything. I supposed they truly are my only actual friends in the universe. I can't count Thog because I made him in my orbiting space lab.

The reason at that moment that I was terribly concerned was that I had no idea where Coranthas was located. Yes, he was supposed be to in Cube Beta-978b, which was within visual site of Phobus. But no he was not there. I had already scanned Delta Five, nope, not there. So, what in the hell did I do? First, I lost the planet Q-7. And now I mis-teleported Coranthas to only Christ knows where. (That's just an expression as far as I know.) How was I ever going to locate Dendrake when I can't pull off a straight quantum jump to my own moon? My game was off.

"So Froth, I know you must have some very important reason for imprisoning me in your cube cell again. I sort of thought these kinds of days were behind me, but could we go ahead and get on with it?" began Phobus.

Maybe I should have just converted him to dark matter right then and there. I needed time to think. *What the hell just happened?* I thought to myself.

"Well, I must come clean with you on something, Phobus. I'm afraid that I might have possibly misplaced Coranthas," I finished.

"That's a good one." Phobus laughed.

"Seriously why did you bring me here? I mean other than just to mess with me?" said Phobus.

"I'm beginning to ask myself the same question honestly," I replied.

"So where's Coranthas?" he asked

"I told you already. I apparently lost him," I answered.

"You lost Coranthas? What do you mean exactly?" Phobus asked.

"Well, you see that cube cell to your left. I had programmed the jump algorithm to drop him right there. But he's not there," I said.

"So, um, where the hell is he?" continued Phobus.

"I honestly don't know," I replied. "He might exist as a Vapor or Wraith now, I'm not too sure if I'm honest about it," I added.

"You converted Coranthas into a Vapor?" asked Phobus.

"Or a Wraith," I answered.

"Nice," he answered.

It became painfully clear to me that Phobus would be no help at all in finding Coranthas, or Q-7, or really with much of anything for that matter. *Why couldn't I have lost him?* I thought to myself. What a mess have I created for myself now. I began to question why I even woke up that morning.

It was clearly necessary for me to leave Phobus in the cell on my moon. At least I would know where he was while I tried to figure out what happened to Coranthas. At least I would not lose him that way. Broth and sustenance would be provided by the drones so he should be good. *If necessary I could have Thog check in on him,* I thought. I should most definitely film that encounter.

I set his cell cam monitor settings to record and reprogrammed two drones to bring Phobus both Broth and food. Then I logged out of the system. I was logged out, but I could see him on my display from my orbiting pod. He was straightening his pants and his shirt, still talking as if I had not logged out making hand motions, etc. I'd be back, eventually. He should be good.

- Interstellar Café, searching for clues

I had not been to the Interstellar Café since the First War's ending. Before I warped space time near Lantos I had the loan shark Tony and the station commander Jok plot a course for the café to head to deep space. Use of the Interstellar Café to observe civilizations' fiery ends had been tabled for now by the newly reorganized Council of Drakar. Though this was the right thing to do, and I agreed with the Council, there was that dark part of me that still remembered my times with the gang partying, and watching worlds perish. Making bets, drinking beer, and consuming Broth. I will openly admit that I can be very complicated.

The Interstellar Café is still a very popular interspecies gathering place for sport, drink, and gambling. I teleported to the station and requested an audience with Tony and Jok. I thought they may know how to find the planet Lantos at that time. The problem would be admitting that I did not. This could be tricky. Fortunately for me, Tony and Jok were only "Plan B."

I absolutely could not allow anyone to know that I lost that planet. But how could I get Tony to get me there without letting him know I couldn't find it? It turned out Tony had no clue anyway. As noted, Tony had been my plan "B." I did of course have a plan "A," but I was not sure currently whether it was going to be fruitful. It had been my "ace in the hole" up until right this moment. I was not certain it was going to pan out. But sometimes great plans require patience, and this proved true with my Plan A. I will explain it all, don't worry.

With my Plan A the story gets even stranger. But I can happily report that my Plan A kicked in right at this precise moment. And I immediately, as if seemingly by magic, located both Q-7 and Coranthas! I love when a great plan comes together.

- Meanwhile, on Lantos, Q-7 System

Sitting at the corner stool of a Podranian bar on my "missing planet" was Coranthas. I could now observe him and learn what I needed. There was a bigger mystery than either the missing planet or the missing Human. So, there was Coranthas, happily clueless. He ordered a Coors Lite. I never understood why he liked Coors Lite. He was always annoyed with me that I had not rescued Heineken from Earth. He looked rather well considering. He was barely phased at all by the circumstance. *Par for the course,* he would think. Happenings like this were just old school for him by this point.

Coranthas took a moment to do a self-awareness test I had shown him many years ago. This was just something he did a lot when he wanted to discern reality from unreality. It was useful to for him to discern dream state from woke state. Ages past, on Delta Five I have given him a diamond-shaped stone from Nectar. He was to keep the stone always on his person. It helped him.

I felt somewhat bad for him that he was struggling. I did care for him. I mean I rescued him from Earth after all. But there was good reason for me to remain in full stealth right now. As I have already hinted a couple times, I was on the trail of bigger matters than these current events. And my Plan A was about more than just finding Q-7. But just to repeat that seeing him struggle, seeing him clutching to my stone, at this moment gave me pause.

I had taught him that when Coranthas found himself ever wondering which state of consciousness he was in he should close his eyes and grab the stone in his pocket and count to ten, breathing deeply. This slowing down of his perception and physical reminder of the stone in hand always seemed to ground him. And I had also secretly ionized the stone. The ionization had the effect of grounding him as well. This ionization required such a quantity of energy for it to isolate atoms to the point where they would discharge, and then eject an electron. As noted, this did several things for Coranthas. It created a neurotheological object for him to focus on in his mind. I never told him about that part of any of this. But I have witnessed him clinging to diamond-shaped stone on multiple occasions. I had other reasons for which I needed Coranthas to be the keeper of this stone but those are for another story. He looked around briefly and then started up a conversation with the bartender.

"What world am I on?" he asked

The bartender shook his head and just laughed handing Coranthas the beer. *This all feels normal for me,* he thought, still clutching the stone. One moment he was hanging with Phobus, or at least he thought he was, then suddenly he was sitting on this corner stool. It was par for the course for Coranthas. *Roll with it,* he thought. It was a decent bar.

Though a Podranian bar, this bar had become a hangout for many Sentient Life forms who had been trapped inside my anomaly. Darlocks, sub-creatures that had served in Dominick's assault teams, undead from the Vampire Guild, and local Podranians, all together enjoying a festive night out. It was quite a site to see if I'm honest about it. Good music, good drink, and food were abundant. Happy smiles, laughter, and good cheer abounded. Coranthas thought to himself that even though he had no idea where or why he was, he would just go with it. Plan A was about to come into sharp focus. I must remain in full stealth as much as I wanted to let him know I was there.

"What the hell?" muttered Coranthas happily to himself, sipping his beer.

"No, this is not hell," a voice responded.

Coranthas looked to his left and then back to his right and there was no one near. He did a 360, looked behind himself. There was no one to have spoken those words. Now Coranthas hears voices. He had been told by many about his condition and that this was part of its manifestation. Coranthas never bought any of that. His firm steadfast insistence was always that these voices are real. In this case he was quite right. Plan A was unfolding.

"Who said that?" he asked.

"Who I am is not your concern. Not yet anyway," the voice answered.

Many times on Delta Five, both I and Phobus had expressed great concern for Coranthas's well-being. We believed that he had gone quite insane by this point. That was why I had given him the diamond not without some serious trepidation. I had kept him alive tens of thousands of years longer than a Human Being's natural lifetime. He reached into his pocket, grabbed the stone, and closed his eyes. With his eyes still closed he took a deep breath, then began to speak back to this voice.

"Are you real?" he asked the voice.

"Whether I am real is not your concern. Not yet anyway," the voice again answered mysteriously.

This was pretty much the way things went for Coranthas these last few decades since the war. He had always been paranoid, untrusting, suspicious, and quite frankly, annoyed by reality. Before I explained everything to him he had lived a very scared existence on Delta Five. But at least he had not yet gone insane. Though this was strange, it was not out of his element. Coranthas has achieved some impressive feats. Remember after all, he is called a leader of many. Don't forget his clever elimination of the Large Master. This situation ironically, is the kind of situation where Coranthas often shined.

"Not yet, huh?" Coranthas asked under his breath, then took a sip from his beer.

His experiences with Sholl-Gar, Phobus, Thog, and the war had taken a severe toll on him. He has some post-traumatic stress disorder going on for sure. Sitting here now, he began to wonder if these last few decades with Phobus on Delta Five playing video games and consuming Broth was just a long dream. If those times were a dream, he probably wished he could go back to sleep and return there. I listened and waited, unseen. Coranthas never, ever lacked courage, though. I always had found this to be one of his most noble strengths. He decided to fully engage this *woman,* whoever she was.

"So, whether you are real or not is not my concern. Going with that, my I ask you what world I am on?" Coranthas asked the voice.

"You are on the planet Lantos in the Q-7 star system," she answered.

"Q-7? Are you serious?" he asked her somewhat incredulously.

"Yessir," she answered.

"The Podranians?" he asked.

Well that explained a lot for Coranthas, at least with respect to the various clientele. It was funny for him to see Sholl-Garian sub-creatures happy and having fun. Those poor bastards had such a ghastly existence on that wretched sand world. Getting sucked into that war and stuck behind my quantum space hole in time, or whatever the hell I did to them all, was the best thing that ever happen to those folks. Hell if this was really Lantos, then he might be safe here, Coranthas thought.

Coranthas allowed himself a brief divergence to ponder that war for a moment. It had been such a great victory, even despite the significant losses we had taken. He also considered how I had managed the political situation related to the wider war to be brilliant. Coranthas always had a way to stoke my ego. He loved the way I had used the Sholl-Garian defense force to fight the wider war for us and Q-7 while we built up the Podranians. And he played a large role in our post war defense build up of Podran. He commanded a large fleet of Podranian starships, always insistant to run the fleet from his ship Witch Doctor One. He had grown to love that ship. Especially after I jacked that thing up.

"So why can't I see you?" Coranthas asked this apparition.

"I do not exist in a similar manner to you, Coranthas," she answered.

"He is going to destroy you," she added.

Here we go. She was about to get going now. This felt very familiar, let me tell you.

"Destroy me?" Coranthas asked.

"Yessir," she replied.

"Who is going to destroy me?" he asked her.

"My husband of course," Rulella answered

"Who is your husband?" asked Coranthas, clutching the stone all the while.

Rulella did not realize that I was behind all of this in its entirety, and that she was helping me find Coranthas's location and the missing planet. She was my Plan A. She had been my Plan A for eons. I just never knew what Plan A was for until I lost the planet. Rulella did not realize she was helping me find Lantos, or that this was all a part of my overall plan. I knew she wanted revenge and had been monitoring me for thousands of years. She was waiting for an opportunity. As perfect as things were seeming to work out something was off though. I could not yet put my finger on precisely what, but something of significance was off. I am usually right about those things which concerned me at that moment.

What Rulella did not realize is that I had been tracking her. I had been tracking her for eons. She was not even aware that I knew of her continued sentient existence. Her thirst for revenge against me could be turned on its head, and she helped me find the missing planet. (via Coranthas) And it also gave me yet another opportunity to mess with her further. But still, like I said, something was amiss. There was a sense of being played by someone. But there was no way it was her. I don't get easily tricked. My radar was up yet I did not have any significant clues as to why.

Let's get back to Rulella though. Cunningly she plotted, never knowing when her opportunity would present itself. Sneakily she went about her plan not knowing that I was behind her moves. But even so as I have stated something greater, something else entirely was afoot. I allowed her to know that I was distraught about losing the planet. I projected the concept into her mind. This was her chance she thought. Rulella was totally unaware of what was happening. And that I would get her to find my missing world for me by losing Coranthas to her. It will make more sense soon. *It was all going according to my plan,* I thought. She would hijack and kidnap Coranthas for me. She would intercept his quantum jump because I told her to do so, and I showed her how. I also planted their destination in her sentience. The reason I planted the idea in her sentience was because I already had learned that Coranthas knew how to find Q-7. I had seen that he knew its location while I was inside his dreams.

Chapter Three

Rulella

I had used my new Model T Photon Wave dispenser to transform Rulella into energy and had planned to scatter her into the Cosmos. The same system may ultimately be used on both Phobus and Coranthas depending on my mood. (Not likely, though; my mood would need to be horrendous.) If I do though, I am considering allowing Thog to execute the conversion process as he is still quite angry with them.

It is important that I document that I do have some regrets related to Rulella and some of my decisions on that matter. She was holding me back at that time. I had begun making so much progress before that relationship. I met her and not long later we were raining nuclear fire on unsuspecting worlds ourselves! All we ever did together was mess with people and stir up trouble. Even so, what I did to her may have been overkill.

I often had wondered what happens to a being's consciousness once transformed to pure energy. The concept is very old, but the technology is solid. This process has been in use for eons in the Zynon galaxy. I have encountered many beings that have been transformed, and I myself exist in an energy form at various times. But what I did to Rulella was quite different. I had thought that her sentience likely would not survive the transformation process. But I also knew that if she did survive it would be possible to discover her then to track her. She likely would not be very pleased with me. So, even though I did not consider her a threat, I determined to locate her if she still existed in a sentient state. And if she did still exist in a conscious state I determined to always know what she was up to. If she did still exist within a mind construct of some form I could still make use of her. Tracking her energy signature was not difficult. But I needed to do experiments to determine if this energy was still sentient, and as a result she was still present in the Cosmos as a Sentient life form.

This was an interesting challenge as it turned out. As mentioned, locating her energy signature and tracking it turned out to be relatively easy for me. But that said, how could I determine that *she* remained sentient without tipping her off to the fact that I am aware of both her location and her sentience? The key to solving the challenge would be close monitoring of the actual subatomic particles that make up her energy signature. Even beings that can transcend dimensions move across different planes existing as pure energy, are yet still made up of *stuff*. (Subatomic particles to be precise.) Everything that exists is made up of matter in some manner including entities that exist as pure energy, Vapor, or even Wraith. Now Rulella did not ascend to her state. She was transformed by my questionable actions. (Again, I have some regrets related to this course of action I took with respect to her, but this is not my current point.) She existed in what is "technically" a higher state, but it was not really "higher" per se, because it was something done to her. In other words she did not attain this state through her own great powers. But here is the point, the very reason I can trace her is the fact that she still, even now is made of subatomic matter. So tracing her was a simple matter of science. But detecting if she remained Sentient? Detecting if she was a conscious being still was a whole different matter. So yes this may be doable, but it would be, as noted, an interesting challenge.

I liked interesting challenges though. So I came up with an experiment that could help me in accomplishing all this.

The Experiment – "The Origins of Consciousness"

Dendrake caused consciousness to evolve in a very specific and slow manner. The Broth initiated the life process yet also included the causality (the code if you will) of all future consciousness. As we have discussed I have always been interested in the planet Earth. For a primitive world they had some of the greatest thinkers. Human Beings were a very curious species which showed the depths of their intelligence. Human religions, philosophies, politics, and writings had always indicated, to me at least, that they seemed to be special people.

Some of their philosophers would ponder the greatest of questions. But one area I had considered of great intrigue was their interest in the origins of consciousness in a very scientific manner. Every known sentient species in the galaxy wonders "why" and "how did I get here," things of that nature. But the humans of Earth took a particular scientific interest in the origins of Sentience itself. They wanted to know how and when they became self-aware. Did it happen before or after the evolution of language for example? They wanted to know if their fellow Earthling creatures like dolphins and dogs experienced their environments similarly. They wanted to understand what creatures like "whales" and "dolphins" were saying to each other. Human curiosity was quite unique in the galaxy. No sub-creature of that wasteland planet Phobus called home cared one lick about what the Zaks or sandworms thought. What was the evolutionary step that catapulted human life to this state of "self-awareness"? They were on to something. Many mysteries of the Cosmos are deeply profound yet stare us all right in the face. Humans thought and considered all these things in the deepest of manners.

Many of Earth's scientists looked at "self-awareness" strictly from a biological evolutionary view. And in doing so crediting essentially the brain itself with being the very canvas of consciousness. They formed attempted explanations of very important matters related to this issue. One long study I examined essentially broke their investigation down to four general points:

Causation of consciousness (the How – Dendrake and the Broth from my perspective)

The "awakening" of consciousness, both on a species level, and on an individual Sentients level (The When)

Perpetuity or temporal (The Big Question, do we live past death, and did we exist before birth?)

The Purpose (The Why)

The "How," the "When," the "Soul," and the "Why" regarding self-aware sentience. These entirely fascinated me. The most interesting thing to me was that as deeply important that these matters are, they are all mostly without explanation, when one is truthful about it.

One theory that I found interesting that human philosophers and scientists debated in relation to the origins of consciousness was the idea of "the Bicameral

Mind". Humans considered this to simply be a hypothesis, but they may have been closer than they thought to the actual truth. This "Bicameral Mind" hypothesis tries to address the "how" question, and the "when" question regarding the development of consciousness. The Broth included Sentience within its encoding. Numbers three and four I consider not only unanswerable but also unnecessary ponderings. Both numbers three and four are hampered by what the galaxy's greatest scientists refer to as the "Mind-Body" problem. I would have to author an entire separate treatise outside of our purposes to cover those matters. Perhaps I will when we are finished with all this.

You see, according to Nectarian writings Dendrake designed a system fully encoded in the Broth. And in this system of interconnected life forms entities would need to be divided into two main groups. A higher and lower tiering if you will. All life forms would be potential food for the energy production of other life forms. This was just part of his life processing system. But the point being that there would be both a higher and a lower tiering.

The long code plan of the Broth brought first primordial life, then advancing life, and then the earliest sentient life. The earliest sentient life did not think and process information in the same way that most sentients do now. It did not experience external stimuli the same way modern sentience does. In fact, the earliest sentient life operated almost exactly as the humans' "bicameral mind" described. Please bear with me, as I am getting to the point of the matter with Rulella. The background information is relevant to how I solved this riddle.

Scientific agreement amongst all the higher species on the known worlds is not always attainable. However, on most worlds with intelligent species, scientists have generally agreed that essential consciousness exists and arises from one's higher brain functions. Nevertheless, most scientists have not been able to solve the *how* part of this. So, the answer remains incomplete. *The Broth did it,* is often said. But early Earth philosophy hit on something with respect to how consciousness might have come about. And remember, they were not aware of the Broth. So though quite clever, they were at a scientific disadvantage.

Here it is in a nutshell from ancient Earth philosophy. The human mind (i.e., Sentient form) once operated in a state where cognitive functions were divided between the *speaking part of the brain,* and the *listening and obeying part of the brain.* They were on to something, and here is why. In the last times of humanity it was theorized that unfortunate humans afflicted with *schizophrenia* were experiencing the world the same way earlier humans who had yet made the leap from the state of the bicameral mind to a fuller state of true self-awareness.

Basically a conscious being in this state heard voices, or so they thought. This was the only way they could process how the brain told them things about reality. These voices were not real voices, but they were how their own brain was communicating critical things about their environment, prior to a true ascendance to full consciousness and hence true sentience. If this theory is accurate, this would have been a state of how the mind worked around the time the Sentient being was developing language more than likely.

I could write an entire series of volumes about how life went from the bicameral mind to modern sentience, and again, perhaps I should. For now I am simply going to explain it in its most basic sense and explain how it helped me determine if Rulella still existed in a sentient form.

Zynon galaxy scientists had often thought that a sentient being which had been transformed to pure energy may yet exist in a sentient state like the bicameral sentient state. Since the being had no actual physical brain any longer, it was thought they would not be able to ascend to any higher sentient state, such as my state of existence. But it was generally agreed that if a being existed in the form of pure energy, or a Vapor, or even a Wraith, in any of those states, they could yet react to external stimuli if remaining sentient.

For me to determine that the energy signature I was now tracking with neutrino scan technology was still "Rulella," it was necessary for me to cause *skips* in time directly in front of the energy's path as it traversed space. Just like skips on a record, these anomalies would cause any Sentient life form, in any state including the bicameral to become confused. My hope was that the energy would show signs of reacting to the odd nature of time around it. Reactions that could not occur in nature without sentience on some level.

So, I rippled space time in her path. It worked. The energy signature began to clearly respond to the ripples in time that implied a state of being self-aware. The energy acted "alive."

I've got her!

As horrible as everything I had done to her was, it still was impossible for me to not be fascinated by her state. I spent the next two thousand years learning how to hear her thoughts, understand her plane, and know her plans. That was a tough one. I was able to successfully glean that her main intention was revenge against me. I tracked her throughout her quest. Ultimately I used both her and Coranthas to locate the planet.

Chapter Four

Dreaming Again

Meanwhile back on Lantos, Q-7 System

Coranthas was dreaming again. Most of his dreams' typical framework remained consistent. The three ominous entities and a dark presence just outside his view, a protective presence, and now a woman on a bar stool clearly in his line of site. There was something beautiful about her to Coranthas, as evil as the whole scenario felt.

Is this the voice? Coranthas thought.

I always made sure to not make my presence known or intervene in anyway. Though I could be present in Coranthas's dreams I did not want to be detected. I mainly did not want to be detected because I was never quite sure what his dreams meant. And worse than not knowing, the entities he is dreaming of were real, including me.

Yes the beings were real just like me and were essentially doing the same thing I was. They were violating the sanctity of Coranthas's dreams. Did they know I was present? I did not know the answer to this, yet. But I always watched. I always listened.

Rulella had led me to find Coranthas, and subsequently my missing planet. (I will explain even more later.) But it is also possible she has helped me solve the greatest mystery of all. I would find out soon enough. It really was a simple trick but carried about by utilizing some immense powers garnered over countless ages. But it was simple, nonetheless. You see, I knew Rulella was glued to my hip always because I was tracking her energy signature. And I had projected thoughts into her being. Now you need to remember that Rulella had great powers too. So, I did in fact truly "lose" Coranthas, but my reasons and plan were sound. I projected thoughts and intentions into Ruella's mind to intercept Coranthas's jump as an act of revenge, which she did in fact successfully execute. But I also projected and planted the simple thought of her destination into her still-Sentient mind, the planet Q-7. Which of course, was my missing planet.

You are likely wondering how I knew that she knew the location of Q-7. Well the fact is that she did not. Coranthas in fact did. I programmed into her mind how to intercept Coranthas, scan his brain, and get Lantos's location and head there. Then I could track her by her energy signature. The reason I knew that Coranthas knew of the location of Q-7 was because of the last times I invaded his dreams. An ominous vision was there in his dream, and he told me Coranthas would know. Not in an audible voice, but via projection into my mind. He also blocked me from retrieving it from Coranthas as I will describe. So here is one of the greatest ironies of all this. Rulella was aware that I could not locate Q-7, and that this distressed me. She knew because I planted that thought into her Sentience. And I also planted the thought of intercepting Coranthas during the jump. But in addition to all that I gave her the destination where to take him. She thought and planned all this because I told her subconscious to do so. So, let us see if you know the next question? You may be wondering why it was that I simply did not scan Coranthas brain to locate Q-7. I would love to tell you that I could have and it was just more fun this way, but that would be a lie. The fact of the matter was I tried. And as I noted, for whatever unknown reason I was being blocked by the presence in Coranthas's dreams. Who he is I am not certain yet, but I have a strong suspicion who it was that was blocking me. In Coranthas's dreams I had tried to scan him for the location many times once I knew that he knew. That is when Plan A entered my mind. Rulella was the only being I was aware of who could possibly read his brain. And perhaps she would not be blocked. So, it appeared, that tracking her all this time would prove fruitful. And I could use her anger and fury to my advantage. There was yet so much more to this however. Though my plan was working I felt dread at that moment. I never feel dread. Well, I needed to check on Phobus and reunite him with the first Thog.

- Drandor Moon Cube cell, present time

"Where the hell is Froth Lord?" -Phobus Uthrates.

It was impossible for Phobus to know how long I had left him there. There was plenty of Broth and Miller Lite brought by the drones. He should have been fine. I sighed, then I checked on him from my wristwatch portal.

I spoke into the Commlink.

"Phobus are you hanging in there?" I asked.

"FROTH!?" He jumped up to his feet

"Froth you there?" Phobus asked, then slipped, stumbled, and fell to one knee.

"Listen Phobus, just hang in there. It's almost done. My plan is just about full circle now," I finished.

"Your plan!?" he exclaimed, exasperated.

He straightened his shirt and pulled it down.

"This? This was your plan?" he finished.

Phobus was annoyed but used to this kind of thing.

"Yes. Stay put," I finished.

At that moment I teleported Thog into the cube next to Phobus.

"Talk to Thog until Coranthas and I get back." I laughed.

Phobus looked over at Thog. Thog had the stare of fire and death, just a mere eight feet away, through two clear cell walls.

"Are you a Thog AI clone?" Phobus asked through the commlink I had set up for them. "You look like version 1.0," he finished.

"I am Thog you bastard," was Thog's reply

"That's not possible, we sacrificed Thog back on..." He stopped himself. Somehow, he immediately knew it was indeed Thog, the "real" Thog. *Oh my god, what fresh horror did Froth Lord do to me now?* he thought.

"Thog!?" exclaimed Phobus with his usual feigned joy. He reached out both arms as if he wanted an embrace.

"Is that really you? Oh, is this true? Dear Thog, it is you!" he continued.

Thog simply stared the stare of death at his old friend and Master. A fire burned in Thog at the betrayal of his two friends in what seemed so long ago. The reality is, I programmed a fair amount their "shared" experiences into all three of their brain stems using my computer. I'm not even sure how much total time the three had even spent on the same world at the same time. For a lot of their remembered "pasts" they were actual comatose in my space lab, temporal lobes connected via a copper connectors I used on drones. It was always sketchy. One time I messed up the cross over cables and briefly, Phobus was Coranthas, and Coranthas was Phobus. I had to restore them from tape.

"Where's Coranthas?" Thog asked. "I need the both of you."

"Not all that sure to be quite honest," replied Phobus.

"What do you mean? You two are never apart," queried Thog.

"Froth Lord mis-teleported him I believe," continued Phobus.

"Wow, that's cool," said Thog.

"A little bit, yeah," finished Phobus looking up and around as he spoke.

Chapter Five

The Q-7 System, Dendrake, and the Beginning of the End

In the 12,400th year after the unnatural birth of Thog on Sholl Gar, a seemingly terrible, mysterious disease began to ravage the Podranians on Q-7. The danger went from small to enormous quickly. This disease made the war seem like a cake walk. The world was quarantined by the Council of Drakar immediately upon the discovery of the Space Virus, as it came to be known. Tom of Podran protested the quarantine as unjust without hesitation. It was clear this situation could possibly escalate rapidly.

This "poor world", I found myself once again thinking. You did not need to be Dendrake to foresee what mess was coming for Podran. Quarantined for a new and deadly virus. Blockaded because of a terrible and terrifying new plague. The Podranians were scared. Hadn't they been through enough already? But it was not just the Podranians who were frightened. The scientists had never seen a disease like this. The Space Virus entered your system and invaded the cerebral cortex of the victim. It immediately hijacked your main stem, then proceeded to replace the being's cells with self-replicated false cells from within its code. It seemed to emulate the "entanglement" aspect of the Broth according to the "scientists" dispatched to the scene. Right at the very moment, just before the victim implodes upon itself, the viral agent bursts itself into the atmosphere, along with the victim's biological matter, spreading itself airborne and space borne. It was an epically horrible scenario. But even so, I was not pleased with the fact that the Council would decide to purge Q-7, yet again. It was quite clear to me that this poor world was going to have to defend itself once more. Fortunately, the gang and I had helped them build up their defense forces both during and after the first Q-7 War.

This was at long last when Dendrake revealed himself to me and explained everything. Though I had come to believe that my purpose was to find Dendrake that was not it at all. Dendrake wanted to use me to set in motion the destruction of the Zynon galaxy and quite possibly the end of all things. You see Dendrake was a lost soul in many ways, it turned out. Legend on Nectar was that he was the Creator of the Cosmos where in which, of course, is located the Zynon galaxy.

But the Cosmos and the galaxy all pre-exist Dendrake, and he simply knows nothing of his own story. He will forever remain a complete mystery. In fact he will forever be the greatest known mystery in the journals of the Zynon galaxy.

It was at this point that he revealed himself to me. It was at this point that he told me all that he did know. Even more importantly and mysteriously, it was at this point that he told me all that he did not know as well. Like the rest of us he had no idea why or how the Cosmos exists. He planted these thoughts into my consciousness.

It was my turn to dream. I never dream. I never sleep. The need for sleep is something that I had overcome so many thousands of years ago. But here I was. For once the subject of a more powerful entity's whims and wishes. I was in fact, asleep, or comatose, whatever the case may have been. I had become so use to Coranthas's dreams, having invaded them so often as I had. The setting and surrounding was in fact his recurrent dreamscape. It was the same.

I was on Delta Five in Coranthas's familiar chamber. This much was certain. I watched Coranthas as he was clearly in state of awe, fear, and wonder as he always was in his own dreams. Of great interest to me was that he was clutching my diamond-shaped ionized stone. That seemed peculiarly un-dreamlike to me. Was Coranthas possibly present in my dream? Inside this dream it seems Dendrake may have pulled him in. And suspecting as I did that this was not a true dream but rather a construct of Dendrake, a projection of Dendrake into my defenseless sub-consciousness, further made the Others' presence unnerving. It was unnerving, but not frightening. A subtle difference yes, but very true for me.

I looked at the three beings, but this time in my dream, their faces were clear. It was the Others. I wondered as I always did in Coranthas's dreams, why they were there. It was a bit daunting that they were now present in my dream. So I looked right back at them. I stared at each one, one at a time, going back and forth from one to another. I made certain that they, each one of them, realized that they produced no trepidation in me.

I never spoke of the Others, but many in the Zynon galaxy would refer to them, including Coranthas. In their lessor minds, the Others were simply others like me. The Others in their minds were other Nectarians. The truth of the matter was that there were no longer other Nectarians. In fact there are no longer Nectarians at all, not even I. You see and it pains me to say it even to these times the entire Nectarian race went extinct tens of thousands of years before the creation of Thog, or the "Unnatural birth of Thog," or whatever we called that thing. I always thought that was stupid. *Not sure why I created that doctrine,* I would often think.

The only Nectarians that remain, exist in a similar state as I. We are no longer Nectarians in any kind of traditional sense. And though the Others exist as I do they refuse to interfere on this plane. They do not partake in our dimension described in these chronicles, at all. Fear of their imminent intervention is ever present for many on many worlds. But it simply will never happen as they have no intentions. The fear of their intervention is entirely unfounded and without merit. And though they had no intentions on this dimension, they would yet be used by Dendrake in his plan for me.

I never saw the point in that unnecessary dimension segregation for which they insisted upon. They disapproved of all my "God-work" I had undertaken. I honestly no longer approved of it myself, but that was all so long ago. But this dimension is fun for me. It's like a playground. I like it here. The people in this dimension, like Coranthas, Phobus, all the absurd Councils and whatnot, were so much more interesting and funnier than these higher dimension elitists. Also, higher plain entities could do great good in lower dimensions for the peoples of the various planets. Though I have also been quite reckless at times in this plane of existence, I have done much good too, no?

It was then when I heard his voice. It was unlike any other voice I had ever heard before. I understood him. That was not the issue. But there was something ominous even for me. The power of the moment was simply my knowledge of who this was. Knowledge that I had inexplicably. Without explanation in my own mind I had no shadow of a doubt who was speaking to me.

"Froth Lord"? the voice began

"I am here," I answered

"Do you know who I am?" the voice responded.

"You are Dendrake," I spoke with certainty

Dendrake began to reveal all to me. He revealed his apparent ultimate purpose for me and his ultimate destiny of all worlds and life in the Zynon galaxy. He had created the Broth and all life on all known worlds. He is responsible probably for all life in all galaxies, though he was not even certain of this himself. If there is another like him, somewhere else in the Cosmos, is entirely unknown, and likely unanswerable. Some questions can never be answered only speculation. He showed me so much all in an instant. He was alone. He had many questions all unanswered. He was tortured internally by many things. Dendrake longed for something he could not attain.

"I am beginning the end-of-life process for all known worlds Froth Lord." he began.

"Starting with Q-7," he stated ominously.

"You spiked the Broth?" I asked

"I spiked the Broth," he finished.

Unknowingly, all of us, Rulella with her quest for revenge, Coranthas being deposited on Q-7, the war itself, and, shockingly, even I, Froth Lord, were pawns, fully used by the ultimate king, queen, and creator of all life, in the plot to terminate all life. It was soon going to be checkmate for all of us!

"Why?" I asked my maker.

"Why?" Dendrake repeated. "Why is the oldest question, Froth Lord. It is my oldest question. You are asking why to which matter? Why am I starting the end-of-life process? Maybe you should rather ask why I started the life process in the first place," Dendrake finished.

"I do not understand," I answered him

"You will at the end," he responded.

"At the end of what, all life? I don't understand," I repeated.

"You will at the end, and you will have your answer to 'why,'" he finished.

For some silly reason at that moment, though totally out of place and context in my dream or this conversation with my maker, I had a quick thought of Phobus and Thog trapped on my moon that popped into my head and had a brief laugh. But then right back to this dream. *I will understand at the end?* I wondered to myself, even within my dream state.

"You are a most interesting Sentient Being. I have watched you for eons and eons. You can be sarcastic, and even evil to a degree, even to your friends. You just thought of your friends and chuckled because you think it is funny that you are keeping them in a prison," Dendrake finished.

It was a fair point he made.

"This plague is a horrendous creation," I said to my maker.

"There are many horrendous creations. Take the Broth for example," Dendrake ominously stated.

"The Broth is the source of all life," I retorted.

Dendrake waited and did not respond right away. I longed to see him. Does he incarnate as I do? *What is he?* I would think to myself. Of course, he read my mind.

"I told you what I am. I expect a lot from you, Froth Lord," Dendrake said.

"You will assist the end-of-life process," he ominously ended the conversation.

I awoke with a shudder. I never shudder. I, Froth Lord, had just met my maker. If I am honest with myself, I had been truly seeking him out my entire long existence. I have been searching for him and longing for this meeting for my entire life.

How am I going to stop him? I thought to myself

Chapter Six

The Q-7 Space Virus

The scientists of the various worlds and councils were concerned. They were very concerned. There was not much debate before the Council of Drakar decided to raise fleets from every known space-faring world to destroy the planet Podran once again. This was necessary to exterminate the Space Plague. Only minimal superficial debate was done. The Podranians had become an accepted member of Sentient interstellar society and had offered much to the galaxy since the first Q-7 War, only to be scheduled for utter obliteration a second time. The council vote was unanimous. I immediately received an automated calendar invite to the bombardment ceremonies on my wristwatch control panel.

No one was glad this was necessary. (Well, except for the Garthonian Empire, the Darlock Vampire Guild, the populace of Sholl-Gar, the Council of Drakar, and maybe a few other planets.) But it is true, no one had seen a Space Virus like this one. The Q-7 Sentients were suffering, and many were leaving their world in utter panic. They all could be carriers of the plague. Sadly, the entire community of worlds declared war and called for the extermination of the Podranians once again to contain the plague. The problem for these sentient species was some of them still had great trouble locating the planet just as I had.

Dendrake explained his plan to me through subconscious injections. He had been assisting me in tracking Rulella. He secretly trained me how to do it. He was the one who implanted into my head the idea of misplacing Coranthas, so I could find Q-7 via Rulella. I had thought that was my idea. He injected the plan that

Rulella would cause Coranthas to end up on Q-7. He orchestrated all of it by mind injection. Somehow, I just thought I already knew that Rulella would send Coranthas to Q-7 because of the dreams. I thought it was me all this time. But it was really Dendrake in control of all things. Someone else masterminding me for once.

Dendrake had caused all the mysterious changes in Coranthas's sentience and consciousness, which had troubled me ever since I rescued him from Earth before the planet's final nuclear concussion bombardment. He did all this with a purpose. He all did this for me. But he did all this for his own purposes, and at the obvious expense of Coranthas's wellbeing. I felt a growing mercy in me for Coranthas. It had always been there. When I rescued him from Earth I had been observing him for some time. I was feeling a bit bad about a lot of the tricks I had played on him at this point.

Dendrake had removed Coranthas's discernment of reality. "Depersonalization-derealization" disorder was the diagnosis the Witch Doctor on Delta Five had determined. We did not realize that it was not a natural illness. Dendrake, all along, was the master of Coranthas's recurring dreams. He was creating a construct using Coranthas as the canvas. He used Coranthas's dreams as a training construct for me. I believe the actual construct is ancient predating Coranthas or even my existence. I did not know it was Dendrake training me to enter Coranthas's mind. He brought the Others to Coranthas's dreams as well. Dendrake was the root cause of much of Coranthas suffering. He did all this to use this "construct," the canvas of Coranthas, as a tool in steering my evolutionary development to that of a Superbeing status. That part I thought was cool I must admit.

Dendrake altered Coranthas's mind to a state at times which emulated that of the bicameral mind. He had a purpose for all of this. He explained to me via mind thought projections that all that I am and can be was because of him. This seemingly all-powerful entity steered my evolution making me the most powerful being in the galaxy aside from he himself. But for what reason? It could not simply be to mess with people all the time could it? He was going to end all life. Why would he do this? *This can't be how things end,* I thought. I believed I can escape to an alternate realm, but the strictly biologicals are going to suffer and perish. Dendrake had interfered with the Others for tens of thousands of years and prevented them from ever interfering with me. It turns out that the Others had been plotting my destruction for many eons but Dendrake held them off me. I found myself thinking that I could have taken them out myself. Did I kick their ass in grade school or something?

But could I stop Dendrake's plan? How could that even be possible? Could I save all life on all known worlds? Nothing short of destroying Dendrake could stop him. *Is that even possible?* I thought. Can Dendrake be terminated as an entity?

Never in my wildest imagination would I have guessed that his final destruction, and relief from his endless existence, was his actual desire and plan all along. As great as his power was he could not kill himself, though he had tried. So he spent nearly two hundred thousand years nurturing, secretly discipling, training, evolving, and empowering a Superbeing. A Super Intellect, with the hopes that I could solve that riddle one day. He told me that he had foreseen that I could destroy him.

The Desperate Assault

It seemed so long ago to me that the planet was "missing." Now we all wished it truly was.

Now per Dendrake's plan, I was forced to assist the attackers at locating Q-7 via Dendrake amplifying across space the location of Q-7 from my mind. (Now that I had found it!) The Broth Virus, or the Space Virus as it came to be known, would be spread far and wide due to this coming assault and subsequent war and the refugees that would spread across the stars. The Broth Virus, perfectly replicating forever via the Broth entanglement, could very well be unstoppable. This could really be it. *Christ!* I often thought to myself.

Fleets from all known worlds are arrived at Q-7 again, per the coordinates broadcasted across the galaxy from my inner sub-conscious via mind invasion by Dendrake. It was broadcast in the open. The roster of the attacking worlds was like the hall of shame. The Darlocks, Garthonians, and Drakarian attack cruisers by the tens of thousands were first to arrive. The Zillerians, the Drandorians, the Sholl-Garians, all arrived with all their forces. Q-7 was about to get lit up. The Darlock Vampire Guild began an attack run. Q-7 was already a suffering planet due to the Space Virus. The Podranians had been greatly weakened but still managed to launch a significant defense force to orbit.

Captain Mulcahee of Q-7 was Commander of Podran Star Command Cruiser One, call sign "Javelin One". He flew into defense position in low Podran orbit rapidly gaining altitude. Several squadrons raced in defensive formations just barely in time for an initial intercept. Their mission in addition to destroying enemy ships was to align the shield satellites array once they were in range. It was a race against time for them.

Javelin One: "Team leaders, Javelin One, report in, over."

Javelin Five: "Javelin Five reporting in, over."

Javelin Nine: "Javelin Nine reporting in, over."

One by one all Podranian defense cruiser units reported in.

Javelin One: "Jeremy do you have comm control of the shield array? Over."

Javelin Nine: "Copy that Captain."

Javelin One: "All teams Jeremy needs cover. Light up anything coming in, over."

Javelin One: "Jeremy, neutrino shields up!"

One by one the Javelin squadron began to pick off and obliterate the closest targets. The Darlocks were in range and if the shield array did not juice up quick this could get ugly fast.

Lieutenant Jeremy Fielder onboard his starcraft shot like a missile almost straight up higher and higher. He was nearing twenty miles per second and maintained full commlink with the raptor satellite array shield. Once the array satellites were in full link alignment he would ionize its field and turn on the planetary defense shield. This was just as I had trained them. The first victims would be those bastard Vampire freaks.

Javelin Nine: "All units, array shields up! Over."

Javelin One: "Roger understand, shields are up."

One by one the Darlock Vampire cruisers began to crash straight into the shield array protecting Q-7. Instantly ionized, de-atomized, then eruption detonated, their ships which made contact were gone forever in an instant. Other ships diverted and attempted to make their escape. Zillerians forces then were next. The Zillerians were obviously new to this as their fleet discipline was horrendous. Nearly their entire fleet flew right into the array shield and were reduced to scattered neutrinos in nanoseconds. There was nothing but spark remnants left of them.

The Guild cruisers also were obviously unsuccessful during the first wave as a Q-7 defense satellite array was able to create an ionized neutrino radiation shield that, as noted, completely destroyed the Vampire ships as well and crashed their older computer control systems. The remaining ships hopelessly raced for deep space. Most were picked off one at a time by the pursuing Q-7 defense force led by Mulcahee. The Darlocks were already Undead so it hardly mattered.

Javelin One: "Okay team, let's clean up the rest."

Javelin Nine: "Copy that."

Both initial squadrons chased off the remaining Darlock ships. The ones still in range were wiped from space. The battles raged above this world in spectacular fashion.

Javelin One: "I'm lining up this bastard Vampire Cruiser. Cover my flanks!"

Javelins Four, Twelve, Thirteen, and Nine raced along, with their commander spraying cover fire.

Javelin One: "Nuking this bitch."

Mulcahee made a direct hit with a nuclear tipped stinger bomb that took out about eleven Vampire Guild cruisers.

The Podrans put up a heck of a scrap. At this point they went on full offensive and went after the Garthonians, with some success I might add. The Javelin squadron's nukes lit up space. However while the Q-7 Defense force was preoccupied with the Garthonians a second large fleet from Drandor came out of quantum leap and began a bombardment of the planet.

The Drandorians had to confront a different issue however. Podranians had, with my help, developed a force shield so strong that it was quite effective against nuclear concussion bursts from space. It would be necessary for a land invasion, but this was not a big worry for them. Drandorian assault Marines are the best there are. The Marines were sent to the surface in smaller neutrino shielded landers which unfortunately could get through the array. Each Drandorian Assault Marine had a skull-mounted video cam which could relay live stream to the café. It would all be live on Channel Nine once the Interstellar Café arrived. The Javelin Squadrons would fly low to the planet and attempt to rake the landing Drandorian Marines. They were successful to an extent when they could engage, but there just were too many landing Marines all over their world.

The Interstellar Café came out of hyperspace at right that moment. Though it had been outlawed to use it at as an observatory for such events, the council voted "what the hell?" It was sent in. The elite of all known worlds began to arrive to watch the Second Podran War. (Later to be known as the First Space Virus War.)

Super elite beings were sitting in their booths sipping Broth and other mixed drinks, watching it all unfold on Channel Nine. The skull-mounted cams on Drandorian Marines were beaming the most intense images of the surface battle. Though Podranians fight hard and are brave they were no match for such a professional, experienced, and disciplined fighting force. Sadly, things were very much back to normal.

I took on human form and decided to do some gambling at the cafe. If we were doing this, *let's do it right*, I thought. The Drakonian Shark Master Tony was running the gambling tables and just generally trying to keep the Broth and beer flowing for the clientele. I put a small bet on Q-7 defending forces their home world but my heart was not in it.

"This is like old times," Tony said

"Yep," I answered.

Tony had wanted to kill me back during the First Q-7 war. He thought I had set him up for a big loss. But heck, I made it harder on my guys by giving up their attack plans to the enemy if you remember. He forgave me after I gave him the heads up that I was about to curve space and time and that they should cruise the café on out of there.

Commander Jok came over to say hello to me.

"This is just like old times," Jok said to me

"Yep," was all I could muster.

With all these new developments, plans, and general revelations, I decided to dispatch Rulella and Coranthas to go get Phobus and Thog. I laughed again for a moment thinking what might be up with those two. They had been there long enough.

- Drandor Moon Cube cell, present time

Thog and Phobus were right in the middle of heated best of seven series of "twenty thousand questions" when suddenly, two pure blue light ionic beams radiated from somewhere above.

"Dude look up!" exclaimed Thog

"Oh shit! Here we go!" Phobus cried out.

Suddenly almost seemingly as soon as it began, it was over. Thog was sitting his face in his palms. On his hands and knees he began groping the ground for his loose lobe tubing. Phobus took a knee and was retching. But the situation was calm at first. Neither of them had ever been this happy to be in Coranthas's chamber.

"Hey guys," said Coranthas.

"Where the hell have you been?" cried an exasperated Phobus.

"I was on Podrania, not sure why," Coranthas finished.

"Froth Lord's wife picked me up," he finished.

"What the hell is Podrania?" asked Phobus, wiping vomit off his face.

"It's Q-7," Coranthas answered. "It's getting lit up," he finished.

"Again? Seriously?" asked Phobus.

"Yep," replied Coranthas.

Suddenly remembering his rage Thog strapped on his Lobe tubing, and began to shoot blue lightning from his eyes at Coranthas. Immediately Coranthas fired up a shield of ions and fire, blocking Thog's frontal assault. Phobus having regained his composure tried to come to Coranthas's defense with his lightning cane. Phobus made a run on Thog, but Thog parried him with a temporary ion flood. Coranthas tried to strike Thog with lightning from his eyes, but that was not one of his strong suites.

"Cut the shit!" yelled Phobus, when Thog got him briefly with a severed Zak stinger he saved from Sholl Gar. (Zak stingers can be ripped out their back side and be used as a venomous weapon. Phobus had natural immunity from all the years on that world, but it stung like a bastard.)

Blasts of ions and photons shot in every direction. Coranthas drones and servants exploded helplessly, being hit from every direction. Each warrior tried to shift each other's time. Each attempted to curve space during their scrap to get the others off balance. The Witch Doctor locked herself in the bathroom.

These guys may not be on my level, but they got some skills.

"ENOUGH OF THIS!"

A shout seemingly from the far corner of the universe. Funnily it was not me this time. It was my ex-wife.

"What are you clowns doing?" Rulella frustratingly asked them.

I had sent Rulella and Coranthas to get Thog and Phobus and to bring them all together back to me. After all that had been revealed and all that was transpiring, I had decided to flip the script, make up with Rulella, and organize the group. We needed to try to head off the Counsel of Drakar on this Space Virus thing. We needed to find a way to help the Podranians again. What a mess this was going to be.

"Thog started it!" wailed Phobus while grimacing and groping at his stinger wound.

"What the heck was that bro?" he finished.

"Knock this off!" Rulella said. "We are getting out of here."

Chapter Seven

Q-7 Wasteland

I, Froth Lord, had felt this pain before. But this was worse. The was much worse by a significant order of magnitude. The Space Virus had killed every single Podranian who remained on Q-7. Though they had waged a truly courageous battle, the multitudes of attack assault fleets combined with the deadly Space Virus, was more than that world could endure. The virus killed more remaining Podranians than the Assault Marines had. They were not yet extinct as a species since many Podranians had headed out as refugees to deep space. Some headed to old Earth since the Podranian home world was now a planet wasteland. Old Earth was a recovered healthy nature reserve and could be colonized by the survivors.

The past joys that we had experienced by partiers on the interstellar café no longer resonated. This virus, this awful, lethal, space virus was now "world hopping" across the Zynon galaxy. The Council of Drakar was hapless in its response. Many of the council alerted all worlds to be on the highest safety measures against the spread. Other worlds rebelled. Some worlds opted for individual rights, as per the counsel of the "Constitution of Worlds," Epoch One. Many Council-Creatures took bribes from the various Sub-Lords of the various worlds. It was pretty much status quo with that corrupt crew.

Some worlds did not believe in the Space Virus. Some worlds thought the council made it up to expand their mining rights. Many thought their gods would save them. In some ways they weren't wrong. (At least in theory.) For the many worlds which worshipped a foreign Sentient, their false god may in fact be on the very council struggling to deal with this plague. Fumbling to deal with it was a more appropriate description. Honestly most of the Council-Creatures were looking into what could be in it for them. Kickbacks were available like candy at that time.

And yet there were other worlds which simply did not care. Their existences were so horrible that they would hear about the Space Virus and be like, "Go ahead, take your best swing." These were the kinds of worlds were the inhabitants often prayed for a merciful direct comet strike. Not even religious type worlds, hoping for a merciful Armageddon. They at least wouldn't have to "go to work" anymore they would say. Life on some worlds was such a drudgery.

The Council of Worlds, Drakar.
Sholl Gar report, 12,400 years after the unnatural birth of Thog

Sholl Gar was a total mess. Not just because of the Space Virus. Also not just because of the first war. It was not just because of the reign of the Large Master, the Young One, Dominick, or the endless Dune Wars. It was more than just the Zak nests, the sulfur skies, and more than just the acid rain polluting the already scarce drinking water. There was so much more.

And even though the near endless Dune Wars had wreaked utter havoc upon this poor world, those nightmares were also not the major reason things were in such horrible condition. In fact the Dune Wars were the least of their problems. Civil unrest, famine, loss of cultural identity, and even just eons of dealing with the sandworms really had brought everyone down as well. It was just not a world you wanted to be on. And things were about to get ugly as the council was not in a good mood. I got my usual front row balcony seats.

Council Chairman, Planet Nine, Sholl Gar system

The Council was more corrupt and viler than ever. What an assortment of Council-Creatures and "Judges" this was. Planet Nine was a world in the Sholl-Garian system. Representatives from Planet Nine often represented the entire system due to bribes and other nefarious dealings. Even the name "Planet Nine" made no sense, as it was closer to the suns than Sholl Gar. Dorian, the current representative to the local system council from Planet Nine began the proceedings. Dorian was a very strange sub-man who always spoke in a rushed, hurried pace.

"Who is the Guardian of the Sholl Gar system at this time?" demanded Dorian of Planet Nine in rapid speech, looking over the top of his pointy nose, spectacle glasses sliding drooped down the bridge to the point of the tip.

"Dominick is dead sir!" answered a drone bizarrely programmed with a brutally intense old Earth British accent.

"And who was Dominick?" asked Dorian, the Chair-Creature.

"He was the ruler of our world and system Sholl Gar," responded the absurd the British drone.

"Ruler of my planet?" asked the Chair-Creature, somewhat embarrassingly.

"Yessir," answered another nearby sub-man.

"How was he killed?" the Chair-Creature asked.

"He died in the Q-Seven War," replied the sub-man.

"What war now?" Dorian asked.

It was truly pathetic he asked that question. An astonishingly sad state of affairs in the galaxy, or at least this system.

"Well sir," he began with a sarcastic tone, "we kind of had a major war not long ago? We lost our entire armed forces, if you remember? Under Dominick?" the sub-man added with an eye roll.

"DEATH!" the counselor screamed.

The sub-man in question was terminated immediately on site. But his point was well made. It was now clear that Sholl Gar had been woefully unprepared for that war and for the war that was now facing Sholl Gar. And they also had no shot against the Space Virus. That thing was going to roast them. And to make matters worse Dorian was a complete jackass.

"Who is our god?" asked Dorian.

"Our god?" asked the backup sub-servant who had been rushed in after Pleebict the first sub-servant had just been terminated.

"Yes. Do we have a god?" Asked the Council-Creature.

"Not too sure to be honest. I'm just being frank about it. According to Pleebict the legends say Phobus Uthrates, or maybe Thog, but I hear Phobus is a bit of a trickster my lord. He faked us all many times, over tens of thousands of years. He lives on some other fancy world now," finished the back-up sub-creature.

"Who is Pleebict?" asked an increasingly confused Dorian.

Terrified, the backup sub-specimen was not sure what to say but continued anyway, fully expecting elimination.

"Well sir, Pleebict was the clerk that you just had disintegrated." He finished speaking with some degree of terror.

"DEATH!" screamed Dorian.

This went on and on ad nauseum. These events with the various committees and councils are just godawful tedious.

"Our ancient holy books say Phobus was coming back to restore all things?" interjected a third, new stand-in sub-creature.

"Well it's clear that didn't happen," finished Dorian.

"So what 'fancy' world do you believe he is on at this time?" asked the Council-Creature.

"There is a legend," the sub-person responded.

"What is this legend?" the Council-Creature asked impatiently.

"Well it is written that he submits to and is the son of Froth Lord, and his servant Thog was sacrificed for our sins," finished the sub-slave.

I got a kick out of that.

"BLASHPEHMY!" was all the Council-Creature exclaimed.

"Well that's what it says!" exclaimed the poor man right before he was slayed as well.

Chapter Eight

My Bad or "Everything You Wanted to Know About the Space Virus but Were Afraid to Ask the Council"

Beings that exist like me have an easy escape. That is partly why I never understood or agreed with the concept of segregating dimensions. Ancient arguments over segregation of sentients had become an obvious horror which was now entirely banned on most worlds. But no serious thinkers in the Zynon galaxy had given much contemplation on the matter of segregation by dimension, or plane of existence. Should an obviously higher being such as myself or even, shudder, Dendrake be segregated by law or statute? Should we be separated by our status? I mean segregating out the vampires might be a good call that should be taken up, but aside from that I would more than likely oppose.

The answer and the reality is that the question is pointless, and without real meaning. There is nothing that can be done to separate us Superbeings apart from our compliance to the separation. The Others choose to be separated. Literally no one except possibly Dendrake could force them into segregation by dimension. (Though I would love a shot to try myself.) "Personhood" as it was recognized commonly remained unaffected. It was irrelevant which dimension or plane of existence a Sentient resides within. A Sentient, physical, energy vapor, or wraith, regardless of dimension retains their personhood status forever. This much is clear.

This creates several interesting issues on the matter as it related to our case. Take Rulella or even me for example. Rulella my ex exists on a plane parallel to the Zynon galaxy. So do I at many times. She did not ask to be transformed to pure energy. That's on me. But that does not change anything. We could debate those things all day and still be facing the same challenges. So, from where therefore do we derive our rights as Sentient Beings? Our personhood is inherent and perpetual as Sentients. At least this much was clear in my thinking. Many Space Tyrants over the eons would attempt to reduce the rights of Sentients, and often they have been successful. (Especially if you consider the bombardments of primitive planets to be a violation of one's rights.) But "personhood" has never been violated as a thing or status for thousands of years. That did not mean much for the humans or for Podranians unfortunately.

Once Rulella and I got back sort of on the same page I spent a brief period making it up to her. Now we see eye to eye. We even understand the possibility of what our combined abilities could produce. We now will work together for only the greater good. But none of this dribble mattered to the poor Podranians, humans, or even to the tiniest ant. Ironically my earliest interest in the Podranians was entirely a completely altruistic venture. I wanted to not only save them but uncover and identify their true god. I thought bringing them into contact with Dendrake would be an amazing advancement for them as a sentient species. Imagine meeting your maker for real as I now had. Consider the emotional and philosophical breakthroughs this could mean for a people. I pondered these things at length. I pondered these things at length.

Boy was I wrong. Dendrake wants to wipe them all out? He literally wants this virus to cause across the Zynon galaxy, a nuclear chain reaction on the genetic level. He wants the reaction camouflaged by false biological markers, to appear as a natural event or evolutionary virus. He wants quantum entanglement to serve as the engine of this Space Virus while it goes about destroying ultimately all biological life.

He sucks, I thought.

So, we got this Space Virus now. It is running rampant across all known worlds, imploding cortexes. It invades the biological processes of all known life forms. It does this because it uses the same genetic components of the original Broth life process. Using the same "entanglement" laws of quantum reality. It cannot be bound by location. The Broth Virus or Space Virus, once loose, seemed entirely unstoppable. All elements of the Broth were created already entangled on the quantum level, forever. The Space Virus's only course was to infect all life on all worlds via the Broth's quantum entanglement. This was now an unstoppable process it would appear.

Beyond that there was another problem. It is not that important considering the bigger picture. However it appears the council Chair-Creature of Sholl Gar system Planet Nine "might" be able to subpoena me for my God-work I did on Sholl Gar. At a minimum that prick might be able to pull Phobus, or even Thog, into their Space Virus probe. Their investigation was going to be such an epic cluster that I could not and would not bear it! *Enough of this!* I thought. That would suck stupendously.

How fucking long ago was that? I thought.

The Council of Drakar was, quite frankly, a clueless and hapless bureaucracy and always had been. As noted the Council members were appointed for life from their home worlds, life which, for some of these species could last ten thousand years naturally. It was pure miracle I had ever convinced them to implement Article 19. And even the Article's implementation was not seen as an act altruistic mercy. It was more viewed as an act of protection of the Deity in question's property.

The Council was always essentially operating in a manner mainly to protect the interests of the most elite members of the galactic community. The Council's main role was to keep many of the civilizations distracted by arranging false flag wars amongst them. This was done so worlds loyal to the Council could mine the warring races' moons and home planets. It was all very corrupt. Planetary invasions often occurred simply as distractions to cover up certain Council-Creature corruptions. They would prove utterly hopeless at containing this Space Virus I feared. I don't even think it was their intension to try. Most were positioning themselves for bribes and kickbacks before escaping to their outer most world getaways. Yes they would appoint committees who would hold endless meetings while the Sentients of the various worlds would suffer their fates. The Council of Drakar provided no justice to any species. It served the elite and their own pockets.

Dorian of Planet Nine Sholl Gar system had always dreamed of being appointed to the Council for life. No Sholl Garian had ever been selected and approved, ever, to the Council of Drakar. I began to wonder if Dorian was trying to angle himself an opportunity. In his truest essence, Dorian was essentially a Sholl-Garian sub-creature.

Dorian on the Council, I thought to myself. *What a joke.* But then I thought about it a little more and I realized he might be a perfect fit for that outfit.

So anyway this council, this absurd bureaucratic galactic body, was going to oversee an interstellar Space Virus investigation. An investigation into an utterly deadly space plague of which they had entirely no understanding whatsoever. As already noted the hearings were ungodly and unbearable as always. The tedious infighting over the Space Virus seemed at times to likely never end. The bitter debate over who was at fault. Entire worlds engaged in bitter finger pointing all the while praying for a quick end.

The situation was seemingly hopeless. This Space Virus will likely infect all life through the Broth. *Dendrake ordained it as such* I was thinking. Now the Council of Drakar is pulling in a special prosecutor due to Dorian's inquiries. The council went through the motions and ordered some bureaucratic medical chief to look at the virus further.

- Medical tent, some random planet

A lab was established for the careful testing of the Space Virus on a random world. Some beings frowned upon trying to do tests on the Broth Virus. What if the tests made it worse? What if a new variant escapes? What if it implodes the scientists' brain stems before any data is collected? "We will select an unsuspecting more primitive species' planet and run the lab from there," it was decided.

Now I had said a "careful" test. This was pure folly. There was quite literally nothing careful about it. Dr. Pwaynoh had been the chief research scientist of the Council of Drakar for nearly one hundred years. No one questioned him on any of these matters. Dr. Pwaynoh was from some wretched world. It hardly matters for our discussions. Whatever he said the Council ordered done. He was a complete tool.

"Doctor you said to put the virus in their water supply correct?" asked a slow-speaking medical assistant.

"Yes," answered the Doctor.

"But this will kill all life on this world Doctor," the assistant stated.

Dr. "P," as he become known commonly during the plague, simply wanted to see how fast a planet would be wiped out. He figured studying it as it wiped out worlds was the best option, and this world was already scheduled for destruction by the Garthonians. He also really just wanted to maintain his newly gained "rock star" status he held with the terrified populaces.

"Just release the plague. I don't have all day," he finished.

- Sometime later, I was dreaming again.

As I have stated I never dream, not like this. Now that I had organized our team, the old gang, I had been feeling better about our chances to possibly stop Dendrake. Of course we would not be able to stop him entirely I reasoned. Nor would we save most worlds. But I figured we could do some good.

As I have mentioned previously I no longer sleep. So dreams themselves are pure anomalies. They creep and invade into normal consciousness for those who have transcended sleep. Once again without real context I was present in Coranthas's chamber. Though all this should have terrified most I always was fascinated with this process. I always was eager to learn all things. For many thousands of years I have been invading the dreams of Coranthas and many others.

So the methodology of how Dendrake was invading my consciousness in a dream state was of the utmost interest to me. I wondered, if reverse engineered, could I do the same to him? I had a strange thought just right then in the midst of the dream. It is strange that I really have never pondered this thought before. But in my mind I began asking myself, *What is Dendrake?* Seriously, what even is he? And all this while I was dreaming. At that moment, in a dream, I wondered where Dendrake himself came from. I had never wondered anything like this before about him.

But nonetheless, this was my concern at that moment within the dream canvas. *Is he a god?* I briefly pondered. What even would make one a god? Am I a god? Many say I am. What even is a god? It was very strange to suddenly ponder one's own status with respect to Deity. For many I am a god in their minds. For many others I am certainly god-like. It was within this context that I began to wonder to myself about Dendrake's origins. My ancient ancestors considered him to be their Deity. My reasons for never believing such a thing was the very fact that I certainly I am not one. I have developed great skills over time yes, but no, not a Deity.

Anyway, though there was no context to speak of in this iteration of the dream, it was still the same dream construct. It was still the same canvas. The three others, faces now clear, Coranthas, and the powerful entity whom I now knew was Dendrake. I still at this point had not figured out if Coranthas was present in my dreams as I had been in his. But I had strong suspicion that he was here.

Also this was my simulated dream, an invasion into my mind, yes, but my dream not Coranthas's. Dendrake had explained the purpose of the construct of Coranthas's dreams and its role in my elevation and ascendence. But what was the purpose of my dreaming? It is not quite the same construct, or was it? Does it still serve in the same way as his vessel? Am I now his vessel? Again, I never felt trepidation only intrigue. Constantly I viewed this all as a mystery I was meant to unravel. I was meant to fully understand it. But I could not explain my reasons for thinking these things.

Then in the dream there was a knock on the portal. Coranthas gets up opens the door. It was Phobus! Phobus had never appeared in any of these visions before. And beyond just that I was immediately certain, through some deeper perception, that it was literally Phobus in a conscious state, being pulled into my dream. Phobus was here with me now. I was not certain Coranthas was present in this construct literally. But Phobus was literally present in my dream. Again I found myself fascinated and in fear of nothing. And I was also fascinated at why I could discern so much instantly. Certainly this was from Dendrake as well but why? At that moment I began to sense it. Power was growing in me exponentially. I began to foresee all to such an extent I never dreamed imaginable. In an instant my understanding of all things began to expand exponentially. Not only was my awareness and recognition of new near limitless information increasing at an astonishing rate, but so was my ability to recognize the implications of all that was occurring. Dendrake was altering me. To the highest degree possible, he was elevating me. Am I a god? Is he making me a god? I was in what could best be described as a trance when I heard Coranthas speak in my dream.

"Um Coranthas, what happened?" asked Phobus

"None too sure honestly," answered Coranthas.

"Okaaaay." Phobus continued with an eye roll. His eyes locked on mine.

"Froth?!" he exclaimed.

Phobus could see me! He knew I was here. Coranthas never did, neither in his nor my dreams. This was fascinating.

"What are you talking about Phobus?" asked Coranthas, clearly unaware of my presence in the construct.

"Wait, you don't see Froth Man?" asked Phobus to Coranthas with a casual point in my direction.

"That's a good one Phobus," answered Coranthas

"Oh kay, well do you have any guac"? asked Phobus

Coranthas left the chamber in search of chips and guacamole.

"He seems well," Phobus added sarcastically.

"Phobus there is literally no way for me to explain to you what is happening here, right now, at this moment. But let's not scatter Coranthas further right now with this confusion," I spoke to Phobus.

"How did I get here?" queried Phobus.

"The last thing I remember I was reorganizing my emergency escape plan while reprogramming a Thog clone, and then all of the sudden I am at Coranthas's door here on Delta Five," he said.

"Who are those dudes?" he continued, casually pointing a hitchhiker's thumb towards the Others while making a "what the heck" face.

The Others just looked at me with full eye contact throughout the dream construct. They didn't faze me. Dendrake still remained silent and hidden in this dream. But his power was immense though unseen. He was transforming me at an ever-increasing rate to a higher realm.

"Don't worry about them," I answered. "I've got this."

"Roger that Froth Man," Phobus replied

"So what's the plan?" Phobus asked.

"I said don't worry about it," I finished.

It was at this moment that Dendrake intervened in this iteration of the construct. He did not speak this time. It was simply thoughts impressed into my subconscious state. He was going to raise my essence to a new level. He began to elevate me to a higher plane of existence. Something astounding was occurring to me right at that moment. In the rush of instant absolutely everything was about to change forever.

At that moment there was an explosion of pure knowledge growing exponentially with my own construct, my own canvas. I began to foresee all things to such an extent I never dreamed imaginable. It is impossible for me to explain but I was suddenly filled with the most powerful foreknowledge of events and of Dendrake himself. I was suddenly entirely aware of things that had not yet occurred. But it was even more than just events. And my mind was being filled to overflowing with thoughts from Dendrake. Knowledge was being planted into my mind and unspeakable works of awe, abilities that were now mine, and I was becoming fully aware of them. And he was making me fully aware of his endless suffering.

"Phobus," I began.

"Yes?" Phobus sheepishly answered.

"Meet me at my Dome," I exclaimed.

"Um Froth man, um, I've not even been at your Dome, dude," he said.

Immediately I conjured up the most powerful spell I ever commanded instantly interrupting Dendrake's invasion into my consciousness. I was not sure where this sheer power was coming from, but I immediately transported myself, Phobus, Rulella, Thog, Coranthas, and, somehow accidentally even "Poor Brandon" from god knows where to my Dome on Nectar.

At first it was entirely unclear to me how this occurred. Then almost instantly I became fully aware of nearly all things. An evolutionary explosion occurred within my intellect, instantaneously and exponentially increasing my mental computational cycles. And then the same runaway process continued, recurring endlessly. Inexplicably I understood all the vast and major aspects of quantum reality, which up until this very moment had remained mostly mystery to me. Dendrake was behind what had just occurred. In one moment I could suddenly see back further in time than I had ever seen before. I saw so far into nearly limitless possible futures observing what appeared to potentially be the end of all things. The end of not just life in the Zynon galaxy but possibly the end of the Cosmos itself. And though it was a clear vision of near infinite futures, it was instantly and demonstrably clear to me that it also was all avoidable. They were all real futures but not all fatalistic outcomes set in stone.

An unparalleled emergence of pure intellect, unparalleled within my long personal story and experience, catapulted me to a state of near limitless bliss as I reviewed what was now available to me. For a moment it seemed that an understanding of the origins of not just Dendrake but all that exists could become known to me. None of my group understood what had just occurred to them. Neither Rulella nor Phobus had any understanding of these happenings. Thog nor Coranthas could function at a high enough level to think clearly about much of anything anymore. Nor would they need to. As for Poor Brandon I simply felt pity. Before my transformation I would have thought, *What the heck happened that Poor Brandon was pulled into this?* But in my now higher plain I saw the reason why even this poor soul was now in my Dome. And I saw pure darkness and evil.

Dendrake wanted to be killed. He has spent hundreds of thousands of years working towards these ends. The Space Virus inherently linked to the Broth as it was, entirely entangled, was his attempted catalyst to bring about his final merciful end. It was bait. It was his attempt to bring about sleep for his exponentially powerful mind, which had never stopped growing in its knowledge, at exponentially greater speed through all known time. His desire for rest, sleep, and death had reached the culminating point where he now had "pressed the button" for my final ascendancy and transcendence, in order so it would be possible even if remotely for me to terminate him. Dendrake was tortured eternally by his own mind. Seemingly perfect knowledge was his and it had tortured him mercilessly. I say seemingly perfect because what mattered most to him he did not know, nor could know ever. Who can tell one like Dendrake the things he does not know? Who could give him the answers for the things that pain him to the core of his existence? Was Dendrake the Supreme Being? This was unanswerable. But Dendrake knew that he was not omniscient. He is not *all-knowing*. He does not know who or what he is and it torments him across the eons. He may have always existed, and yet he does not know! It was more than he could bear. What can end this existence?!?

- The "Button"

Dendrake had created the "button" through hundreds of thousands of years of preparation. Preparation of the one to come. He used the Broth, the Construct, all life, and all his power to bring about a being with at least the potential to slay him. The entire purpose the Broth and all life was to somehow raise someone, some *thing,* that could kill him. He could not kill himself! Dendrake was patient knowing the ascendance of me was critical, and had now finally in his mind set the final plan in motion by pressing the "button."

There was now one very big problem for Dendrake's plan however. There was a stumbling block yet. Even before my final ascendence I never would have thought it right, proper, or desirable to bring about the death of one like Dendrake. And now in my new freshly higher state, it was entirely clear to me that killing him was not on my agenda. The great irony in his elevation of me was that in my higher plane of existence I simply would refuse to kill him. Killing one like Dendrake? How could one even ponder such a thing I would think. Dendrake is likely the most important fact of the entire universe unless one figures out how he got here.

I needed a plan. And instantly the entire plan in all its fullness became clear. And it also was entirely clear that Dendrake, wherever he is right now, knows all that I am thinking and planning. So, my plan was going to need to be something special. It was going to have to fool the unfoolable. I would not kill Dendrake, but this plan needed to be perfect, a masterpiece.

But Dendrake, knowing all my thoughts and all my plans, then planted his thoughts and plans into my mind. It was in this moment, this moment of both vulnerability and immense power, that I contrived "The Lie." One of the powers being granted to me, literally bestowed to me by Dendrake, may allow me to plant false projections into Dendrake's mind. But first I would read his mind. At that moment I did not know if I was invading his mind, or he was inviting me in. Not knowing whether he was allowing me to do so I partook in Dendrake's own self-conversation within his canvas, the construct of his mind. He showed me how to enter!

- Fatalistic Causality Loop

Dendrake, in his near omniscience foresees my yet planned series of quantum anomalies, the most powerful vortex ever created, before I even dreamt them up. In fact viewing his mind, experiencing his thoughts, was how I learned what I was going to plan. You see he foresees it in his mind. And in his construct I am granted access to all that he foresees. I could literally see what I was going to create right inside Dendrake's foreknowledge. There was almost a loop of fatalistic causality to it. I see what I will do in the future inside his mind, then I plan it. He is showing me my future so that I can attain it. Not only is he showing me what I will do, but he is also importing how I will do it as well. He believes that the combined power of the vortex I will initiate, the quantum singularities that he foresees me creating, with his own powers fueling them, that he may finally be able to terminate his own life. He sees the combination of my planned anomalies, of which I now am aware by viewing his foresight, and his mighty powers. He also knows the trap he foresees me setting. His plan will be to override my planned tricks, and finally, mercifully, end his existence.

But he also knows, and again he is allowing me to see this, that he could fail. It is what he has always known. He has tried before but he alone cannot do it. He showed me now in his mind how he foresaw my greatness, and how he made his plans. Dendrake created the Broth and hence all life primarily to bring about my own existence from among all Sentients. Quite literally, in his mind, he was showing me that I am the very reason that anyone exists in the galaxy. He told me in his mind that I was a real god. Am I?

He also knows entirely everything I was thinking. He knows the "lie" I had just contemplated and was planning to attempt. He may risk it he was thinking, and I was reading his thoughts as well. He may risk my plan succeeding just for the off chance and hope that it ultimately fails. His plan is self-termination with the combination of our vast and immense powers, and he does not care who he brings with him into non-existence. So Dendrake plans to empower me and allow me to spin up the most frighteningly powerful anomalies and singularities the Cosmos has ever seen to bring about his end. My ascendance was near completion. I had my plan. I had my lie. He was aware. It was now a duel.

In my plan if executed properly, I would catch, ensnare, and confine the most powerful known being in existence inside a state of disposition where he is momentarily not only happy but, in a state where he is beyond content lasting for all eternity. If I can bring him to such a psychological state of joy, and then trap him there for eternity not only would I not have to kill him, but I would save him from the torment he so much wants to escape. And I figured out how exactly that would be instantly. Dendrake hit the "button," transcended me at the exact right moment, with the purpose of giving me the ability to kill him. Almost a physician-assisted suicide if you will. But he has created a way for me to save him also, and he realized it not. I will explain my plan later. But first I would go stop the Space Virus. It was going to be quite simple for me now.

"Rulella."

I spoke for the first time since the group had made the quantum jump.

"Yessir," she replied.

"Keep everyone safe. I will be back," I said to her.

"Quantum entanglement is a physical phenomenon seen in the itty-bitty most part of the quantum realm." – Earth science journal, twenty-first century, eons before the unnatural birth of Thog

Stopping the Space Virus was not even a chore for me now; it was an utter joke honestly, and my newly relative omniscience told me clearly that Dendrake knew it would be easy for me to stop. What about the millions of planets already wiped out I thought? What about Q-7? None of this mattered to Dendrake. This was not to say that he was purely evil in his acts, but he was entirely indifferent. His only desire since even before he created the Broth, was to bring this day about. He thought he might had done it finally.

Stopping the virus simply required me to have control of the Broth in the same manner Dendrake always had and still has. As powerful as I now was Dendrake still, even right now, had to allow me to stop the virus. He had to allow me the control of the Broth. And though his entire plan was to create a Superbeing so powerful that Dendrake could be destroyed by him, even now, he still would have to allow it.

Anyway I now share a common state with the Broth itself. I am now part of the entanglement. And with the ascendance from Dendrake "pushing the button" and my new entangled state with the Broth on the quantum level I spoke the Space Virus into extinction. Inside my own mind I was able to visualize the physical properties of the Space Virus on the quantum level such as position, momentum, polarization, and location. I was able to simply speak an irreversible wave function collapse which in essence reversed the course of the Space Virus. I was able to do this because I was now one with the essence of the Broth just as he is. I could see the saved of futures of countless worlds all in one moment due to my acquired levels of foreknowledge. They were saved. Saved for now.

It had become simply within my power to speak the virus into history, nonexistence. And it was gone forever. Though I understood all fully, it still fascinated me to no end. I was given full credit for the extinction of the Space Virus. My first thought was how absurd it was to give me any credit. I simply told the Space Virus to go away? Dendrake granted me that power.

The Space Virus was no more.

The Council of Drakar ordered an immediate end to Dorian's special prosecutor's inquiries. Dorian was destroyed immediately at the meeting on site.

Chapter Nine

Coda

Coda: something that serves to round out, conclude, or summarize

I had thought my plan needed shielding from the one who can see all things. I had thought it was pure genius. Not only my ultimate plan but also how I shielded it from him; pure genius I had thought. Remember, the canvas of Coranthas's dreams, and even my dreams in my previous realm, was a training construct made by Dendrake. It was made for us to exist within without ever knowing what was occurring, and experience all things Dendrake wished. It was hard to know who was fooling who at this moment. Each new moment was more enthralling than the last.

And remember there was no real "time" in the canvas. There was no real "when." Being present in the canvas was being separate from time, sort of. It was the infinite beyond the infinite. And he trained my mind and prepared me. He prepared me for when once outside the canvas, at the exact right moment he would "push the final button." This he planned would not occur until all the pieces were in place. All the pieces in place that would ultimately cause me to choose to kill him. For all his foreknowledge he seemed to have not seen something. He reasoned and foresaw that I would believe that I needed to kill him to stop the Space Virus. At least that was my thinking.

But I was able to stop the virus once I became fully entangled with the quantum nature of the Broth. Did he somehow not foresee this as he foresees everything else? Or did he know and there was yet still another trick waiting for me?

Even in my new higher plain of existence I could not know, even now, for certain.

But for some reason my plan still felt entirely sound to me. I'm going to make him ludicrously happy, even for one moment in space time, then ensnare him forever within that moment. Here is how I was going to do it.

It starts with the canvas. It starts with the canvas of Denrake's own mind. In an instant after eons of training me within my own mind and the minds of countless many others Dendrake coded me with the knowledge of how to enter his mind. He did this because he foresaw this could be how I killed him. Using my now nearly limitless intellect I was able to think thoughts of killing him, while stealthily not planning to do so, and in fact forming my plan to trap him. There was no way for me to know for sure this would work however.

It would be precisely because he "knew" that I was about to kill him, that he would momentarily become delirious with joy. In that state of foreknowledge that he finally, mercifully, after near infinite waiting, was about to exist no more, would experience a contentment beyond a contentment any other life form could ever experience. Only the Superbeing Dendrake could ever possibly reach the state of bliss he will reach at that moment of his imminent death.

The other truly ironic component will be that my intrusion into his canvas construct, the invasion of his consciousness, the creation of a "dream state" within the greatest dreamless Superbeing, would be the very thing he trained me to do to him. I could only trap him within his *own* super mind. It will only work ironically, *because* he is the ultimate superbeing whose canvas is like no other. This was the ultimate coda for Dendrake.

Now was the time.

- The mind of Dendrake

Dendrake did not sleep. Like me he never slept and was dreamless. He never had slept to the best of his knowledge, as much he would have liked to sleep. He could create near endless "canvasses" of reality. "Multi-verse" small boxes of illusion, false points in time, fully separate from time. He could put himself in these canvasses for his own purposes. He foresaw me making my plans. He read my now transcended intellect and mind. Dendrake had planted this idea and given the knowledge for me to enter the canvas of his own consciousness. He foresaw through my thoughts, my planning to trap and "kill" him in his own mind, bringing his endless horror to a final ending. He also foresaw my planned trick. Dendrake would risk it for the potential reward.

At that moment I keyed an algorithm into the control panel of my wristwatch and beamed instructions to Thog. He was to never at any point lose track of Coranthas's coordinates once we are inside the Construct. I can handle myself.

- The Ingress

The time had come. Finally I entered his construct. Dendrake detected, sensed, and saw that I, Froth Lord, though I was pretending to believe that I was undetected had entered the fullness of Dendrake's conscious mind. Of course I knew that Dendrake detected me. That was all part of my ingenious plan. But it was also part of his plan as well.

I had managed to pull off the seemingly impossible, maybe. Before my ascension this would not have been possible at all. My now higher intellect was seemingly near limitless. It allowed me to project a mental state, my thoughts, readable, viewable by Dendrake, but in a camouflaged manner. Part of the reason this was possible and would be successful was that most of the plan to kill Dendrake looked precisely the same as the plan to ensnare him in the blissful state forever. Using my newly attained highest intellect I could shield and protect the final step of the actual plan from Dendrake's foreknowledge, possibly. My new higher intellect could project false foreknowledge into Dendrake's conscious mind, or so I hoped. Dendrake would foresee me, "omnisciently," but falsely, killing him. Dendrake would believe he is about to be killed and would hence reach a state of utter joy and contentment just prior to being ensnared forever in that state.

At first I appeared to move cautiously through Dendrake's canvass. The false dream state, for which Dendrake showed me how to catalyze in him, was very calm but eerie. I purposely built the canvass construct to show my inexperience, possibly lacking creativity, but it was done by me with intent. This was not hidden from Dendrake. Dendrake saw that what I was doing was on purpose. It was not relevant to him. I had quickly learned how to master shielding some parts of my thoughts from Dendrake by projecting, strongly, other thoughts amplified to Dendrake. (Or so I thought.) In some ways this was like a friendly duel. Not unlike the way Phobus and Coranthas would go at it with their pathetic powers in comparison, but similar in a sense due to their relative parity.

The three others looked over at me this time. I was here. I pulled Coranthas into the canvas, not because I needed him for myself, but in part to continue to fool the unfoolable. I need the canvas to be exact. I felt bad bringing him into this. Thog was to continuously monitor his location.

As Dendrake felt closer to his ultimate desire some of his intellect and guard were weakened. I scanned possible futures and saw the one I was attainting to achieve. I sensed Dendrake feeling an increasing anticipation. The kinds of antici-pation one has when expecting joy, but also simultaneously fearing disappointment. *I would not trap him until the joy was pure bliss* I thought. After all I had spent eons wondering, looking, and wanting to meet my maker. There was a sadness I felt that my maker wanted to end his existence so thoroughly. At one time I wondered if I could change his mind. But now that I had ascended I realized and sensed fully that nothing would have changed his mind and brought him joy enough for him to desire his continued existence. Yet here I was, about to ensnare him in a state of contentment only ever remotely possible for a being like Dendrake to experi-ence. I was giving him the greatest gift ever given. Yes, it was ultimately a devious trick. Yet it would be the greatest thing ever done for Dendrake. The intense irony that he would be so greatly angered by an entity trying to bring him limitless bliss was not lost on me.

As my plans were nearing the moment of execution something in the canvas changed. I felt no fear, just fascination. The room in a moment was no longer Coranthas's chamber, not that it ever was. No one was present in the room apart from me and an unseen Dendrake. The room was now transformed entirely. It evolved inside his mind canvas at first to a very familiar hallway. I instinctually began to walk towards this corridor and then breached the entrance. The gateway from Coranthas's chamber now opened into the upstairs foyer of my childhood home on Nectar. It was a very surreal experience even for me with my long history of such things. Knowing this was Dendrake's construct for me, and seeing my child-hood home hallway, made me pause in wonder for a moment. This was new to the dream construct. Never in Coranthas's dreams did I see my past. Then I heard them. I heard my parents' voices clearly. Fascinated, I moved down the hall-way toward what was clearly my old bedroom chamber. It was a very lovely house, which for me, was filled with amazing and fond memories. Both my parents had long since elevated themselves to another plane eons earlier. It was most Nectarians' preferred path of life and existence. Cases like me who opted for this existence have been extremely rare. In all honestly, I knew of no other Nectarians who have chosen the path I have. I knew of no others who choose to remain attached to this plane. I wanted so much more than to simply leave the realm of my youth. They called me unnatural, but for me, it was the exact opposite. I have explained that I like it here on this plane of existence. This plane is where we come from, where all sentience comes from. Unnatural long life was a result of my choice and power. But even so, a Nectarian could exist for millennia under normal circumstances. *I may have ascended, but I was at home in this plane,* I thought.

I heard their voices as I neared my childhood room. I heard all our voices. It was my mother and my father. The discussion was regarding my future. We were debating my ten-year-old life's path. They were discussing my plans. I was arguing with them. I wanted to play baseball. My father never was angry, but he was upset in the construct of this memory, which is precisely what this was. This was an actual memory from my mind.

But why this memory? I wondered. It was not an accident, and the brilliant side of me was determined to understand what Dendrake's point was with bringing this experience from my past to bear. I think he was showing me something. For whatever reason he was reminding me that I was in fact different. For example, why did I love Earth so much? In this example we were arguing about the human game of baseball of all things.

"He spends too much time on Earth already!" exclaimed my father in an unusually angry expressive tone for him. "Just because the boy can strike out every hitter he faces does not mean he should," he finished.

I could see myself, baseball glove on one hand, ball in another. I could not make out my face in the dream construct but it was obviously me. I could remember in the construct like it was only a moment ago. I remember arguing that I could strike out of every batter, and my father would so wildly argue how that was not a good thing but a bad thing.

"I also can hit a homerun every time," my ten-year-old self quipped sharply.

"That is exactly my point! You do realize you are not one of them. If you are not careful they may suspect you are not one of them," he would interject.

"They could not do anything to me," I quipped with an arrogance to my father that surprised me. It was a surprisingly emotional experience for me to watch this moment. I never think about them other than in respectful awe. I don't usually think in a nostalgic, melancholy-type manner. I have never found such emotions to be useful but I still had emotion. I wondered at that moment, while in Dendrake's canvas, if my parents still existed.

"You won the ribbon for your paper describing the reality of the existence of dark matter beyond it being a mere gravitational anomaly. You were nine! The council of mentors has declared you an official prodigy of galactic sciences. Enough of this baseball! Enough of this Earth stuff!" finished my dad. I had forgotten how much I loved him. It has been quite literally tens of thousands of years since I had seen him in a state as real as this.

"But he loves Earth stuff so," my mother chimed in. She had always nurtured my love for humanity. We had taken human form as a family and spent adventures on Earth many times over the years. Earth was a stunningly beautiful planet. My father would often say how good the humans had it and how they simply had no idea. And that their world was a paradise among worlds. You see families and peoples like ours were wise and not like the Garthonians. My father obeyed the ancient oracles of first contact to the letter of the law. No one on Earth was ever to suspect who we were really were. And we never told anyone about the existence of humans or Earth. As far as we knew we were the only ones in the galaxy aware of them.

That was the main reason he hated my playing baseball in the ten-year-old summer leagues. It was not that he did not want me to have fun or to enjoy discovering humanity. He did not want us or any advanced Sentients to endanger them. So many years ago Thog would ask me to tell him about Earth and I would tell him it was a tragic situation, if you recall from Coranthas's writings. I was holding back most of what I thought when I answered them. I was holding back most of what I felt inside. I had learned to be clinical, even analytic about Earth's fate. I even became cold and hard about the fates of other worlds as a result for a time. It was how I could manage the horror of what was done. To this day it is likely the most traumatic and most impactful historical fact of my long existence.

"That is beside the point," he retorted. "He needs to stop going down to Earth. I don't understand his obsessions with it," he went on.

Their voices started to fade somewhat as I walked further down the hallway. They muffled into the background as I walked a bit further in the construct of

Dendrake's sentience. I could still hear them in the background as though behind me, falling further and further back as I walked.

"He loves baseball!"

"I don't care. He will be the greatest quantum scientist in the galaxy!"

"He is a boy!"

"This love of Earth is unnatural and dangerous," was the last thing I heard my father say as their voices faded.

It was hard to discern, which was why I walked on. Though this diversion was certainly unexpected and interesting, it served no purpose and did not distract me from the real reason I was here. Nor did it distract me from the fact that I was inside the canvas of Dendrake's mind. Now there was another portal that in my childhood home led to a great external upper outdoor foyer type ramada. As I entered through the portal the entire canvas once again changed form entirely. I entered what was rather than the foyer expected, a giant sphere-shaped plane-tarium style vast space. A space with no form and in complete darkness at first.

It was transformed into a 360-degree enveloping "sphere-like" giant chamber, with no floor, no walls and no ceilings. At this very moment I remembered my anomalies external to the canvas and I began to activate and set all that was to come in motion. I began to unleash them just outside Dendrake's mind. Swirling black holes, quantum singularities, and the vortex of the elements began to rage outside the construct.

Inside this new realm that was my surrounding, the interior of the canvas, the depths of the mind of Dendrake began to light up with stars and brilliant distant galaxies. It was astonishingly beautiful. Time was now slowing within the canvas, due to my series of anomalies happening outside and surrounding this construct of simulated time. Only in this canvas could I make Dendrake subject to time ironically, since the canvas was outside of normal space time. And now I was slow-ing that abnormal space-time at an infinite rate, endlessly.

Slowly and with great subtlety, the stars in this firmament begin to dim. The brightness of these distant galaxies, beautiful nebulas, and super clusters began to fade. It was soon approaching total and absolute darkness. Approaching pure black even while my anomalies continued to spin up around the construct. I had pushed my own "button" and there was no stopping it. I even wondered if I could even stop them if I wanted to. The depths of his presence had never felt nearer. I was in his mind, or a construct, created by me and him within his mind. For the second time I would soon hear his voice. It was more like a projection of his thoughts to me, but audible. Then at that moment right before me, Dendrake took on human form. I joined him in the common state he chose.

Again for me, there was only fascination. For the second time I was meeting my maker. This time it was so personal. He could be anything he wanted, anything that had ever existed. He could make a new thing to be. He could have been a galaxy himself if had chosen. He looked so normal quite honestly. Unimposing and even gently he stood before me. He wore essentially a long dark but purple looking robe. He had greyish hair and stood roughly the same height as I in my human form.

We stared into each other's eyes at this moment. I was inside his mind, and he was joining me there inside this incarnation of himself, a purely simulated construct. What seemed like a long period of false time passed by before he spoke to me.

- The King's Pawn

"I have known you from the very beginning. In fact from before the beginning," he began.

"Known me?" I asked my maker.

"You have been known by me through my foreknowledge of all things," he said.

His disposition was very calm and even kind.

"I have known for all time, all time since before the Broth was formed and even far, far before that," he finished.

The anomalies were now raging outside his canvas. I had pressed my button, and as I said there now was no stopping it. Space and time were bending and curving violently around this construct while we interacted. Black holes, curved space, every trick I knew with my higher intellect was fully engaged. Creator and Creation alone together in the canvas and construct we both had built. He read my mind.

"I am not your Creator Froth Lord," he said with slightly more ominous tone.

"No?" I replied.

"I created the Life Process, then I foresaw you. It is different. I have many questions for you," he said.

Questions for me, I thought to myself. *Semantics,* I thought, he is my maker. The Broth was created by him. All life that exists in this galaxy comes from the Broth. I began to wonder if my plan was doomed to fail. I always knew there was that chance.

"What questions do you have for me?" I asked with sincere curiosity.

"Why did you love them?" he asked.

Love who? I thought to myself. This being is omniscient, so I must love someone, somewhere. Was it Phobus? Coranthas? Thog?

No way.

"Love who?" I asked

"You know who I am talking about," he replied.

"Honestly, I am not sure—"

Before I could finish the thought, "SILIENCE!!" he thundered.

Immediately his form changed in a whirlwind before me! Atoms and elements swirled within the sphere. The appearance of a vast sea of electrons flew around and between us both. The darkness exploded with light. The galaxies surrounding me lit back up as bright as a supernova then flew out of their places in the firmament of the construct. Thunderous claps echoed throughout the canvas of Dendrake's mind. As if they were physical the construct walls shook, rumbled, quaked, and collapsed outward. Still in total darkness within our canvas his appearance expanded to one of vast enormity. He became as tall as the sky, seemingly ready to burst forth from the construct. His eyes were bright red emeralds glowing with fire. His fist was like a wrecking ball or a rampaging moon all itself. He banged that fist to an invisible floor causing such a thunderous clap yet again.

Then as intensely quick as this had begun things darkened once again. The thunderous sounds became quiet. The silky blackness returned. And now once again standing before me was Dendrake, transformed back to his stately calm human form. Now I sensed the full range of my powers were at work, circling our reality ferociously almost as if a powerful wind outside your home. I had catalyzed a thermal runaway phenomenon where one process continues to catalyze other processes approaching infinity, finally resulting in an uncontrollable escalation, the ultimate anomaly of all anomalies. The singularities I had set in motion stirred and built upon themselves and their own power. *This was damn cool* I thought. It was a decent vortex. There was always the possibility that I might not make it out of here too.

I was still deep in a state of fascination with both Dendrake's transforming and the runaway conditions I had created, when I heard him speak yet again in a calm and stately manner.

"Your move, Froth Lord," Dendrake spoke.

He had both human-like arms extending in the "behold" position. Instinctively I looked down to where he was indicating that I should. There before us was a magnificent, beautiful chessboard with the most exquisite chess set. The pieces were astounding in their crafting. The kings wore wonderous robes of silky appearance, one in white, one in black. They seemed lifelike, though they were not. Sixty-four squares setup for battle. Thirty-two pieces in their start positions. He sat down across this invisible surface where the board was laid. I was white. It was my move.

Instinctively I did the king's pawn opening, the Napoleon attack. As absurd as it sounds I immediately moved the piece. Seeing the chessboard and myself being white, I kind of lost my bearing of all that was occurring in that moment. I moved that pawn forward without the slightest hesitation, as if I had no other concern in the Cosmos other than this chess match. All those matches with Coranthas he never could handle the Napoleon attack, though he defended properly from the outset at times. The Napoleon attack was named after an old, ancient human dictator from planet Earth. There was much literature both historical and fictional, regarding Napoleon which I had rescued along with Coranthas in Earth's final moments. I had already read all of it. Though he was not a great player I found the Napoleon opening to be my favorite. I could not remember the last time I had ever lost a chess match. I was now in a match of wits, a chess duel, with the maker of all known life.

Meanwhile legions of black holes working together swirled the elements of matter and time around the construct of Denrake's false dream. They created the most powerful vortex likely ever in existence until this very point. Time was nearly stopped in the canvas. I briefly had concern for Coranthas in that moment, remembering he was in this construct somewhere too. It was Dendrake's move.

It was Dendrake's move, yet his now gentle stare remained focused straight into my eyes.

"You did not answer me," he said.

"Why did I love humanity?" I asked.

"Yes, I want to know why," Dendrake declared.

I thought about what he was saying and realized immediately that it was true. I had loved them. Now pondering this question, it occurred to me that I did not have a good answer.

"I don't know," I said.

"I do," he said.

We began to carry out the most interesting philosophical, scientific, and surprisingly emotional conversation I had ever experienced. Likely the two most complex thinkers in all existence over all time, past, present, and future, began to raise to each other the very questions that address the most fundamental issues. We raised the very questions that vexed each other over the eons. Traditionally when I have approached philosophy I have never sought to arrive to settled positions. I had always felt such a lofty goal to be preposterous. Ultimate answers would never be reached. Ultimate conclusions were merely more speculations. Dendrake saw all that much differently. It was fascinating to me.

The study of philosophy has always been more than just a thirst for knowledge for me. Dendrake asked me questions that supersede simple matters related to the theories of understanding. We both "knew" a great many things. But Dendrake was more troubled by what he did not know.

"I love their early thinkers," I would say.

"Rubbish, all," he would reply.

I explained to him my love for both Aristotle and Plato. The ones credited with Earth's early Western thought. Their methods I believed to have contributed to the building up of the greatest human thought. And I explained to him that human thought had impressed me deeply, surprisingly though it were, to my core.

I explained to him that for a primitive species they practiced logic in a manner while even quite young as a civilization that often made me emotional.

The storm outside the construct was now echoing inside the canvas of Dendrake's mind. Again, I hoped Coranthas was okay.

I was staring at the board knowing all my next moves depending on each that he would make. Dendrake moved his king's pawn to "e5," blocking my pawn. This was a sound response, but it was the move I fully expected. It was the move Coranthas's would make by almost rote. It was a "safe" move.

I immediately moved my bishop from his home base "f6" to "c4." This was an obvious setup for which even Coranthas would begin the proper defense. Though the Napoleon attack was obvious to skilled players, even if defended properly, I knew how to execute the attack through and around such safeguards. I already somehow through a new power, knew his next move. And it was not the right one. It was not yet a proper defense.

As my anomalies roared around us he moved his knight from "b8" to "c6," blocking nothing. There were multiple other proper defenses he did not take. *He can't possibly suck at chess,* I thought.

Then our conversation got straight to the heart of the matter. Dendrake began to spill it all. It was an intense dance between him continuing to train me, granting me powers (like my new foresight), and him lamenting his very existence. He was deeply scarred. Though he had brought me this far, I was not the same as him. Which was the source of his greatest pain. He was alone with respect to what he was. And he did not know what he was. He told me how I had what he can never have. Knowledge, at least a comprehension to how I came to exist. I retorted to him by suggesting that I do not truly know anything in the same manner he does not. And the reason this would be true would be because he did not know where he came from; therefore all ultimate origins still elude me. I argued that he being my maker, and not knowing his own origin, was just as deep an existential crisis for one like me and the rest of all life. He did not agree.

"You know who and how you are!" he would thunder. Once again transforming his appearance in a frightening vulgar display of power. The elements around him swirled into a frenzy. Once again, he appeared as tall as the emulated sky above us.

"DO YOU SEE IT YET!" he bellowed.

I could sense what he sensed now. He was bestowing mighty powers onto me even further. Powers that would transcend me even more vastly. He was putting thoughts into my head. I began to see and understand more. I *was* going to kill him I now thought. He is making sure of it. I do not think he was ever tricked. And now he is making me do his bidding. I sensed his increasing joy. I tried right at that moment to see his future, but I was not quite able to make it out.

I moved my queen from "d1" to "f3." I already knew he would not block me. And now I figured out how he planned on thwarting my plan. He is about to make me hate him. But I had one trick left.

In music a coda is defined as a passage in a musical work that brings a piece, a song, an opera, or just a movement towards an end. It is often defined as an expanded cadence driving toward a purpose. This was now Dendrake's coda, separate from the long song, it was a section with an altered structure. Some of the greatest music of all time would have the most emotional codas leading to great fade out emotional endings wrapping up their greatness. I hid my emotion from him as I sensed his rising. Dendrake had seen my projected cause of his death. It would never have been believable before my sudden ascendance. Never possible before when Dendrake pushed his button.

Dendrake moved his bishop to "c5," which blocked nothing and left me with check mating him in my next move. And I fully planned to make it so. At this moment he unleashed his plans to its fullness. Dendrake filled me with a sudden canyon of hate for him, a hate for him so deep, so shocking, that it was hard for me to comprehend. In one long moment he showed me all the horrors of all the wars, all the murders and all the rapes. He showed me all the terrors, all the abuses. The worst things any being could ever see or do or imagine. He showed them to me at once. He showed me all the suffering of the past and what he would do in his future. He showed me all the corruption.

"I DID ALL OF IT!" he screamed in a thunderous evil wail.

Then he showed me the most awful thing of all. He showed me what he planned to do to all Sentient Life forms. He showed me how he had allowed me to stop the Space Virus. And how easy he could cause great suffering by his will. He showed me his plans for all life, including those who until now I had yet known how much I loved. The torture he would do to Thog and Phobus. The horror and torment he would cause Rulella, for whom I suddenly felt nostalgic protective compassion. And worst of all, the suffering he had planned for Coranthas. He drilled into me his plans for Coranthas to such a depth that I could not bear it. Coranthas would suffer in the endless trap I had set for Dendrake in the construct forever, and it would be my fault! My trap would ensnare the one who until this moment I did not know, was the one I cared for the most.

"IT'S YOUR FAULT!" he thundered.

My anger grew to a rageful hate as he spoke filling my head with thoughts that all the horrors ever committed were arranged by him. They were arranged by him and purposed by him. All the suffering in all life spawned from his Broth.

All of it was so he could make me HATE him at the exact moment I had planned to trick him. So that I would not trick him but kill him!

"You saved Coranthas. Look at what I will do to him in here. Look at all the evil *YOU* have caused Froth Lord!" he screamed in a now evil, echoing ghastly wail.

Such horrors awaited the universe if I did not kill him. He showed them all to me.

Suddenly his appearance was more like a snake. No longer was he in human form. Even with all this it was also clear to me that Dendrake was filling me with a higher love as well. He was not doing this to spread good and mercy. He was not doing this to cause anyone peace. He was showing me all his evil and filling me the highest love any being could have. This was so I would kill him. I would have to kill him to spare all others from his horrors. *The most loving act I could ever do would be killing him,* I now thought. (Knowing he would foresee that thought.)

At this moment Dendrake had succeeded. He had flipped the script. At this moment I was in fact going to kill him. And it was not out of hate. It was not out of revenge. He continued to pump the horrors of his plans so that I would kill him out of the highest love for my friends and all others. The very love that Dendrake himself was bestowing. His joy raced to infinite joy. A deep sense of contentment came over him. He now was experiencing the full foreknowledge that I was going to kill him. And it was no longer a trick. And hence he foresaw it. His merciful end was finally near.

But like I said I still had one trick left.

At the very moment that Dendrake reached the highest state of elation possible, awaiting and anticipating his imminent death, achieving his coda, I would trigger the final series of anomalies unlike any rips in the universe or time I had ever done prior. The anomalies in space-time already occurring, combined with my nearly endless curvatures in space, creating a whirlpool, not unlike the power of the largest black holes have now encircled the canvas. Now I combined all these anomaly effects with the fact that the canvas construct itself exists purposefully separate from time. These combined reality natures locked the canvas of his consciousness forever in a moment of time. Of the utmost irony existing in the canvas of Denrake's dream state consciousness is the only place where he can be frozen and locked forever, for all time. Outside of the canvas he exists separate from any concept of time. Though within the construct there was no true time, time was being "emulated" by me and him to bring this phenomenon together.

At this point it was a real struggle for me to return to my plan not to kill him. The danger to all existence and all life is so high that I had truly thought I must do it. The hate I felt was so strong. He had created the Broth and all life because he wanted me to kill him. He was the great cause of all the horrors of Sentient experience, explicitly so I would hate him enough to kill him at the exact right moment. The immensity of this evil is still hard for me to comprehend to this day. And yes, I was taking a tremendous risk to leave him trapped. Honestly, I was not sure I could have killed him anyway.

But now he was trapped!

Inside the canvas I can now keep him in this emulated time. Time is now slowing exponentially within the canvas until it nears infinity of slowness, essentially frozen. Dendrake will be entirely distracted by two things at that moment.

I had one shot at this.

Queen to bishop's pawn, takes pawn on "f7." Checkmate!

Firstly, he is now in the highest state of bliss of any being that ever in all of existence, likely will ever achieve right at this moment. It will fully keep him unaware of both the fact that he is stuck in the realm of emulated time, and that time, in this canvas has been locked, or in other words, slowed down to an infinite state of slowness or again essentially stopped.

And secondly, my true and powerful thoughts of how I was going to kill Dendrake set the trap. I believed I was going to kill him for just long enough, during a stopped moment of eternal time. It involved the very same anomalies I am using to ensnare him. Dendrake will now never know or suspect that he is NOT about to perish. Instead he will forever then exist in a state of perfect bliss without end in stopped time, trapped in time. And though he could if he became aware, escape with ease, he will never do so. He will never do so because he will be forever in the state of perfect bliss. He will be imminently expecting his merciful end which never will come. And by this anticipation for an imminent end I will be causing my creator to experience endless perfect joy. This above all else is the greatest achievement I will have ever accomplished.

This is the greatest feat I will have ever achieved. (To this point.)

Checkmate!

- Dendrake's Collapsing Canvas

It had taken hundreds of thousands of years to reach this point. The construct was now collapsing around me. I had other pressing issues to deal with now that I had trapped Dendrake. After my ascendance, I had the power to stop the Space Virus by my word. But now, even exponentially more powerful, I might not have the power to get us out of here. Death had clearly not been Dendrake's purpose, but was my and Coranthas's purpose to be trapped eternally here with him? It wouldn't be bliss for us. Well, at least we'd have the chess board.

The construct started ripping apart rapidly as all things seemed to be collapsing now as I ran to get Coranthas. Though this was someone else's dream state I needed to retrieve Coranthas, or he would be stuck forever as well. The illusion of the sphere was gone now, and I was suddenly back in Coranthas's chamber. In human form I dashed down his hallway looking for him.

Again I stopped and looked at the Others in the construct, and even with all my knowledge I was like, "I don't get them." They are of no use whatsoever. They looked at me, utter chaos shaking and collapsing construct around them. What do they care? They are not even in this realm. All these eons in this construct and I finally just pondered them more deeply for really the first time, though briefly.

It began to dawn on me. *What the fuck are those guys even doing here?* It is just weird how some thoughts finally come to you.

It didn't matter. I made my move. I lit up Dendrake's place like a Christmas tree with fission lightning streams for ten seconds ionizing his immediate surroundings back in that sphere in the construct closing the lock. Until now his entire general area had been quarantined from all the blasts. Just then Thog beamed me Coranthas's location within the construct as I had asked of him. He had managed to keep a lock on him the whole time.

Into my wrist commlink I began to speak.

"Nice work Thog!" I spoke loudly.

"No worries Froth Lord," said Thog.

Dendrake was in perfect peace awaiting imminent non-existence. He had never experienced anything like this before. There was this overwhelming feeling of joy within him. Being so emmeshed with him in this construct I could sense it. *I got him,* I thought to myself. Rejoicing even, was not too strong a description of his condition.

But he was approaching neither his demise nor his salvation. Yet within the same emulated stopped time his bliss quintuplicated over and over exponentially, within the same plane of existence in the construct. The depths of his peace and contentment in that moment trapped in his construct are impossible to over-state.

I had invaded his dream. I had invaded Dendrake's construct. It had worked! And I had become so powerful. More accurately, he had bestowed upon me pow-ers unspeakable. Yet it might not be enough.

My series of anomalies, though under any normal circumstances would have had no impact on him whatsoever, caused Dendrake, the most powerful being ever initiated (maybe) to lose touch with reality. It worked well.

But there was a problem. Coranthas and I had to escape. And I had yet to lo-cate him. It was possible it was too late as the combination of all my anomalies bent time over upon itself fully. The encircling of the construct with so many black holes, and dimensions of anti-matter whirlpools, the entire bending of space until it curved entirely back on itself, all combined to worry me I might not get us out of there.

"Thog. Resend his signal!" I yelled into my wristwatch comm.

"I can't find him!" I screamed.

"Stand by," Thog's voice came across my comm.

"Give me just a couple seconds here," he finished.

Then I saw Coranthas. He was sitting there amongst all the chaos and all the destruction. The whirling forces of the universe. He was an unaware pawn in Den-drake's infinite plan. *Was I the king's pawn, or was Coranthas?* I would ponder within myself. It was Dendrake's fault, not mine, I thought at first. I looked at Coranthas, and he was clutching the diamond shaped-stone I had given him so long ago. He was counting to ten. Seven, eight, nine, ten, he would count. Then he would start again at one, two, three, continuing in this endless loop, clutching the stone, trying with all his mind and power to discern reality. This struck me with such a deep sadness at that moment. To think Coranthas with his condition of not being able to discern reality, that he might be stuck in this time stopped vortex, but NOT in a state of bliss. He would stuck here in a state of torment just as endless as Den-drake's state of bliss. He would be counting to ten, holding his anchor stone, end-lessly waiting for the trick to work but it never would. As deep was my love for him now had become I realized that I MUST get him out of here at all costs. This was not the right time for this emotional reaction. Everything that I had done to him flashed before my mind. Suddenly all the things I had done, good and bad, all the countless times Dendrake and even I had pulled him into these constructs pressed into my thoughts. It was not just Dendrake. I was guilty too. He continued to clutch the diamond-shaped stone, and struggle with figuring out his own reality. I brought him here to help me fool Dendrake. This was my fault. I was going to get him out of here. I briefly considered using the power of the stone but remembered how dangerous it was for me to yield it. I needed another way.

Coranthas thought he was dreaming. I just grabbed him. I looked around and just decided we need to make a quantum jump. He kept counting to ten even as I held him in my arms. But even this was a problem considering the extent of quantum anomalies. Had I not thought this through? I quickly scanned for a solution. I needed a jump target that was close enough but not within the outer walls of my anomalies. This was necessary so that Coranthas could survive and still be in a realm from which his brain could rebound. This entire experience in the construct was no longer about trapping Dendrake for me or killing him for that matter. It was now entirely about saving Coranthas.

This jump we needed to make was totally different then teleporting to the moons of Drandor. The nature of reality here would really be a problem for quantum leaping for a being like Coranthas. He would surely not survive a jump of great distance under these extraordinary circumstances. We could not target Sholl Gar, Delta Five, or Earth. They were all too far him to survive the jump intact from this vortex. Even I might struggle. And Thog was too close to the anomalies. He was going to have to worry about his own escape.

Surrounded by the collapsing walls of Dendrake's canvas I spoke into my wrist commlink.

"Thog! Phobus! Do you guys read!" I yelled into my wrist commlink. I was becoming desperate, not for love of self, but for concern of my best friend. As powerful as I now was, inside this vortex of mine and Dendrake's creation I was going to need the boys to help us. They were going to need to save us, to save even me.

"Thog! Phobus!" I screamed in near horror, horror because of the depths of my love and fear for Coranthas. I looked around and the collapsing canvas of false time.

"THOG! PHOBUS!" I screamed into my commlink.

Right at that moment of utter chaos I heard a faint crackling coming through on the watch comm at first, then it got clearer, then I could start to hear it. I heard music coming through. I could make it out clearly now.

Witch Doctor One: "Over there! Over there!" Phobus was singing along with the song.

Witch Doctor One: "Hey Froth man! I have to say I love Coranthas's old Earth tune collection." (Amazingly, it was Phobus).

"PHOBUS?!" I yelled into my commlink.

At this moment, the construct started to collapse.

Witch Doctor One: "Send the word! send the word! over there!"

"PHOBUS?!!!!!" I yelled in desperation.

Witch Doctor One: "The Yanks are coming! the Yanks are coming!"

"PHOBUS?!" I screamed again into my commlink.

Witch Doctor One: "Hey Froth Man! I am cruising by looking for Coranthas. The Witch Doctor said he disappeared, Phobus out."

"PHOBUS! Beam me your gamma coordinates to my watch!" I screamed.

I immediately scanned space. A leap to his ship was possible if he was not already within the anomaly boundary. And I might be able to teleport Thog to him too. I was hit by a wall of joy! There it was, Witch Doctor One, cruising through the Gamma Seven quadrant pass. It was in range just barely, and outside of the outer rim of my trap but close enough that Coranthas should survive. Immediately I quantum leaped us to the shuttle Coranthas in my arms. I couldn't believe we made it!

Chapter Ten

Aftermath, Planet Earth, Yosemite, some years later

"Dude what the fuck? Seriously?" complained Phobus

"What now?" asked Coranthas sarcastically.

"What in Dendrake's name is that smell?" finished Phobus.

I enjoyed these camping trips. This was the first time I was going to reveal to Coranthas that he was literally on planet Earth. After everything Earth really was a lovely world. *I might even build a cabin here,* I thought.

"What world are we on?" asked Poor Brandon.

"Earth, I think," answered Thog.

"Earth?" asked Coranthas, surprisingly.

"Yes dear Coranthas," I answered.

"Okay," Coranthas answered. "I am from Earth, originally, correct?" he continued.

"No, of course not," answered Poor Brandon.

"It's okay Brandon," I intervened.

"Yes," I answered.

It had been a very long time since I had ensnared Dendrake in the canvas. My "crew" was not even aware of the actual circumstances apart from Rulella. I had always known Rulella would exist forever as pure energy. And I had been proven correct that she would continue to exist with Sentient self-awareness, whether in form of energy, gas, vapor, or even as that of a Wraith.

Rulella amazingly, after all this time, and with the near limitless power I now wielded, still wanted to give me grief for the eons of trouble I had caused her. But I had a turned a corner after all this with her. I "loved" her I guess, if that is a real thing?

My love had faded some since the ensnarement, but I suppose I felt it, but the most important thing to me ultimately, was that for some reason, she was fully aware of what I had done to Dendrake. That alone was fascinating to me and likely had caused our reunion, and would maintain our full reconciliation. Even I, now the second-most powerful being in the universe, had to admit that I had a hard time understanding women.

"How did I get here?" asked Poor Brandon out loud while roasting smores.

Poor Brandon was utterly clueless about what had happened in the past several thousands of years. He had no idea how or why he had been pulled into this millenia or series of events, both small and large.

"Dendrake tried to use you as some kind of beacon," I answered. "You actually no longer exist." I explained.

"Don't worry about it." I finished.

"A beacon?" asked Coranthas roasting his marshmallow.

"Yeah. I'm honestly not sure why but it had something to do with Phobus and Sholl Gar. Most other things are clear for me to decipher since I ascended, but this for some reason remains murky," I finished.

"I no longer exist?" Poor Brandon indifferently asked, trying to keep his hot dog on the fire stick with just six fingers total and one eye.

"Nope," I answered.

"That's kind of cool," said Thog.

Thog then walked over to Coranthas and Phobus. I decided to pay attention to this bit.

"So hey, Coranthas. Hey Phobus. How you guys been?" began Thog.

"Hey Thog. What's up?" Coranthas asked.

"Not much," Thog answered.

"Well, I did have a couple questions for you guys," he finished.

"What's up?" Coranthas asked while roasting a hot dog.

"You're from Earth, right?" Thog asked Coranthas with an annoying tone.

"Dude yes, I am. I think we have been over this a million times," Coranthas finished.

"What's the point? All the secrets are behind us now," Coranthas finished.

"Yeah dude, we're on vacation here," added Phobus.

I was ready to step in if needed.

"Well back on Sholl Gar, when you sacrificed the Son of Froth Lord...um, me? For the sins of all Sholl-Garians, as a substitutional act of reconciliation? Remember, as an act of atonement for the sins of all worlds?" Thog asked.

"Ah yeah. It was something like that if I recall, duh," answered Phobus with an annoyed tone while staring at the campfire.

"It was supposed to be some kind of substitutional pardoning of all life, no?" Thog asked.

"I don't know," answered Phobus, the god of Sholl Gar.

"Heyyy...I think it was just for the sins of Sholl Gar bro..." said Coranthas.

"Froth?" Phobus deferred to me.

I just kept watching and listening. I loved when they talked theology.

"Dude let me handle this," interrupted Coranthas.

"So Thog, you're pissed Phobus killed you, right?" asked Coranthas.

"Wouldn't you be?" asked Thog

"He'd have welcomed it," added Phobus still staring at his hot dog on the stick.

I was loving this.

"Maybe," answered Coranthas.

"Do you remember all that crap you did to us, and that happened to us before Froth Lord admitted he was messing with all things?" Coranthas asked.

"Possibly," answered Thog.

"Okay," Coranthas finished.

"Do you remember defending Sholl Gar with Phobus all those years?" he continued. "Countless frontal assaults against Phobus's defense perimeter?" asked Coranthas.

I was starting to follow where he might be going with this.

"How do you know any of that was real?" Coranthas began.

"Froth Lord has already told us the truth about all that stuff," he finished.

"I only backfilled some history holes Coranthas," I interjected.

"Yeah I get it but Thog was never real. You made him in your Space Lab you said."

"okay," I said, hoping to see where he was going with this.

"None of it matters, but Thog is pissed because we slew him happily, but the thing is, he is just a fake life form anyway," Coranthas added.

"Hell you cloned me like five million times already right?" Coranthas asked.

"Not quite," I interjected.

"Okay but that is not the not point. Why are you mad Thog?" finished Coranthas.

"Sorry to interrupt you guys. I mean I know it's important and all, but Thog is there any chance you could scratch my low back?" asked Phobus from out of left field.

"I just have this itch and I just can't quite get there. Do you see where I am pointing?" Phobus continued.

Almost like a computer program or obedient pet Thog could not stay angry or resist his old master. He reached to Phobus's back and scratched. Thog simply dropped the entire matter, and all was forgiven.

"So Froth Man, what is deal with Dendrake now? We all set Froth?" asked Phobus.

"He is trapped in a state of eternal bliss," I answered.

I supposed Dendrake was right about one big thing at that moment. He never had free will before, and most certainly does not have it now. No matter what state of bliss he was in, in the stuck, stopped moment any trace of free will that he might have had prior was now robbed of him. Was it possible he did not detect or foresee my trap or is not aware about it in that stuck moment? There was never a question in my mind that he could escape if aware. Perhaps he is aware, but the trickery that created his bliss did something more than just trap him. Perhaps he is consciously content and happy and chooses to not change that. The answers to these questions would elude me for now.

"So what was his main deal?" asked Phobus. "Why did he not want to exist anymore?" he asked.

These were strange questions coming from Phobus. It is not that the questions were particularly deep, but the discussions they would produce certainly could become so. Philosophy was something I did not speak with him about too often.

"Dendrake is a seemingly omniscient being," I began. "Dendrake has a perfect foreknowledge," I said.

I had always believed that this would be the case for the one who created the Broth and all life. However after I ascended and entered the canvas of his mind I was able to see it all.

"He was tormented by the question of free will." I continued.

"You see through foreknowledge and foresight, and seeming omniscience, he knew about all potential futures. Now after my ascendance I have been bestowed by Dendrake a lessor form of foreknowledge. I can scan near limitless potential futures. But I cannot identify the fatalistic, certain-to-occur future. Dendrake can," I continued.

"Too much brew Froth Man?" asked Phobus in his typical way.

"He sees all possible futures Phobus. But it goes beyond even that. He also sees the future that will in fact occur. This does not mean that all the 'potential futures' which are not identified as the one which will occur, are not just as real as the one that does in fact occur. It does not speak to that; it speaks to the immensity of Dendrake's omniscience," I finished.

What I meant by this was that Dendrake saw every single possible outcome of all futures, and they were literally real outcomes, even though beyond just seeing those his foreknowledge could identify the one that would occur.

So Dendrake therefore struggled with free will. Could the future he foresees *fail to occur?* Was he only able to choose to make the Broth? Could he choose as an act of his will to not make the Broth even after seeing its creation and all life it spawned through his perfect foreknowledge? When viewed this way through perfect omniscience it seemed that he had no free will. This was a key part of his torment. It was probably the very core of it.

But even beyond this torment, was the torment of the fact that he did NOT have perfect omniscience. As powerful as he was, and as perfect as his foreknowledge, and all-knowing cerebral capabilities, he realized it was not possible for him to be omniscient. A truly omniscient being would know with certainty, and perfect peace, where he in fact came from. Which he did not. He would know what came before him. Dendrake did not. He would now all origins. He did not. Dendrake would also know, if truly omniscient, whether these questions even mattered. All these he could not know. So rather than do what my more limited newly attained knowledge and foreknowledge did for me (bring me perfect fascination), it brought Dendrake deep dread. The kind of dread that haunts one in the darkest places.

The kind of dread that causes utter despair. Despair magnified exponentially and near infinitely because of who was experiencing it. So like how it was impossible for any being in all existence to ever approach the perfect state of bliss Dendrake was now existing within; no being could have ever or yet ever will experience the sheer darkness that Dendrake's dread brought upon him through his imperfect omniscience. His desire to end his existence would eventually make sense to me when examined in that context. At that moment I found myself wondering once again where did Dendrake come from? I realized I must not ponder that for too long, or risk creating for myself a potential burning need for answers that rather than bring me the joy of fascination, descend me into the pit as it did for my maker.

I explained one more time to the group that Dendrake would never want to escape the construct ever, due to the vast, inexplicable, near impossible level of his perpetual contentment. I explained to them that though Dendrake aspired to non-existence that I had given him eternal bliss instead. I explained to them the irony that his anticipation of imminent death combined with the near endless power of his mind had established for him the highest level of happiness any being could attain, ever.

"In other words, Christ help us if he ever gets out," chimed in Phobus

"Everything's fine", I answered him

He wasn't wrong. Anyway, I looked up at the stars. Earth was a nature reserve at this time not polluted by the typical exploits and byproducts of advanced civilization. I sure hope the resettling Podranians don't destroy this world.

I leaned in and spoke to Coranthas.

"Earth truly is a beautiful planet," I said.

Coranthas would not be going back to Delta Five. We had created a ranch complex for him and his drones not far from this very location. Even with all my powers I could not heal him from his "depersonalization-derealization" disorder. Coranthas persistently experiences reality as if bicameral like in a perpetual dream state, always questioning what is real and what is not. Coranthas does indeed hear some voices that are not real. I often would reread his chronicles and journals, and often wondered how much of his issues were because of me. I saved him from this world so long ago. Now I am giving it to him. The Podranians are going to check in on him from time to time as will I. I have spoken to Tom, the leader of the Podranians. He will be watching Coranthas for me as well.

Coranthas looked over at Witch Doctor One over on the hill.

"You really grew to love that ship, huh?" I asked

"Yeah after you souped it up for the first war," Coranthas said

"Does her owner know where it is?" I asked.

We both smiled and kind of started laughing.

"No," he added.

She was busily scouring the galaxy on star buses in fury trying to find Coranthas.

"Do I ever have to go back to Sholl Gar?" Phobus asked sheepishly.

"Yep," I answered.

Phobus had long neglected his solemn duty as Deity to his home world of origin. He would be returning to make all things new. Thog would be going with him, risen from the dead as his "Lessor Lord."

"It will be like old times for you two," I said to him.

"Oh god," answered Phobus.

"I forget is this his second or third coming?" asked Thog

That got a good chuckle from the group.

A while later I went over to the edge of the hill to look at the beautiful stars. For a moment I did wonder about Dendrake yet again. I thought of the construct and the canvas. I wondered if it possible that Dendrake had found happiness and contentment even if he did not realize how or why, forever. I considered the trap and how his state of "bliss" would perpetually be dependent on him never realizing the truth. *Can a being be happy in a state of being forever deceived?* I wondered. In the state of true ignorance of the reality of the trap I believed he would remain content. And hence I had done him a great and wonderful act. Though it is true that it is impossible to know. And though I can scan many futures none are set it stone. We will see if I am ever able to discern his mystery. For now, I can see nothing.

I took a couple of moments to further ponder him, and then turned and looked back at the group. Coranthas was off to the side. He was sitting and seemed almost in a trancelike state. At first I was not sure what he was doing. But then I noticed he was clutching my diamond-shaped stone in his hand, counting.

241

Chapter Eleven

The Constructs and The Broth

Ageless Eons Ago

It was not possible for Dendrake to know how long he been in existence. He had long since given up the idea of understanding where he had come from. No longer did he bother with questions or thoughts related to his own origins. He was envious. He was in pain. When he thought about the vast, extensive life he would create from nothing, emanated from his Broth, he felt bitter jealousy. Even though most life forms would never know where they had come from he still knew where they came from, and he was still envious because he knew. He was envious knowing that there would exist self-aware Sentient beings who at least could possibly discover who had made them. In many ways he was like a child.

He was envious of the Nectarians in whom will be given this knowledge. He often wondered why he will do so. Why would he make that choice, the choice to make them so great?

Did he even have a choice? he would wonder to himself for eons. His seemingly omniscient foreknowledge tormented him. It tortured him to know for example, everything about Froth Lord eons before he even had created the Broth.

If he foresees all things then where was his free will? How could he fail to create The Broth when he foresees it? Even then he already knew about how he would manipulate and shape all events for the life created by his Broth. How then did liberty fit into this? *It did not,* he thought. He spent near seemingly limitless ages trying to avoid creating the Broth. He agonized over it. But he foreknew he would create the Broth.

So, he created the Broth.

Though he had tried he was unable to end his own torment. Of all his powers one thing was forever seemingly out of reach. Rest for his exponentially powerful mind was always out of reach. He did not sleep like his life forms did. His mind construct did not stop learning. He learned at exponential rates, always and forever, always approaching infinite knowledge. Most super-intelligent entities that he would foster through the Broth would deeply enjoying thinking, analyzing, learning, and decoding the mysteries. But Dendrake was bored by thinking.

And Dendrake was tired. He had already unwrapped every secret of the universe that he cared to even as uninteresting as it all was to him. And he did not care to bother trying. He found it all so tedious. Even as his knowledge continued to exponentially expand at ever-increasing speed he never once found an ounce of joy in any of it or anything. He saw countless galaxies. Vast stretches of super-clusters of the Cosmos. He had so much power, so much knowledge yet knew nothing about where any of this had come from. Did he have a beginning? Like any other Sentient he could not remember back past a certain point. But in his case, there was no one else to tell him what went on before, even if there was a "before." There were no peers, no beings, no teachers not that he needed one. Even with the vast knowledge of how things work. Even knowing what everything was made of and how it all held together, he was alone. And there are not many things worse than being completely alone.

Even with all the despair there was one thing he pondered more than any other. There was one thing he obsessed about above all else. One thing he would spend near endless time considering. He had foreseen the greatness of Froth Lord. He will be unique amongst all life forms his Broth will bring about. Remember he had seen way past by a matter of many eons all that is recorded in these chronicles regarding Froth Lord. What Froth Lord becomes ultimately is nearly without explanation. We do not touch a fraction of his ultimate story. But Dendrake saw all of it. From the perspective of Dendrake the entire future might have well been in the past already.

Dendrake saw that Froth Lord was the most super intelligent of his life forms, but also that he could be sometimes cruel, sarcastic, funny, fearless, yet also he could be kind and altruistic. He would strangely befriend the most pathetic life forms. He would enjoy the company of the least likely beings. Some things he would regret for millennia. He would torture himself over sins of the past. Yet he would be at his greatest in the care of his friends.

He could also at times mistreat others terribly. But he usually felt bad later. He usually made attempts to make up for things. Dendrake foresaw all of this. His only question was that of fate. If he foresees, is it a fait accompli? Could the future he sees fail to occur? Could it be altered? He spent many eons considering these questions before creating the Broth. That is when he hatched his ultimate plan.

Froth Lord can kill me, he thought. *I will make him the greatest of all beings, and he will figure out how to kill me. I will convince him to kill me. I will make him hate me.*

Immediately he began to build the first construct. The construct was his first creation, the first canvas of many.

Dendrake already knew what creating the Broth would entail. As ludicrous as it may sound, the construct was a much more involved creation than the Broth. The Broth essentially was encoded with a life process, a life process which immediately would kick into action, and all its potential outcomes immediately become inevitable if given enough time. In infinite time all life outcomes would occur in all galaxies. The Zynon galaxy would just be the first. But the quantum entanglement which Dendrake included in the Broth code, allowed him to have control of all Broth-based life outcomes forever. This also felt to him like a contradiction. Did he control the outcomes? Or did the Broth itself? He had no answer.

The construct was very different. It pre-existed the Broth and hence all life. The purpose of the Broth was entirely Froth Lord centered. But not primarily about Froth Lord. The constructs were to be used by Dendrake to bring about his own merciful end, via what would become the near limitless mind of Froth Lord.

But Froth Lord will try to trap him, ensnare Dendrake, in the construct he foresaw. This is inevitable. Dendrake foresaw all of it. But as he had pondered before are all foreseen futures set in stone and fate? Will Froth Lord's plan, foreseen by Dendrake, succeed? Or could Froth Lord be himself tricked in a similar fashion as his future scheme to trick Dendrake? Froth Lord's plan was indeed clever Dendrake would surmise. Even with seemingly omniscient foreknowledge, this question could not be answered. But one thing was certain, Dendrake must try. He must. So he needed the constructs. And he needed The Broth.

And he made them both so.

Worlds, The King's Pawn

The End

Addendum

- The Life and Times of Michael Garrham, Tens of Thousands of Years Earlier (Froth Lord's Notes)

Michael Garrham stared at the chess board on his screen. It was nearly five p.m. Friday at the end of a long and tedious week at this miserable office. "Chess.com" was his only salvation in this dreadful existence. He was very careful to have his work-related computer materials open on his machine so he could switch his screen quickly away from his current chess match. Michael kept an ever-vigilant eye on his manager's corner office to always be sure the coast was clear.

He was playing white this time. His opponent was from some Eastern European country called "Latvia" or something. Unfortunately for Michael he had not been able to focus on the match as much as he would have liked and was getting his butt handed to him. *This guy always beat me,* he would think to himself. He could not remember ever beating him. His opponent began a DM chat with him off to the side:

"You should resign the game. I have you. Don't make me go get three more queens," the chat read.

He was quite correct. Michael was defeated, but sometimes you could win on time or even get a stalemate. But this was not one of those times. Not against him. Also it was very frowned upon to not resign and try for a tie or stalemate. Professional chess players would never do such a thing.

Michael resigned the game, logged off the site, and began to pack up his things. It was Friday night he happily thought. Even so, this did not necessarily mean anything special for Michael. Sure it was time off from work. There was time to play chess online and perhaps some more video games. He would always have a couple Heinekens as well. But he was alone, and he had no friends to make plans with. All his contacts were chess players from all over the world.

Michael turned on cable news. He never really cared so much about events that were being reported. He just liked the "white noise" of having cable news on in the background. It reminded him of being at the airport or something. Normally he did not care too much about the news but last month there had been truly tremendous excitement. The president of the United States and many other world leaders together released statements that planet Earth had been contacted by extraterrestrial civilizations, plural. Michael was not even sure if he bought it at all, but the chaos that had ensued globally was entertaining to say the least. Many cultures, especially the hyper-religious cultures and cults, read this like it was the end of the world. Many simply refused to accept it. The government was lying to "disprove God," some said. Eschatology, always somewhat popular in the United States especially, made a huge comeback over the past month. Preachers were in their glory. Mike would even pull up some of the really hyped-up ones on YouTube. Even with all this entertainment, it was still a good battle on chess.com that Michael cared about.

He sat in his recliner with his laptop booted up and opened a Heineken. Just at the precise moment he had found an opponent he heard something out of the corner of his consciousness. At first he ignored it. King's pawn from "e2" to "e4" he opened not paying attention to the TV anchorlady. But then he heard the first horrible reports coming in on cable news. At first he tried to ignore it because he had already led with his king's pawn and was trying to set this guy up. But very rapidly it became impossible to ignore. The anchorlady was screaming and going completely crazy. America was under devastating attack.

"What appears to be nuclear explosions are occurring all across the East Coast!" an obviously terrified and traumatized anchorwoman declared. "Reports are coming in from all over." Thinking this must be a joke he checked every channel. All the networks were screaming about the nuclear assault. "Is this the Russians?" screamed one anchorman. Another ranted about the North Koreans.

Michael lived in the Midwest of the United States. He immediately arose to his feet to go to a window to look at the world. Though he was apparently not yet near an immediate ground zero target, the night sky, which should be dark, had a glow emanating from nearly all horizons. As fear and terror started to take over he once again did a double take when he heard the news lady. She was going apocalyptic now.

"THE ENTIRE WORLD IS UNDER ATTACK! THE ATTACK IS COMING FROM OUTER SPACE!" she screamed.

Not long after the TV and power went out. The sounds of destruction and devastation were becoming worse and worse, and now the entire Earth was starting to light up like a massive inferno. Now the night sky looked like the brightest noon summer day. Michael was now a bit concerned. The earth began to shake right under his feet. What in Christ's name is happening!?

The ground was now shaking so hard that the structure of Mike's apartment surely would collapse any moment. Suddenly all the windows of his building shattered in an instant, broken and breaking glass exploding in all directions. A very hot and strong wind could now be felt pouring into the dwelling. The last thing Michael remembered prior to passing out was what appeared to be a man in a white robe suddenly and inexplicably standing before him in the darkness. This apparition reached out to him during all this chaos and fast-moving destruction, and spoke, "Don't worry Michael, everything's fine". Then Mike faded out to black.

That man, that apparition, was none other than Froth Lord, and Michael was to become our hero Coranthas. Froth Lord removed Michael from the planet Earth having chosen him, after years of scorching him on "chess.com," including earlier that evening. He erased Mike's memories to spare him the torment of knowing the fate of his home world. And brought him to a compound built for him on "Delta Five" handing him over to the Witch Doctor's care. "Delta Five" as it shall be referred to, is merely a code name. For obvious reasons, we shall not reveal his true location.